Praise for Jen

Ace, Marvel, Spy

"Jenni L. Walsh captures the thrill of being on the court in a vivid and detailed portrayal of Alice Marble's rise to sporting greatness, as well as her struggles to fulfil her dreams both on and off the court. *Ace, Marvel, Spy* is a smashing success."

—Billie Jean King, sports icon and equality champion

Unsinkable

"Walsh's latest (after *The Call of the Wrens*, 2022) is a heartfelt tale of two women in two times. *Unsinkable* joins the ranks of other spy novels written in this vein, but Walsh's prose truly allows the reader to enter the mind and heart of each character, bringing their motivations, flaws, and desires to light . . . Walsh skillfully crafts two well-rounded characters who grapple with internal and external conflict, and yet who honestly earn their resolutions."

—*Booklist*

"An intriguing and thoroughly original novel merging the maritime journeys of Violet Jessop—a very real person who survived three separate shipwrecks—and the fictional Daphne Chaundanson, a brilliant young woman invited to join Special Operations during the dark days of World War II. In author Jenni L. Walsh's expert hands, separate tales are seamlessly woven together to create a remarkable dual-timeline narrative. *Unsinkable* is about the bravery of women and the stunning lengths they will go to protect others. It is a heart-stirring story of women who risk everything in order to claim their proper place in this world. Walsh takes readers on an exhilarating voyage of danger, sacrifice, and ultimate triumph."

—Lynda Cohen Loigman, *USA TODAY* bestselling author of *Two-Family House, The Wartime Sisters,* and *The Matchmaker's Gift*

"With elegant prose and superb attention to detail, Walsh pulls you instantly onboard this beautiful tale of two determined, whip-smart, and truly unsinkable women. I was intrigued from page one, both Violet's and Daphne's stories sweeping me along through every harrowing moment until that perfect twist and captivating ending. A must-read for fans of unstoppable, courageous women."

—Noelle Salazar, *USA TODAY* bestselling author of *The Flight Girls*

"Jenni L. Walsh spins an incredible tale of survival and heartbreak in this riveting novel. Inspired by true events, the rich historical detail and tense plotting make for an unforgettable read. Historical fiction lovers, add this one to your list!"

—Sara Ackerman, *USA TODAY* bestselling author of *The Codebreaker's Secret* and *The Uncharted Flight of Olivia West*

"A stunning dual narrative spanning some of the marquee events of the early twentieth century. Violet and Daphne are compelling heroines of the first order, and one cannot help but root for their triumph from the first page through to the seamless, satisfying conclusion. Walsh is a master storyteller, and *Unsinkable* shows her skill at its best. Not to be missed by anyone who loves historical fiction and resilient heroines."

—Aimie K. Runyan, bestselling author of *The School for German Brides* and *A Bakery in Paris*

"An extraordinary story of two extraordinary women. Jenni L. Walsh expertly weaves together Violet's and Daphne's histories—Violet is real, Daphne an amalgamation of several real-life women—to craft a historical novel that is vivid and enthralling. There is intrigue and bravery, duty and love in these pages, and readers will keep turning them to the very end, eager to learn the fates of these two inspiring women. A joy to read."

—Kate Albus, award-winning author of *A Place to Hang the Moon* and *Nothing Else but Miracles*

"I fell headfirst into this historical fiction tale featuring two powerful and resilient women, Violet and Daphne. Walsh seamlessly weaves together fact and fiction in a dual-timeline narrative that keeps the reader guessing, culminating in a satisfying conclusion. The courage of both main characters lingered with me long after I turned the final page. I am so looking forward to whatever Walsh writes next!"

—Amita Parikh, bestselling author of *The Circus Train*

The Call of the Wrens

"In *The Call of the Wrens*, Jenni L. Walsh chronicles two volunteers in the Women's Royal Naval Service during the First and Second World Wars. Spanning decades in a story that is both epic and intimate, *The Call of the Wrens* is an original and compelling tale of sisterhood and strength."

—Pam Jenoff, *New York Times* bestselling author of *The Woman with the Blue Star*

"What a lovely surprise. The heroines in Walsh's latest can be found racing around war-torn Europe on motorbikes, relaying secret messages and undertaking daring missions as part of the real-life women's branch of the Royal Navy. There's also giddy romance, family secrets, and shocking twists, making it an absolute treat for historical fiction lovers."

—Fiona Davis, *New York Times* bestselling author of *The Magnolia Palace*

"The lives of two women in two different world wars collide in unexpected ways in this powerful exploration of the British Women's Royal

Naval Service, commonly known as the Wrens, a daring group of real-life women who were instrumental in both World War I and World War II. Laced with triumph and tragedy, bravery and redemption, this tale of finding oneself in modern history's darkest hours will break your heart and put it back together again, all in one delightful read."

—KRISTIN HARMEL, *NEW YORK TIMES* BESTSELLING AUTHOR OF *THE FOREST OF VANISHING STARS*

"*The Call of the Wrens* by Jenni L. Walsh is a beautifully written gem of a historical novel, shedding light on a little-known group of women, the Wrens, during both world wars. Walsh skillfully entwines the stories of Evelyn and Marion as they journey to find their voices and, ultimately, their calling. I was completely captivated by this richly drawn portrait of strength, survival, and love."

—JILLIAN CANTOR, *USA TODAY* BESTSELLING AUTHOR OF *BEAUTIFUL LITTLE FOOLS*

"In *The Call of the Wrens*, Jenni L. Walsh has woven a wonderful tale inspired by the real-life women's branch of the United Kingdom's Royal Navy. This dual-timeline novel features two courageous heroines, Marion and Evelyn, roaring around Europe on motorbikes during both world wars. Thrilling missions, family secrets, romance—it's all here. We need more books like this that show the remarkable contributions made by adventurous women during the darkest of times."

—ELISE HOOPER, AUTHOR OF *ANGELS OF THE PACIFIC*

"In *The Call of the Wrens*, Jenni L. Walsh lends her remarkable voice to the little-known, intrepid women of the Women's Royal Naval Service, women who revved up their motorcycles and risked their necks to heed Britain's call to win the world wars. Packed full of action and with a heart-wrenching twist, Marion and Evelyn's story reads like a battle cry for anyone who's had to fight against other people's expectations and find her own place, and her chosen family, in this world."

—CAROLINE WOODS, AUTHOR OF *THE LUNAR HOUSEWIFE*

"With a winning blend of adventure and romance, Walsh highlights the bravery and intrepid spirits of women destined to forge a path beyond the restrictive expectations of their era and circumstance. A winning treatise on courage and sisterhood, *The Call of the Wrens* will have fans of Kate Quinn and Erika Robuck rejoicing with each compulsively readable page."

—Rachel McMillan, author of *The Mozart Code*

ACE, MARVEL, SPY

Also by Jenni L. Walsh

Adult Fiction
Unsinkable
The Call of the Wrens
A Betting Woman
Side by Side
Becoming Bonnie

Middle Grade
Operation: Happy
Over and Out
By the Light of Fireflies
I Am Defiance
Hettie and the London Blitz
She Dared: Malala Yousafzai
She Dared: Bethany Hamilton

To Emma,

ACE, MARVEL, SPY

A NOVEL OF ALICE MARVEL

JENNI L. WALSH

Ace, Marvel, Spy

Published by Harper Muse, an imprint of HarperCollins Focus LLC.

Library of Congress Cataloging-in-Publication Data

[[CIP TO COME]]

$PrintCode

This novel is inspired by the memoir of Alice Marble. After reading, you *may* want to continue with my author's note.

Lindsay, thank you for your endless tennis knowledge as this book came together page by page and match by match.

Chapter 1

Now

San Francisco Gazette

Monday, September 16, 1940
Has Tennis's "Best in the World" Gone as Far as the World Will Let Her?
SAN FRANCISCO, CALIF. - It's been quite the impressive few years for our hometown girl, Miss Alice Marble. Only days shy of twenty-seven years old, she has racked up an impressive list of accolades. Winning eighteen Grand Slam championships. Holding a place in the World Top Ten. The top-ranked US women's player. Earning the title of the *Associated Press* Athlete of the Year. Being named the "Best Dressed Woman in Athletics." Gracing

the cover of *LIFE* magazine, donning the tennis shorts she designed, to boot.

Marble is at the peak of her game on and off the court, stretching her vocal cords as a nightclub singer while maintaining an unbroken string of twenty-eight tournament victories, which most recently included making quick work of Helen Jacobs in two sets (6–2, 6–3) in the National Championships in Forest Hills, New York.

But what comes next for San Francisco's own? With the war knocking at our door and competitive tennis on hiatus until further notice, Marble may be all dressed up in one of her designs with nowhere to go.

lice licks her finger and forcefully turns the page.

A Shifting America

SAN FRANCISCO, CALIF. - With the war ongoing overseas for over a year, America is shifting. President Roosevelt has declared a state of national emergency. Embargoes are in place for scrap iron and steel exports for all destination other than Great Britain and Western nations. Plants across the country are changing their assembly lines from trousers, cars, and toys to uniforms, planes, and ammunition.

Churchill's impassioned "blood, toil, tears, and sweat" speech may not have been directed at us Americans, but we've unofficially answered the call. Which, as of today, includes the passing of the Selective Training and Service Act. All men between the ages of twenty-one and forty-five are now under conscription. This marks the first peacetime draft in our great country's history. Will our fathers, sons, and uncles cross the pond to officially aid our Allies in the war? We pray the answer is no and Hitler's troops will meet their end soon. But for now, our men are required by law to prepare.

With a sigh, Alice lowers the newspaper. She knew the war was coming. Hadn't *he*—she won't think his name and drudge up all those memories—predicted it? But now to see the state of the world so clearly in black and white . . . it takes the wind out of Alice, while also igniting a fire inside of her.

"What is it?" Alice's coach asks, eyes never lifting from her nails, transforming them with each swipe from bland to a tasteful mauve.

The women sit across from one another at their kitchen table, two mugs of steaming coffee between them.

Swiftly Alice folds the paper once, twice. "I feel as if I should be doing something."

"We have practice in"—her coach checks her watch—"Two hours."

"No, that's not . . ." Alice shakes her head and starts again. "I've just read about myself."

"Is that so?" The question is said facetiously, eyebrows lifting, leathered forehead crinkling.

Alice goes on, ignoring her coach's mockery. "And I've read more about the war."

Again, her coach's eyes remain trained on her nails.

Alice rises the intensity of her previous sigh to a huff. "I feel like I should be doing something of greater importance than hitting a ball back and forth over a net. Seems I won't even be able to do that anymore."

"Are you hurt?"

"No."

Alice's coach shrugs.

"I'm serious."

"Fine." Her coach screws the cap onto her polish. Her short, blonde hair has grown grayer in recent years. Most likely on account of Alice. "I understand the war has disrupted tournament play. Wimbledon isn't happening this year. But the real question for you is what could be more important than keeping your tennis game sharp while you wait for it to resume?"

"Well," Alice says, licking her lips. Her mind and heart careens back to years ago when there'd been *him*, someone she'd almost fought for. But right now? "I'm not certain. But an act passed today." She taps the newspaper, as if needing this proof. "Men are required to sign up for the draft."

"I read that too."

"Okay, well, America joining this war feels inevitable. Helen Jacobs said she's enlisting in the WAVES."

Alice's coach smiles. "Was this before or after you whooped her butt on the court at Nationals?"

What's louder than a huff? Sticking to one's guns. "I'd like to do my part. Serve, you know."

"You *do* serve your country. Every time you step onto a court, even if it's during a meaningless exhibition match, you take people's minds off the war. You give them a show. A great one, if I say so myself. You belong on the court. Entertaining. It's what you do best, Alice."

It *is* what she does best. Alice can recognize that, and how her name being chanted on the courts is a currency for her. A way to feel valued.

Seen.

Respected.

A way to belong.

Tennis is all she's known for the past decade—since she was seventeen, a face ripe with acne, built like a fireplug, no tennis skills beyond hitting the ball as hard as she could, and a desire to prove herself so strong folks couldn't help but sit up and take notice of her.

Chapter 2

Then

July 19, 1930
British Columbia Clay Court Championships

Alice growled deep in her throat, from both pain and frustration. She'd won the first set of the match. Her opponent had taken the second, which swayed the game's momentum in the other player's favor. Now they were going into a third and final set after a ten-minute break.

At a limp, Alice followed her opponent off the court and toward the dressing room. She didn't know the other player's name. Not because Alice thought herself above the girl. In fact, it was the opposite. Alice's opponent was spit and polish. Wearing a uniform Alice drooled over, which made her own middy blouse and long, white pleated skirt appear frumpy. The other girl was likely born with a silver spoon in her mouth and a top-of-the-line racquet in her hand. Alice didn't know her opponent's name, because whether it was Jane or Judy or Jennifer, it wouldn't have meant a lick to Alice. At only seventeen years old, but, more importantly, having played for only two years, Alice was too wet behind the ears to know the who's who of tennis.

In fact, she was too new to know much of anything about tennis. She only picked up a racquet to begin with because her oldest brother, Dan, insisted it was more ladylike than playing baseball with the boys.

"You can hit a tennis ball just as hard as a baseball," Dan reasoned.

Alice could.

With her first swing, she fell in love with tennis. She became obsessed with the satisfying *thunk* of the ball striking her racquet. How rewarding it was when her timing was on and she hit it perfectly. Or when the ball went exactly where she wanted it to go.

More than anything, Alice coveted being in control.

She glanced again at her opponent. The other girl was chatting with her coach, strategizing while changing into a new game blouse.

Alice sat alone. Her shirt stuck to her with sweat.

Feeling inferior was an emotion all too real to Alice off the court. But put her on a court . . . now, that was the great equalizer. It didn't matter that Alice's background was more humble. Both girls had a racquet, the same out-of-bound lines, and a net to hit the ball over. At the end of the match, whoever played best won.

Alice so badly wanted that to be her. The biggest problem she faced going into the third set: her heels were on fire. Which, frankly, made being the better player damn near impossible. She blew out a breath and tucked her short, blonde hair behind her ears, repositioning on the bench, seething in pain. A moment later, another person dropped beside her.

"Miss Marble?"

She nodded to the man.

"Let me have a look at those feet of yours."

"You're a doctor? You look like one."

It was the white hair, bushy eyebrows. The stethoscope around his neck also helped.

"Thank you, I suppose," he said with a smile. "Now, off with your shoes."

"It won't be pretty," Alice warned him.

"I once drained an abscess as big as my hand."

Gingerly she removed her battered shoes. Alice's socks already had holes from overuse. Now they were also bloodied. While she removed them, the doctor made a clucking sound. When he set his eyes on her bare skin, he sucked in a breath through his teeth.

"Sweetie," he started, stopped. He shook his head. "You've been playing for days with blisters, haven't you?"

At this point, the days had smushed together. But it was the finals of the British Columbia Clay Court Championships, and Alice had played three rounds, a quarter final, and a semifinal to get there.

Frankly, she still couldn't believe the Northern California Tennis Association invited her to go as their representative. Yes, she'd won a few junior tournaments to get on their radar. But she was just a kid. A kid without a coach or tennis club. Without a sponsor and all the fancy equipment. Without any real tennis knowledge besides to hit the ball as hard as she could when it was blasted over the net at her.

Originally Alice almost had to reject the invitation. An answer she would've delivered through tears. Her family, now that Dad had been gone a few years, barely had the money to buy new socks, let alone send her to another country, even with the tennis association giving her a stipend of seventy-five dollars to go toward her expenses. She didn't have the heart to ask her ma for the rest. Instead, Alice did the odd job. Jobs, really. And she sold her old glove and bat. Still, she'd come up short.

Then a mysterious envelope arrived in the mail—no sender, hence the mystery—with three twenty-dollars bills inside. With that very generous donation, the measly amount Alice had earned, and the association's stipend, she'd been able to make the trip north.

And now that she was at the Jericho Club, she couldn't blow it. She'd come too far and still had so much to prove. There was just that little problem that she could barely walk, let alone run.

"Can you fix me up, Doctor?"

He pressed his lips together. "Miss Marble, your blisters are infected, badly. I'm surprised you've made it this long. And as a medical professional, I am bound to tell you that it's unsafe to continue playing."

"I just need enough bandaging to get me through this last set. Can you do that?"

To prove a point, he gently pressed gauze to her heel. Alice cringed and tears sprung to her eyes.

Someone shouted a warning that the match would resume in two minutes. She rolled her neck, feeling defeated, feeling angry, feeling like she was going to let down everyone who believed in her.

Truth be told, Alice didn't know where the idea came from—a stroke of brilliance, perhaps—but she asked the good doctor if he had any scissors in his bag of tricks.

He did.

Without a minute to spare, she hacked at the heels of her shoes, cutting out a square shape in both.

The doctor's bushy eyebrows were sky high.

"Tape?" Alice asked him.

It was the best she could think of to keep on her backless footwear.

"Well, I'll be," the doctor said, shaking his head as she wrapped the tape in figure eights around her ankles and the bottoms of her shoes. Alice hoped that response meant respect as opposed to thinking her a foolish kid.

All she could think was, *Well, I'll be finishing these games, this set, and this match.*

Alice jogged back to the court. She could do that now without wincing. That was already a victory. So was the fact it was her turn to serve. That gave her an advantage as she'd much rather be the one slamming the ball over the net than the one receiving it. And slam she did, taking the first game. She even won the second game, despite her opponent whacking the balls at her. Four more to go.

Alice could run, jump, stop, and start better now. Back in Golden Gate Park, she always played on dusty asphalt courts, the only courts available to her in the public parks. This was her first time on clay, and she didn't hate it. Despite the surface being slicker and it being harder to find her footing on the gritty surface—hello, blisters, as she slipped around—the game moved slower. And now, with her modified footwear, she was making it to most balls pain-free.

Someone shouted her opponent's name. Henderson. Alice's attention caught on it. No one knew her name. No one was shouting it. No one was in her corner. Maybe someday that could all change.

If she worked hard enough.

The ball came off Henderson's racquet. Alice zeroed in and ran, sliding over the clay, it moving under her feet, as if she were skating, trying to time her swing perfectly to return the shot.

Henderson handled it, approaching the net.

So did Alice.

They exchanged a series of rapid-fire volleys until Henderson unexpectedly lobbed the ball at Alice, sailing over Alice's head, forcing her backward. She leaped up and connected with the ball with an overhead that cracked like thunder.

Men were the ones who smashed the ball. And in the short amount of time Alice had been playing, she hadn't seen a lot of women leaving their feet.

"It's unladylike," she'd heard an older stuffy lady say at one of her early tournaments.

Did Alice care?

Nope.

Why wouldn't Alice jump if it meant reaching the ball and winning a point?

The ball zoomed over the net, much to the crowd's delight. Maybe things were changing and tennis was becoming less stuffy.

Alice's point.

Alice's game.

Henderson won the next.

Then Alice.

Eventually they were tied 6–6. And tennis had a pesky rule of winning by two.

In the end, Alice did.

She fell to her hands and knees, her ridiculous bare, bloody heels pointing to the sky. But she'd done it. She'd won her first tournament on foreign soil. And all she wanted was more, more, more.

Chapter 3

How remarkable to return to California from Canada with the victory—and $6.37 left over from her stipend.

Alice's mother always taught her to pay it forward. Or in this case, pay it back. Alice still didn't know who her mystery donor was, so she returned the six dollars and change to the tennis association who had believed in her. What a feeling, one that made her want to play tennis morning, noon, and night.

She couldn't. School. But Alice played whenever she could, both at the public courts and at local tournaments when her ma could afford the entry fee.

Alice was over the moon when the tennis association came calling again as summer vacation began. This time they wanted her to go east. Like, all the way across the country east to New York to play in a few tournaments before the big shebang at the National Championships at a place called Forest Hills.

She swallowed hard at the thought. The opportunity was huge. So was the distance. Then her stomach dropped at the practicality of being able to go. Her family's financial situation still hadn't changed. Her dad was gone forever. Her mother still had Alice, a younger brother, Timmy, an older sister, Hazel, and two older brothers to look after, even with Dan and George both working full-time. They dropped out of school a few years ago to do just that. And, unbeknownst to Alice until recently, Dan had been pulling extra shifts since she'd won up north.

"When the next big tournament came along, I wanted to have the money ready for you," he said. "It's a great help that they're paying for you to get out there and to put a roof over your head. But I can take care of the rest."

"Dan . . ." A thick throat kept Alice from saying any more than that. But with her oldest brother, she really didn't need to.

"Ma . . . ," Alice said when it was time to leave for the train station. Her mother had tears in her eyes and Alice reminded her, "God bless, angels keep."

It was a prayer Alice's ma had taught her when she was little. Over the years, the prayer had shortened to those four words, but it began longer: "God bless us, and angels keep us safe from harm."

Alice's mother nodded. "I'll write you every day." But then emotion overcame her. Alice wasn't sure if it was fear or pride she saw on her ma's scrunched-up face as her mother muttered, "My baby girl . . ."

But as she managed the long train ride to New York's Grand Central Station, as she retrieved her bags and navigated an underground tunnel to the Roosevelt Hotel, and as she signed her name on the hotel's ledger, she'd never felt older. Never more like a fish out of water too.

The hotel was fancy. So was her suite, with its high ceiling, floral walls, and other details and embellishments Alice didn't have the names for.

A bellhop delivered her bags with a smile. All but hearing her ma's voice in her head, Alice pressed a dime into his hand.

"Not necessary, Miss Marble," he said, returning the tip. He dipped his head. "Good luck on the courts to you."

Alice had a feeling she'd need it. Tennis was more than just a physical game; it was mental. Anger, frustration, or self-pity lost just as many points as an ill-timed swing. Alice learned that early on. And as she lugged herself and a tennis bag to the stadium at the West Side Tennis Club, her hand tightened on the strap. If Alice thought the hotel was out of her league . . .

She blew out a breath, reminding herself that being intimidated wasn't her style. Alice was cocky, almost to a fault. The kind of girl who lettered in softball, basketball, and track at her high school, who waltzed onto a court without the heels of her shoes.

Feeling less-than? Not feeling like she belonged? That was something new, a whole different ball game to navigate. Alice's opponents were bred for the game and lived at ritzy boarding schools and attended tennis academies. But once they stepped onto the court, they'd be equals. Right? The great equalizer? That was what she'd always told herself. But this time felt different. These eastern girls were good—and knew their way around a grass court. Would it feel similar to the asphalt court Alice was used to or the clay courts from Canada? She had no clue.

During warm-ups Alice watched them, bottom lip between her teeth, fighting to keep her jealousy at bay as the other girls worked with their coaches. Yet there was Alice, having no one but herself. Fortunately she had a photographic memory, and she used it to mentally collect their movements, hoping she could use some of what they were being told in her own game.

A mooch. That was what she was. Nothing more than a beggar swiping leftovers from someone else's plate. Alice groaned; wasn't that the mental thinking that could hurt her during a game? She may've gotten into tennis because her brother put a racquet in her hands. But now that she had a grip on it, she wanted to be the very best. She needed to prove herself. She needed to exceed expectations. And now, in New York, she needed to make the fact that her brother had worked overtime for the past year worth it.

In her first match, Alice won the coin toss, choosing to serve first. With her serve, she tried to pull her opponent out wide, but the other girl handled the return with no problem. On grass, Alice's delivery was slower, the bounce lower on account of the softer surface. Alice tracked the ball high as it whizzed back at her. She swung overhead with all her might. And whiffed, coming up short, the ball going over her racquet and the power of her missed swing leaving her off-balance.

Alice shook it off; she wasn't the tallest player. In time, she'd know what to jump for and what was beyond her reach. For now, she refocused, despite the reaction from the crowd not making it easy for her. Nor did the coach's very loud jeer that his player had Alice on the ropes. She was certain her cheeks were flaming red as she threw the ball up in the air to serve again.

Her opponent returned. Alice returned with a backhand, gripping her racquet so tightly her knuckles were at risk of bursting through her skin.

Hard. Hit it as hard as you can. Pray it's too fast for her.

In a blink, there was the ball again, nearly bringing Alice to her knees to hit it before a second bounce. By the time she recovered, the ball was back on her side—Alice nowhere near it.

Her opponent looked to her coach. He mouthed something. Something Alice couldn't make out. But whatever he said, the other girl nodded and returned to play with a steely resolve. Then, too quickly, the match was over.

Alice's cheeks were so hot at that point her skin could've been on fire. She'd lost 1–6 and 0–6.

Alice heard the grumblings. How *she* was the junior champion of northern California.

She didn't think it could get any worse. The universe laughed at that. Alice had come east for a string of tournaments that would culminate with the National Championships at Forest Hills. But when Alice reached this final, monumental tournament, her name was nowhere to be seen on the lineup. Did the powers that be not think her good enough? Even though she'd been invited to come east to play in *all* of the tournaments?

Alice wanted nothing more than for the earth to open up and swallow her whole.

Instead, a special meeting was called. Alice didn't know by who. And—for the first time in the blasted history of Forest Hills—they did a new draw with Alice's name included.

Only, Alice couldn't help questioning if it was a pity entry. Did the tennis association actually want her included?

When it came time for Alice to play in the first round, she couldn't get her head in the game. Her first appearance at Nationals ended right then and there. She lost in the first round and couldn't bear even stepping foot in the dressing room afterward like some imposter. Instead, she blended into the stands, head in her hands, and watched some *real* tennis players. Maybe she'd learn a thing or two. Or a million.

"The papers are going to be brutal," she heard a woman sitting beside her say.

Alice closed her eyes; she'd been recognized, and she let out a snort. "Wonderful."

"They're going to call you husky. And slow. And say how you weren't worth all the trouble to get you into the tournament. They'll say to go back to California."

She lifted her gaze to the woman and muttered, "Is this a pep talk?"

The older woman smiled. "I'm husky. I'm from California. And I, too, have lost in the first round before"—she leaned into Alice, a surprising intimacy—"Three times."

Who was this woman? Helen Moody was the only player Alice knew, that all tennis hopefuls her age knew.

"Three times?"

"Don't make me admit it again. It was a long time ago. But listen—you've got a lot of tennis ahead of you. Get yourself a good coach. Work on your ground strokes, consistency, and strategy. Figure out how to use all that power of yours."

For the first time in hours, maybe even days, Alice smiled. But she couldn't bring herself to say the words *I can do that.* Not when she couldn't afford a coach and the sting of losing was still so fresh.

"This is just the beginning, Alice. One day you'll be playing at Wimbledon. When you do, take notice of the words above the entrance."

Alice sat straighter. "What do they say?"

She leaned into Alice again. "You'll see for yourself."

Chapter 4

Alice settled into the theater's seat, her shoulders relaxing. Dan was beside her. She'd been back from the "tournament that will not be named" for a week or two. Maybe three. What was time when you'd lost all direction?

She'd graduated from high school with no immediate plans.

Her tennis career might be over before it ever truly began.

And . . . she didn't know what was next, beyond a blissful hour and a half of Marion Davies in *Going Hollywood*. She was more than ready to be transported to Tinseltown.

Dan shifted toward Alice. "Tell me what she said again?"

She scrunched her brows. The opening credits were still rolling.

He prompted, "The tennis champion."

Oh. Her. *That*. Alice licked her lips. Heat crept into her body as she thought about the powwow she had in the stands after getting demolished on the court. Mostly because she hadn't known who she'd been talking to, until another player told Alice after the fact.

"It was Mary K. Browne."

Whose name Alice *should* have known considering the superstar had won the US Championships *three* times.

"And she said you could have a lot of tennis ahead of you? Yet you haven't played in nearly a month. You've never gone that long without playing."

"That sounds very judgmental."

He shrugged. "Just getting the lay of the land, Allie. You know I'm your biggest fan, but . . ."

"But what?"

Someone shushed them, which was completely unnecessary; the film hadn't started. Alice shot a glare at the husher and focused again on her brother.

"But you need a coach we can't afford to keep going. You said so yourself. So if that racquet of yours is only going to collect dust in the meantime, maybe it's time for a backup plan. I wish I had the chance to finish school." He raised a palm when Alice opened her mouth. Not that she knew what she'd even say. An apology? He originally dropped out because of their dad's death, not on account of her tennis aspirations. He went on, "You *can* continue classes though. Why don't you apply to the University of California? Sit for the entrance exams, at least. You can try for a scholarship. It's an easy commute, so you can live at home while you complete your education and give yourself some more time to see what you want to become."

A tennis player.

The best *tennis player in the world.*

In an instant, the thoughts erupted in Alice's head. In the next second, she was on the verge of a cold sweat in the already chilly cinema. She'd been the biggest negative Nancy about tennis since returning home, all because she wasn't sure how she'd ever compete with those east coast girls without a coach. Could she do it on her own? She had the drive. But how far could she go being self-taught?

Dan was staring at her for a response. What had he even said? Something about her future? It wasn't something she wanted to think about in this moment. Being at the movies was her escape. She wasn't poor here. There was no one to prove herself to.

Instead of answering about her future, Alice threw a useless fact at her brother. "You know, Marion Davies always wanted Bing Crosby as her co-star in this film, but Mr. Hearst, the money behind the film, said no because he didn't like Bing's singing style. But then the director, Raoul Walsh, and the composer, Arthur Freed, convinced him. And now"—she gestured to the film, Bing appearing on screen—"Here he is. It's amazing what the right connections can do."

Dan shook his head. "Read that somewhere, did you? That memory of yours is unparalleled."

"In an interview," she said under her breath. Then she gestured again, this time a flapping of her hand, telling her brother to pipe down. If only her mind would quiet too. But Dan had gotten inside her head. Did he not believe in her? Is that why he suggested Alice sit for entrance exams? Was she the only one who saw tennis in her future? Maybe having a backup plan wasn't the worst idea in the world. So much for her cockiness. Alice apparently left that on the grass in New York.

To: Ms. Alice Marble
From: The University of California

Dear Ms. Marble,

On behalf of the University of California, I am pleased to offer you admission as part of the entering class of fall 1932. This offer is being extended to you as a result of your outstanding secondary school records, entrance exam scores, and a fascinating thesis on the character of Eliza Doolittle in George Bernard Shaw's play "Pygmalion."

As a student of the University of California, you will follow in the footsteps of distinguished scholars who've studied at one of the world's premier universities, forge lasting friendships in your quest for intellectual growth and paving your way to a bright future.

Furthermore, you have been invited to interview for the Regents' and Chancellor's Scholarship. Please contact the registrar's office to schedule your interview time. To complete the enrollment process, please submit the included forms.

Again, congratulations and welcome to the University of California!

Sincerely,

Robert Gordon Sproul

Robert Gordon Sproul, B.S., L.L.D., President of the University

Standing at her mailbox, letter in her hands, Alice let the words sink in. She'd been accepted. Dan would be pleased. But was she? The opportunity to interview for help with tuition was good. She twisted her lips and began choosing her steps up the broken cement steps toward her white frame house.

Ma would be pleased too.

Alice bobbed her head. *College.* She considered it further. Alice had tried not to give it much thought after she applied. Since then, it'd been months of sporadic tennis on her beloved asphalt courts, lots of downtime reading, picking up the odd job like folding clothes at a boutique, helping Timmy with his homework.

She'd been on the courts all morning, where every whack, smack, and crack off her racquet filled Alice with life. But would she ever be good enough to play on grass or with the hoity-toity girls from the east?

She adjusted her bag over one shoulder and eyed the letter again.

Congratulations.

Alice needed the universe to give her a clear sign. Was this letter it? She turned the knob on the front door and stepped inside, calling out, "I'm home," and immediately stopped in her tracks. "Oh."

They had company.

Chapter 5

Seated on the Marbles' couch, legs crossed at her ankles, the woman looked prim and proper. A sleek bob perfectly in place. Nails painted a tasteful light pink. Blouse and skirt without a wrinkle. Somewhere thirty to forty, if Alice had to guess.

Dan was perched on the edge of their dad's old chair like he was ready to jump up at any moment and show their guest to the door.

The woman smiled.

Alice wasn't sure what to make of her. She wasn't their typical drop-in, not that they entertained much company.

"Alice," her mother said, standing from where she sat beside the woman on the couch. "This is—"

"Eleanor Tennant," the woman said in a British accent, on her feet in a wink, her hand extended.

Her handshake was firm, exactly as Alice expected from the put-together looks of her.

Alice turned to her ma, prepared to follow her lead. When her mother said nothing, Alice sat on the closest piece of furniture: an ottoman. She placed her tennis bag on the floor. Not knowing what to do with the college acceptance letter, she folded it and left it on her lap.

"Alice," Ms. Tennant said, taking her seat again, "it's so nice to finally meet you."

Finally? Alice smiled, not knowing how else to react.

"You see," Ms. Tennant went on, "you've been on my radar for quite a while now. I'm a coach."

"A tennis coach," Dan interjected, as if the explanation was needed.

Alice's mind whirled at the mention of that vocation as she again tried to gauge her ma's reaction: lips pressed together. It was an expression that wasn't entirely out of place. Her mother often held her tongue. And her opinions. Alice often did the opposite. Of both. "And you're here because you'd like to coach me?"

Ms. Tennant smacked both hands against her thighs. "That I am."

The prim and proper woman had some bite.

Alice's mother cleared her throat. "Having Ms. Tennant as your coach is something we began to discuss while you were out, sweetie."

In Alice's chest, her heart began to beat wildly. Her very own tennis coach. With her eyes, she tried to communicate with her ma: *but the cost.* How could they ever afford it? And why was this woman knocking on her door after Alice's horrible performance in New York? She leaned forward, edging herself closer to the conversation. "And?"

"And," Dan said, "it's a lot to consider."

"That it is," Ms. Tennant said, "so let's keep considering. Alice, I've a plan for you and me."

The way she said it contained such confidence that Alice was ready to agree to anything this woman offered. Instead, Alice pumped the breaks and tried to remain levelheaded. "I'd like to hear what you have in mind."

Alice glanced again at her ma, who seemed more relaxed at the mention of a plan, the clasp of her hands not as tight.

Ms. Tennant did a snap point. Alice almost laughed. "Smart girl. Many of the tennis families move to Los Angeles. It's where the coaches are. We can play comfortably all year. But I know that's not an option for your family, Alice. So what I propose is a unique partnership that makes this not only realistic but also affordable for your family and, for me, more accommodatable. Every few months you'll spend a few weeks with me in Los Angeles to practice together. Your mum will owe me nothing. You'll earn your court time by helping me train my other students and by helping with my secretarial work. When you're not with me, you'll be here with your family. I've tapped some contacts and I've arranged for you to take on clerical work at Wilson Sporting Goods. They'll pay you forty dollars a month, and they've agreed to a liberal leave policy for when you're with me in LA."

Alice's mouth hung open. Ms. Tennant had figured it all out. Tennis. A job here. A job there. No need to disrupt her entire family. A means to make it all happen. A fully realistic path forward for Alice to play tennis at a higher level. Everything she wanted was within her reach, handed to her on a silver platter. Still, Alice was astonished, made evident by her response, "I don't know what to say."

"You'll say yes, of course," Ms. Tennant said in that English accent of hers.

Alice chuckled, the sound gobbled up by Dan's stern voice. "I'd like to hear more about what makes you qualified to coach someone with Alice's potential. Why should we pick you?"

As opposed to all the other coaches lining up at their door? His words should've bolstered Alice, but they only made her feel self-conscious, when the real question was why Ms. Tennant wanted to coach *her*.

"Because I see potential in Alice. Have seen it since she began winning those junior tournaments. Her ground strokes are lacking. We can work on that. But she's powerful. She's got quick feet. She's got heart." Ms. Tennant trained her no-nonsense gaze on Alice. "When you lost in New Yor—"

"You were there?"

She shook her head. "No, but I have many friends who were. Mary Browne, for one. She told me how you didn't bury your head in the sand. You went to the stands and watched the other players. You *wanted* to be there. Most players who were embarrassed the way you were would have been out of there faster than you can say Jack Robinson."

Alice scrunched her brows.

"Just a saying my parents used to say," Ms. Tennant offered. "Anyway, I see something in you. I have for a while. You're all shiny and new, ready to be molded into one of the best tennis players this world has ever seen."

"Alice *will* be the best, nothing less," Dan stated.

Ms. Tennant smiled, then tapped her pointer finger against her other hand. "We need a win at Nationals." She tapped two fingers. "We need to get Alice on the Wightman team. Not necessarily in that order." Three fingers. "We go after Wimbledon. That's the end goal. She wins Wimbledon and she's the best in the world. Would you like that, Alice?" She winked, not waiting for a response, and said, "When I saw my horoscope the other—"

Dan groaned.

Ms. Tennant pressed on, "When I saw how it said to take the leap with an unturned stone . . . well, I knew it was time to put this plan of mine in motion. So here I am."

"Ms. Tennant," Ma began.

And Alice knew what she was going to say next. Her mother didn't put any stock into astrology. She also hated overpromises. After her dad's car accident, the doctor professed he'd recover. Then he got pneumonia. They lost him on Christmas Eve. Alice cleared her throat, also clearing away the vivid memory she wished her brain could let go. "I can do it, Ma," she insisted.

"See," Ms. Tennant said, "that is the exact attitude I am looking for in one of my players. Reminds me of myself. I've never been timid about going after what I want. A Taurus through and through. Case in point, I'm here." She grinned. "When I was twelve, I stole a tennis racquet. I know, I know, shame on me. It all started because I saw a woman carrying it as she walked down the street. She looked confident, strong, and I felt compelled to follow her. She ended up getting onto a horse-drawn bus, but I didn't have the fare."

"Let me guess, you snuck on?" Dan asked in an even voice.

"I like you," she said to Dan, an effective way, Alice noticed, to dismiss him while also complimenting him. "No, I ran right alongside the bus until she got off at the Golden Gate Park. A place I know you're familiar with, Alice. Where you yourself got your start. I watched her play, enamored. And I just had to have her racquet for myself. The first racquet of many. The others I've paid for." There was that wink again. "Do you know who that woman turned out to be?"

Alice honestly didn't have the slightest clue.

Ms. Tennant's voice rose to a level way too high for their modest living room. "Mrs. Golda Meyer Gross, one of the top women players at the time. After watching her play—and boy, could she play—I was convinced I could play just as well. That's why I needed the racquet. Once I had it, I played whenever I could on the public courts. Playing anyone who'd go against me. Most were better.

Good thing, too, because that's how I learned. It's also how I got noticed by Maurice McLoughlin."

At Alice's blank stare, she explained, "A former National Champion. We'll brush you up on who's who, don't worry. Well, Maurice McLoughlin offered me two gigs, both at the Beverly Hills Hotel. As a hostess and as a coach. Douglas Fairbanks Sr., Enid Storey, Norma Talmadge, and Marion Davies . . . Oh, I see *those* are names you know, Alice. You like the films, huh?"

Alice hadn't realized how her face had lit up.

Ms. Tennant laughed. "I give all the big stars private lessons now."

Dan nodded. "So you've only ever really been a coach?"

"Again, a hard hitter, aren't you, Daniel. I played too. There was a time I was ranked third in the country behind Molla Mallory and Marion Zinderstein." She pointed a finger at Alice's brother. "A very close third."

The room was silent after that. Would Dan put this woman to the test again? Would their mother finally chime in? She'd never been against Alice playing tennis, not really. She'd just been leery of the cost of it all. Ms. Tennant had an answer for that. But Alice's mother may not be keen on her baby girl living with an English woman she'd known for all of fifteen minutes.

Alice repositioned in her seat, the university acceptance letter crinkling in her lap. Without a second thought, Alice slipped it beneath her legs. Out of sight. Out of mind. No place in this conversation.

If her mother said yes, this piece of paper would be forgotten faster than she could say Marion Davies. Alice's hands found a prayer position. She existed on bated breath. Her future hinged on a single word. She couldn't even look at her ma. But she heard her—loud and clear.

"I think this all sounds agreeable, Ms. Tennant."

It wasn't a single word, but it was certainly the right set of them.

"Fabulous," Ms. Tennant said with an honest-to-god fist pump. "It looks like my investment is paying off already."

Alice cocked her head. "What do you mean?"

"I told you you've been on my radar for a while, caught wind of your name after you started winning those junior tournaments. A girl who played on the same public courts I did once upon the time. Alice, I'm the one who sent you that anonymous donation. And please, call me Teach."

Chapter 6

From the second Alice accepted Teach's offer, she felt indebted to her new coach. Actually, Alice's stomach flipped upside down at the thought that she'd been indebted to the woman longer than she even realized.

Alice couldn't let her down. Or her ma, her brother. Herself. Anyone.

Before Teach left Alice's house, she caught her mother trying to steal a private moment with Teach. "I'm putting my daughter and my trust in your hands, Ms. Tennant. Make her the best, just as you said you would. Give her what I can't, no matter what."

Alice resisted the urge to throw herself at her ma, to hug her, to thank her, to assure her mother that she had done more than enough. But she knew she wasn't meant to hear her ma's words, and she blinked away the emotion.

A few weeks later, Alice was in a taxi, having just disembarked from five hundred long miles on a bus. It was her first visit to Teach. Alice's knee wouldn't stop bouncing.

The taxi stopped in front of a small brick house. Alice shouldered her bag and soldiered her nerves before she knocked on the door.

"Alice!" Teach said in greeting. "Aren't you glad you only have to make that trek a few times a year?"

Alice laughed. "Tennis is worth it."

"That's the spirit. And frankly, I'm glad you're the one who said it. From here on out, tennis is life. Many sacrifices will be made. Understood?"

"As long as none are chocolate," Alice said playfully. Teach only stared; a quip wasn't what her coach wanted to hear. She quickly course corrected. "Yes, ma'am," then busied herself with removing her coat. She slung it over the back of the couch.

"I own hangers and have a coat closet for that, Alice."

She stumbled over something that came out as, "Right, of course, sorry, okay."

Teach was already walking deeper into the house toward a tiny kitchen. "Dinner's at six. No sweets after seven. You'll have a curfew. To be determined. Some people need more sleep than others. At the breakfast table by seven. No chocolate. I'm kidding. I'm not a tyrant. But listen to this next one. This next one is serious. No boys. They're only a distraction. Tennis first. Always. Oh, this is Gwen. She's my sister."

Alice fumbled to put her jacket away while she leaned to the side to get a view into the kitchen, trying to match Gwen's name with a face. Alice didn't see this phantom sister until she joined the women in the kitchen. Gwen sat at a table, focusing on a crossword and grumbling under her breath, "Ellie and her rules."

"Don't call me that," Teach admonished.

Gwen chuckled to herself.

Teach checked her watch. "Why don't you go make yourself at home. Second door on the left. Dinner's in one hour. Don't be late."

Alice wouldn't dare.

She began to turn, but Teach's words stopped her. "One more

question, Alice."

"Yes?"

"My rules. Are you okay with them?"

"Will they make me the best tennis player in the world?" Teach nodded. "Then yes."

"Good answer."

***

"Again," Teach demanded.

Alice blew out a ragged breath and checked her anger. Was she overjoyed to have a coach? Absolutely. Was actually having a coach—one who was blunt and tireless—an adjustment? Yup.

At this point, Alice had been serving for the past hour. Without, it felt pertinent to add, Teach bothering to return a single ball.

"Listen, Alice, you have wonderful ball sense and game instincts. However, strategy . . . we need to work on strategy. The serve is the most important shot you have for three reasons. You know them?"

"Because I'm in control."

She held up one annoying finger and stared at Alice, waiting for number two.

Alice's shoulders rose and fell. "I don't know, Teach. What are the others?"

She added a second finger. "You get two shots at a serve before losing a point." And a third digit. "Your serve sets the precedent for the rest of the point. Right now, your serves are all over the place. I'm going to return this one, though, okay?"

"About time," Alice said under her breath. She bounced the ball, preparing to toss it up in the air. She'd just started the motion and . . .

"Wait!" Teach screamed.

Alice nearly threw out her back.

"What shot are you planning on doing after I return the ball?"

"I don't know."

"Well, you should. You're in control, remember? You said so yourself. That means before you even throw the ball up, you should know where you're hitting it, what I'm going to hit back, and what shot you'll hit in return." Teach cocked her head. "Name the shots for me."

"This feels like school."

Teach raised a well-plucked brow. "Then you should do fine. Your brother boasted about your good marks. Now, if you don't have the ability to choose the right shot at the right time, you won't be successful on the court. Period. Done. The end. Put a fork—"

"Please, stop."

She put a hand on her hip. "I'll stop when you know as much as I know. So go ahead and tell me all the shots in your arsenal."

"Forehand, backhand—"

"Uh-huh, uh-huh. The ground strokes. Which, I'll say, need work. Your serves are decent. Your hand-eye coordination and footwork are better than decent. But your ground strokes are terrible."

Alice's brows crinkled with annoyance at her coach's candid evaluation of her. "Volley," she said, deadpan, wanting this little lesson to end so she could finally serve the ball.

"Yep, volleys at the net."

Alice blew out another breath, her agitation growing that Teach chimed in after everything she said. "A serve." Alice quickly added, "Overhead." She wracked her brain, bringing to mind a match from New York. "A lob."

"Okay, not a bad start. Then of course we have all the variations of top spin, flat, slice, inside out, inside in." Teach gestured in a circular motion. "Being you're right-handed, what we need is for your forehand to be your best shot. If you get the ball on your forehand side, your chances of winning the point greatly increase. That means when you serve, I want you to plan for your next shot to be a forehand. Let's perfect that first. Later we'll add more to your arsenal."

Alice nodded. Bounced the ball. "May I serve now?"

"I don't know what you're waiting for," Teach said, but with a sly smile.

Alice rotated the ball in her hand, readying to toss it.

"Wait!" Teach demanded.

"What now?"

"Your shirt is untucked."

"So?"

"In," Teach said pointedly.

Alice grumbled, but did as her coach asked.

Finally, Teach let her serve, and, *finally*, they played.

Alice won three points. Teach won nothing. Alice had her at 40–0.

"Now," Teach said, "don't get overly cocky. Forty-love is a pivotal point in any game. Either you're a point away from winning the game, set, or even the match. Or you're the one with the egg, and you're a point away from losing."

Alice scrunched her brows. "Forty-love? Wouldn't thirty-thirty be more important? You're tied. It can go either way."

Teach sighed. "It's a dangerous point, yes. But I'm playing chess, not checkers. In our case, you're the one who's up. You could be bold and take chances. But if you lose this point, you give me a foot in the door. That may be all I need to kick it down. To get in your head. And stay there. Tides turn fast in tennis. Pivotal," Teach said, stressing the point. "It's do or die time, Alice. Forty-love can make or break you."

This time it broke her.

She tried to remember what Teach drilled into her head as they played, to plan her second shot. Move Teach side to side. Use her position to take time away from Teach. Vary her pace. Push Teach deep behind the baseline. But Alice was off her game. Teach had *her* doing all those things. And when Teach won by two, with Alice still at forty, Alice stormed off the court, frustrated, defeated, feeling as if it was only a matter of time before she was without a coach . . . again.

Teach said nothing as Alice left the court. But as Alice peeked over her shoulder at her coach, the tightness of Teach's lips spoke volumes. Alice knew tennis was equal parts mental and physical. So when Alice returned to the court the next day, she stayed put, even when Teach showed her frustration with twisted lips.

And when she muttered.

And ran a hand through her hair.

A week passed, then two.

More muttering, more twisting, more mussing.

"What?" Alice said eventually. "I'm obviously not doing what you want."

Teach sighed. "It's not that. Not exactly. You're improving."

"Could've fooled me."

Her eyes seared into Alice's, so much so that Alice had to look away. "You *are* improving. But something is off. I just can't quite put my finger on what it is."

Teach closed her eyes, shook her head, turned on her heel. Then she whirled back, a newfound energy behind her gaze. "I've an idea."

***

"We're off to see the wizard, Alice."

"Excuse me?"

Teach snorted, clearly amused with herself. From the driver's seat, she glanced at Alice. "There's someone I want to watch you play."

"So you're not giving up on me?"

"Not until I earn my sixty bucks back."

Alice rolled her eyes, though inside she was feeling a large amount of relief. As an afterthought, she asked, "Does this wizard have a name?"

Teach didn't respond. Figured. But Alice quickly realized from their surroundings that whoever this so-called wizard was, he or she was a big stinking deal. In Teach's Buick they climbed and climbed a narrow road, switchbacking alongside the Pacific, until they reached a mountaintop estate surrounded by countless acres of woods, groves, and orchards.

A valet quickly ushered them from the car, the automobile swiftly disappearing from the round drive. Eyes wide, Alice waited for whoever was to greet them next. She hadn't been expecting an older man. Lanky, balding, extremely tall. Piercing gray eyes that immediately began piercing into Alice. Most decidedly not a disembodied head. "This her?" he asked Teach, his intonation giving little away if Alice was what he expected or not.

"The one and only," Teach said. Now her voice was upbeat. Or perhaps *hopeful* was a better word.

"Let's get on with it, then."

At that, the man—who hadn't yet told Alice his name—led them to his tennis courts. "Show me what you can do, Miss Marble."

Teach jogged to the other side of the net. The wizard sank into a lawn chair. Alice served, then immediately recovered behind the baseline, awaiting Teach's return. Alice had set herself up for a forehand down the line. But Teach was expecting it from her. Alice hit it back. Teach hit. Alice won the point. And they went from there—for about ten minutes—before the wizard unfolded from his chair to his full towering height. Without a glance in Alice's direction, he crossed the court to Teach, Alice's return barely missing him. Teach let the ball bounce past her.

The man shook his head. "That wasn't good tennis, Eleanor."

Alice's mouth fell open. Which she then quickly and firmly shut to grind her teeth. He saw ten minutes. Ten. That was it. And sure, she hadn't been playing great lately, or even right then, but she was still *seventh* in the country. Who was he to make such a remark after seeing so little of what she could do?

In fact, Alice intended to show him a little more . . . specifically how outraged his comment made her. She chucked her racquet; it soared over the court's fence and landed in what she hoped was a precious-to-him citrus grove. A few oranges plopped to the ground.

Teach frowned.

The man seemed nonplussed. Alice guessed a multimillionaire didn't care about a few ruined oranges.

Then Teach gestured toward Alice in a "come on, give her a chance" type of manner.

"No," Alice muttered to herself. He was watching her as some sort of audition to see if he wanted to help coach her. She felt it in her gut. And Alice's stomach turned over at the thought. This man clearly wanted nothing to do with her. The feeling was mutual.

Teach set her calculated gaze on Alice, asking, "Do you know who he is?"

"No." And she hated how disrespectful her answer sounded, especially in her cold tone. Alice's own embarrassment cooled some of her steam.

"This is Harwood White. He's truly a wizard, seeing what I

can't when I get stuck. He's helped me with some of my former top players." Teach was about to tick them off. She didn't disappoint and ended with Ruby Bishop. "Do you remember her, Alice? If my memory doesn't fail me," she said mockingly with a tap of her temple, "Ruby beat you at the junior championships. Hmm."

Mr. White choked on a laugh but quickly recovered. "All right, Eleanor, as subtle as ever. You'd said she's a Libra?"

Teach perked up. "Sure is. Alice is a fighter. Plus she was born on the twenty-*eighth*."

She said the eighth with emphasis. Teach once said something about eight being a powerful number.

Mr. White's head bobbed and, when he spoke, he muttered, as if he were giving himself a pep talk. "Excellent sportsmen. Perfectionists. Steadfast with their goals. And eight. A good omen. A good omen, indeed." He clapped his hands together. "I'll watch her some more. See if I can pick out what you're missing."

Alice hadn't expected this change of heart, especially after she targeted the man's citrus. But now both Mr. White and Teach were beaming at her and she found a smile budding on her own face. "I guess I'll go get my racquet?" she said, still a bit unsure. "I'd like the chance to fix whatever I can in my game."

Mr. White nodded curtly. "On one condition."

Alice wasn't dumb enough to say, "anything," but she gave him an, "I'm listening."

It almost got another choked laugh from him. He crossed his arms. "My condition is that you do what I say. No fussing. I won't tolerate any more sass. No time for it."

Alice swallowed. How much did she actually need this man? She already had one coach telling her when to sleep, when to wake, what to eat. She was surprised Teach didn't count the number of times she chewed her meat. But Teach's expression communicated that they needed this man—the wizard. Alice already owed Teach too much not to give this a try. So she bit the bullet and stuck out her hand for Mr. White to shake.

Chapter 7

"Your grip is part of the problem," Whitey said matter-of-factly. It was what he asked Alice to call him.

"My grip?" She looked down at her hand around the racquet's handle. It looked fine to her. "I didn't know there was any other way to hold it."

Whitey rotated the handle a quarter turn in her hand.

"Ew. That feels weird."

He raised a brow.

She said no more.

"Okay," Whitey went on. "Before, you gripped as hard as you could and hit as hard as you could. Am I right?"

"Yes, sir."

"Don't call me that."

A hint of a smile emerged on Alice's face.

If she wasn't mistaken, Whitey had the start of a grin too. "That's not how we want you to generate power, though," he said. "Hold the racquet loosely. Just two fingers and your thumb around the end. You'll have more muscle and less spin on the ball. It'll do wonders for you on grass courts."

Alice wanted to shrink away at the mention of *that* surface. She felt sure Teach had told him all about her lack of skill there. "It still feels weird," she mumbled about the grip.

He shrugged. "It'll take time. How about we try hitting some balls?"

Teach lobbed to Alice while Whitey instructed her.

"Step into the ball."

"Full swing."

"Follow all the way through."

"Get to the net."

"Ruby Bishop beat you at the net."

"Stay there."

"Nope. Don't hit the ball."

"What?" That stopped Alice.

"Meet the ball, Alice. This is a game of control, not a game of strength."

She scrunched her brows, the ball bouncing past her. "But you said we were changing my grip because it'll give me more muscle."

He pressed his lips together and Alice quickly said, "Let's go again."

"That a girl. Look. The control will come. What's important is you're creating as much power as you did before, but with less effort."

Alice nodded.

"The control will come," Whitey assured her again. "With practice."

"That I can do."

"Now pretend I'm Ruby Bishop. Get to the net."

Alice did.

They practiced for hours, until Alice was certain she'd collapse if she hit one more ball.

"Ruby wouldn't stand a chance if you played her again," Teach said afterward. They were in the car, heading home. Teach beamed, a literal glow coming off her at how pleased she was. "I knew that man would fix you." She bounced her hand off the steering wheel. "Your grip. Didn't see it. But your new hold will do wonders against someone like Bonnie Miller."

"Who?"

"Junior champion of Los Angeles. Her serve and forehand carry a lot of topspin. The ball bounces high. Gives her opponents an easy shot every now and again."

"Tell me about the other girls I'll play against."

"Thought you'd never ask," Teach said, clearly happy with her protege.

Helen Jacobs, a formidable serve and a strong, consistent backhand.

Sarah Palfrey, a clever player with a great net game.

Helen Moody, Herculean legs, a mighty swing—especially on her forehand—but less-than-stellar footwork.

Kay Stammers, an aggressive leftie with a good forehand.

Teach went on and on. Carolin Babcock. Sylvia Henrotin. Midge Van Ryn. Dorothy Bundy. Josephine Cruickshank. Dorothy Workman. Gracyn Wheeler. The who's who of tennis. All of them vying for the same accolades.

Alice committed each and every detail to memory. She'd use it to beat each and every one of them.

San Francisco Gazette

Saturday, July 22, 1933

Marble Plays It Like a Man!

SAN FRANCISCO, CALIF. - After a poor showing at Forest

Hills, then disappearing from the tennis world entirely, Miss Alice Marble is back. And with a bang!

Word is Marble has been training with dynamic duo Harwood "Whitey" White and Eleanor "Teach" Tennant. Whatever they are doing is working, while also turning women's tennis on its head. It appears Marble has not only adopted an aggressive serve-and-volley style generally reserved for the boys, but she's also hung up her skirts in favor of mid-thigh shorts. This is the biggest shake-up in women's tennis clothing since 1920, when Miss Suzanne Lenglen traded in her long skirt, petticoat, and high-necked blouse for a one-piece sleeveless dress. It comes as no surprise the rest of women's tennis followed. Will that be the case with Marble's new style sense, along with her new game?

The tennis world cannot wait to see.

Next up for Marble is her second trip east, first to play at the Maidstone Club as a qualifying tournament to win a spot on the Wightman Cup team. If she does, she'll play in the international Wightman Cup itself. Then Marble will get another shot at the National Championships at Forest Hills. The last time Marble played on grass courts she left with a stained ego, but here's wishing Miss Marble all the success this time around.

"You're a shoo-in to make the Wightman tournament team, Alice," Teach assured her over the phone.

"Say it again?" Alice said, wrapping the cord around her finger.

"I will not. Every second of me calling you in New York costs me an arm and a leg. Yes, you'll be playing on grass. Yes, you're still perfecting your new game. But you've been winning and you're damn good. They'd be lucky to have you."

They being the American players who competed annually against England's team, a women's rivalry that'd been going on for over a decade. This year it was the United States' turn to host after bringing home the cup the past two years in a row.

Alice smiled, not because Teach stroked her ego, but because Teach knew Alice needed to hear it all again. The only thing better would be if Alice saw her coach's face while she said it. But Teach had stayed behind when Alice went east, not being able to take the time off from teaching. Alice understood that, especially when Teach supported her through the income from those lessons.

"Okay," Alice said, following the word with a long breath.

She looked down the long hallway of the Maidstone Club. A stern-looking man with snow-white hair had his eyes focused on Alice and was walking at a clip in her direction. "I think I have to go."

"Yes, go, go. Telegraph me once you have your schedule."

"I will." A few of the other girls already had theirs and Alice had been waiting to receive hers. The line went dead just as the man stopped in front of Alice. "Miss Marble, I assume?"

"Yes, sir."

"Mr. Julian Myrick," he said down his nose, which would've had a greater effect if they weren't nearly the same height and if he didn't have a large smudge on his glasses. But Alice knew the name. He was the chairman of the Wightman tournament committee, the one who signed the letter inviting her there.

"Of course, how are you, Mr. Myrick?"

"Very busy.

Alice clasped her hands at her stomach.

"I've many players to talk to." He produced an envelope from inside his breast pocket, handed it to her, and punctuated the exchange with a nod before continuing on his way.

Alice quickly opened the envelope to find her schedule. She made a sound she couldn't identify.

"Mr. Myrick! Mr. Myrick," Alice called, chasing after him, a response that appalled him if the curling of his upper lip was any indication. "Um, sir, I believe there's been a mistake. This has me playing both singles and doubles in a three-day span."

She pointed to the schedule as if it were his first time seeing it. He'd look. He'd laugh at the oversight. It'd get fixed. All would be right in the world again. But that was not how it went. "Yes, that is correct, Miss Marble," he said instead. "Mrs. Moody has afforded you the honor of playing with her in the doubles."

Alice cleared her throat. "Yes, and it's quite the honor. But three—"

"As I've said, I've other players to talk to, Miss Marble. Do not make me regret your invitation here."

"Of course," she said quickly, her heart pounding at an alarming rate. "But perhaps I could only play the doubles with Mrs. Moody in this qualifying tournament then?" *And save the singles for the Wightman's Cup next week*, she left off.

By the way his nostrils flared, he understood Alice's implication, which she realized too late Mr. Myrick interpreted as audacity at suggesting he undergo another draw for his tournament.

Mr. Myrick let out as exasperated huff. "You are counting your chickens before they hatch, Miss Marble." He said her name as if she were diseased. "In order for you to qualify for the Wightman Cup team, you first have to prove yourself by making a good showing here in both singles *and* doubles."

But all those games in three days? And why both singles and doubles? Alice couldn't help herself from one last retort. "Is anyone else scheduled to play as many games?"

If looks could kill . . .

"Miss Palfrey and Miss Babcock have no need to do so. They come from a long line of tennis players."

And Alice didn't. Her stomach sank, squeezed into a knot, and she teetered on the edge of being sick. She knew it'd accomplish zilch to remind Myrick how she'd won two singles tournaments to Sarah Palfrey's solitary win. Same with Carolin Babcock. But she'd already pushed too far, as evident by the rising color in the tournament director's cheeks.

"Furthermore," he said between his teeth, "I will be the judge of who's to play. Not you."

He said nothing more. Off he stormed.

Alice stumbled backward until her heels hit the wall, needing the support of it. Playing both singles and doubles in a three-day period . . . The third day could be four matches alone if she made it to the finals in both. Alice didn't know how she'd pull it off.

***

"Anyone else dying from this heat?" Alice asked the women in the dressing room. There was about twenty-five of them in the tiny space, but only a few of the girls were clustered in Alice's corner. Last time she was in New York, she was so intimidated by the pedigree of the other players and by her lack of a coach that she didn't even notice the hellish humidity. But this time Alice pulled at her neckline.

A few of the girls laughed. One was slowly shaking her head, a look of total disbelief on her face. "Honey, I don't think it's the weather getting to you. I think it's how much tennis you're expected to play."

Alice cringed. "Yeah. That. Mr. Myrick hates me."

Carolin Babcock chuckled. Her curly, dark hair certainly got the memo it was humid. "It's because you wear shorts."

Alice cocked her head. Maybe. But it was more about where Alice came from, and she knew it. But she didn't want to admit that to these other girls. Why put the idea in their heads if it wasn't already there? Bad enough it was in Alice's.

"What'd your coach say about it?" Sarah Palfrey asked. Somehow her slick, dark hair was defying the weather.

Thinking about Teach didn't make Alice want to cringe any less. "I haven't telegrammed her yet. Steam would blow out of her ears if she knew what I'm up against. I'm relieved she's not here, actually. Carolin, what's it like having your ma travel everywhere with you?"

Carolin raised her brows. "She's out of earshot, right?"

They all laughed. But laced within Alice's lightheartedness was a tinge of jealousy. Carolin came from money, the granddaughter of a banker who was so rich he had theaters named after him, and her father was able to uproot the entire family and move them to Los Angeles so Carolin could focus on tennis.

"So you're going to do as Myrick says, Alice?"

"Huh?" Alice said, distracted by her thoughts.

Sarah tried again. "Myrick . . . are you going to play all the matches he wants you to do?"

Alice shrugged. "What choice do I have? I want to make the Wightman team."

"What about Helen Moody?" Carolin said, lowering her voice despite Helen not being in their dressing room. She always requested a private space. "Are you excited to play with her? One would think Myrick would be nicer to you since *Mrs. Moody*"—she said the name in a hoity-toity voice—"Requested you specifically as her doubles partner."

One would think. Alice shook her head, then admitted, "It'll be interesting. She's the only player I knew of when I got my start."

"Word is she has a hurt back," Sarah added.

"Get ready to do all the work," Carolin said.

Alice pulled a face.

"Yeah, good luck with that, Alice," Sarah said with a sly smile. "But not too much luck. I want to make the team too."

Carolin rolled her eyes.

"What?" Sarah questioned.

"You know what," Carolin insisted.

Alice sure didn't.

Carolin went on, "There's no way you're *not* making the Wightman team, Sarah, when your coach is Mrs. Wightman."

Sarah's face wrinkled up in annoyance. "It's no guarantee."

Was Alice's jaw on the floor? She wouldn't be surprised. She hadn't known who Sarah's coach was. Teach had never told her, perhaps because she knew Alice would immediately feel . . . what? . . . slighted, intimidated . . . that Sarah had this very clear leg up.

Once more Alice was reminded that she came from a very different background and circumstances than her peers. She also reminded herself something else: the court was the great equalizer.

And for the first two days, that sentiment rang true. She won her first matches handily—and without the sun completely draining her. This third day, though, she'd play semifinals in singles and doubles and, God willing, finals in both as well.

In her singles match, Midge Van Ryn . . .

A right-handed baseline player with a game that was based more on technical skills and accuracy than on power . . .

took Alice to three long sets before Alice put her away. It'd been hot as Hades. Walking off the court after Van Ryn, Alice's temples pounded to the beat of her heart. An official approached her. "Miss Marble, Mrs. Moody is waiting for you to warm up."

"Right," Alice said. She'd known the turnaround was going to be tight. But, bloody hell—as Teach would say—she barely had time to change her clothes before she was back on the court for the doubles semifinal with Helen, who didn't look impressed by Alice's so-called tardiness. Alice resisted an apology. None of this was her doing. Instead, Alice suggested they start loosening up. Immediately Alice recognized two things.

The first: Teach had been spot-on. Helen Moody had killer instincts and an unreadable demeanor. The press even called her "Poker Face."

The second: the rumors of Helen's back injury weren't fiction.

Alice's stomach twisted into a knot. Facing two of England's top players, Betty Nuthall and Mary Heely, would be a formidable match as it was, partly because Teach hadn't provided reconnaissance on either of those ladies. But Alice knew Helen Moody usually brought a mighty swing, strong legs, and less-than-stellar footwork. And this time, a hurt back. That'd make her swing not as mighty and her footwork even less dazzling. Alice soldiered herself for a battle.

A battle that went to three challenging sets, where Alice pulled most of the weight. Legs heavy, arms dead, head spinning, they won, but it took Alice a few seconds to even realize they had. Without missing a beat, Helen began strutting from the court, her face turned toward the cameras.

Alice stumbled after, hands shaking, gaze wobbly, skin on fire, knees weak. Like an apparition, a reporter was suddenly in front of her. "Nice work out there, Miss Marble. You ready to do it all again in an hour?"

"An hour," she parroted.

Someone took her arm, saying something about getting Alice out of the heat. Then she was inside. Cold towels were on her forehead. In slow motion, the wall shifted into the ceiling. Voices hovered by and over her, the words *singles final* cutting through the din of noise.

Alice still had her singles final to play.

In less than an hour.

She couldn't quit. She wouldn't let Myrick's ridiculous schedule and his prejudice against her on account of her humble beginnings beat her. She owed it to Teach and her family to give this everything she had.

Alice sat up, dots appearing before her eyes. "I'm fine," she said. "I just need some tea."

Tea, a sugar pot, and milk were placed in front of her. Alice poured in sugar until an attendant took the pot from her.

"Eat some toast," another attendant suggested.

"Yes, okay," Alice said.

She answered the same when she was told the match was beginning. She stood on her side of the net. Alice's opponent, the name escaping her, stood on the other.

Everything hurt from fatigue. Alice wished the problem could be solved by cutting off the heels of her shoes. But there wasn't an immediate cure for exhaustion. Dehydration. Whatever this was.

Alice yanked at her shirt, pulling it away from her perspiring skin. Then she awaited her opponent's serve. At first, it didn't come. Instead, the woman approached the net, leaned over it. Alice stayed on the baseline. Still, her opponent mouthed, "Are you sure?"

Alice nodded.

The game began.

The woman made quick work of her.

Winning the singles final went down the drain.

Qualifying for the Wightman Cup team likely going with it.

Yet Alice still had the double finals to play with Moody.

"Miss Marble," an official said, immediately leading her inside. "I don't think you should play anymore."

Alice shook her head just as the devil himself joined them. "She has to play," Myrick said. "A crowd has come to see Mrs. Moody play and I won't disappoint them."

Alice rolled her eyes. Even that hurt. But she'd play.

In the dressing room she clumsily changed into her fourth outfit of the day.

She was led to Helen's side on the court. Helen said nothing.

"We love you, Alice," someone in the stands called. Similar sentiments followed. Many spectators were on their feet.

Alice raised an arm, thanking them for their support, emotion welling in her throat. For the first time she felt seen, appreciated.

But if any of them thought she'd miraculously pull off a win, they were sorely mistaken—and that feeling was the pits. So was the fact Helen and Alice lost in two straight sets, no need to play a third and final one. In a blink, Helen Moody was gone. A hand was around Alice's waist, guiding her.

Someone called out, "One hundred and eight, Miss Marble. You're remarkable."

She didn't understand.

The person holding her up clarified. "That's the number of games you played today, Miss Marble. Four matches, eleven sets, one hundred and eight games. All in nine hours on the hottest day of the—"

That was the last Alice heard.

Chapter 8

Now

October 12, 1940
Sherry Netherland Hotel, Manhattan

Sounds of imagined bombs explode in Alice's head, a testament to how strongly she feels pulled toward the war in Europe. Only men have been conscripted so far, but it's not stopping women from joining up. Tennis friends like Helen Jacobs are volunteering. There are rumors of the Roland Garros Stadium in Paris, where Alice has played, being used as a *centre de rassemblement*, an internment camp where so-called political dissidents and foreign nationals are being detained. London is bombed day and night, the press calling it the Blitz.

It makes Alice sick. All of it, along with a sense of helplessness about all that's being lost. Especially with what she just read in today's paper. The All-England Lawn Tennis Club has been bombed.

It's where Wimbledon is held. She grips the newspaper tightly, so tightly she wouldn't be surprised if ink stains will forever be a part of her skin.

After the onset of the war and after this year's Wimbledon was cancelled, the All-England Lawn Tennis Club underwent a transformation. The car parks became vegetable gardens and housed pigs, chickens, ducks, geese, and rabbits in makeshift wooden shelters. Fire, ambulance, and first-aid groups occupied many of the club's buildings. Regiments marched through the main concourse where the best players in the world once walked.

Then yesterday, she reads, the German bombs sought to destroy tennis's longest running and most prestigious destination. Two explosives struck the golf course at Wimbledon Park. Another landed at the club's entrance. A fourth flattened the club's tool house. But the final one unsettles Alice the most. A bomb careened straight through the roof of Centre Court.

She throws the paper down. She leans away. She swallows roughly. And Alice feels it even more, a pull toward the war to avenge what she loves most. Tennis.

She's sent care packages to her English friends. Still, she's idle to do anything of real worth. Alice sighs and taps the paper with her finger. And decides to do something about that pull.

The door to the US Army enlistment office flies toward her as she tugs. Alice's enthusiasm is on full display.

Inside, the room is lined with enlistment posters and landscapes. She recognizes Mount Rushmore before focusing on a man behind a desk.

"Hello, soldier," he says in greeting.

"That's the plan," she says.

He introduces himself as a sergeant and gestures toward a seat across from him.

"I'd like to volunteer for the WAVES."

"That a girl," he says, removing the pencil from behind his ear, then proceeds to ask her a litany of questions. After a standard inquiry about her health, his pencil stills.

"Miss Marble," he says. At this point he firmly places down his pencil. Never a good sign.

"What is it?" Alice is used to Teach. She shoots straight from the hip. But this sergeant is rolling the words around his mouth.

Finally, he sighs. "The thing is, Miss Marble . . . And I know this is going to sound funny being you're only newly twenty-seven—"

"In my prime," Alice cuts in.

"Yes, a top tennis player."

"*The* top."

He nods. "I have no doubt you can run circles around most of the men. But the problems you've faced with your health in the past classify you as unfit *now* for the US Army."

Alice grinds her teeth before opening and closing her mouth like a fish, until all she can do is repeat the word. "Unfit?"

"I'm sorr—"

She waves off his apology. "Do I look sick?"

"It's not how I'd describe you. No, ma'am."

"Yet I'm being penalized for something from *years* ago?"

He taps his finger on a list of health conditions, specifically on hers from once upon a time. "Unfortunately my hands are tied. I'm sorry."

Alice stands abruptly, her chair screeching. "Then my hands will do a world of good with the navy."

She hightails it out of the army's recruitment office and stomps the thirty minutes it takes to reach the navy's. The cool air and the fact there's a wait inside the office does her temper some good. By the time Alice is sitting across from a naval officer, she's written off the whole shebang with the army as a fluke. "I'm here to serve."

"Wowee," the officer says. "Miss Marble in the flesh."

"In tip-top shape, straight off of winning the National Championships."

She gives him a winning smile, only for her muscles to tense when he slides a health questionnaire in front of them. The tendons in her neck are likely protruding when he, too, after asking her the prerequisite questions, puts down his pencil. "Miss Marble, it'd be my pleasure and honor to see you in a navy uniform but—"

"My health history precludes me."

He licks his lips. "I wish it didn't. I've no doubt you'd make our country proud."

Alice is on her feet. Einstein once said how the definition of insanity is doing the same thing over and over again but expecting different results. Still, Alice tries the Marines, then the Coast Guard.

***

"Not as you had hoped?" Teach asks as Alice walks into their hotel room, pausing in the small kitchen area where Teach is lighting the burner. After winning Nationals at Forest Hills, they decided to stay in New York for a while longer. Teach's sister, Gwen, holds down the fort in Los Angeles. Back home, her family will have to go a bit longer before Alice is able to see them again. Her ma insists she understands, even saying, "I knew what I was getting myself into when I said yes to Ms. Tennant, baby girl."

Here in Manhattan, Teach has been busy running clinics and

speaking to various groups on "The Will to Win." And Alice has been . . . floundering, not entirely sure what to do with herself. To stay in shape, she's still on the court every day. Sometimes she assists Teach with her lessons. Sometimes she takes Spanish lessons for something more to do. Mostly Alice has been pining for a way to get involved in the war. That door was just slammed closed, multiple times.

"Don't act like you're not cheering inside," Alice says bitterly. If an opportunity doesn't include tennis, limits Alice's tennis, or interferes with Alice's tennis, Teach isn't a fan. Even with Spanish lessons, Alice had to argue with Teach, explaining how knowing the language could help if she ever plays against a Spanish speaker like Lili de Alvarez, who, unrelated, was one of the women who paved the way for Alice's decision to wear shorts on the court. In an earlier Wimbledon, Lili showed up in a "divided skirt." The *Associated Press* claimed "the costume, despite the freedom of movement it gave, was not very becoming." Alice claims it was practical.

"Well," Teach says, cracking an egg to fry. She pauses. "Would you look at that. Two yokes. We have some good luck coming our way."

Alice shakes her head.

Teach raises a brow. "Fine, *I* have some good luck, if you're not interested." The egg sizzles and Teach wipes her hand on a towel before precisely folding and hanging it again. She joins Alice in the bedroom area. "I won't lie that the armed forces rejecting you to kingdom come doesn't work to my benefit. L.B. Icely has been calling me daily about you."

"The president of Wilson Sporting Goods?"

"The very one. He wants to discuss setting up a pro tour for you."

"So no more competitive tennis?"

"Alice, there *is* no competitive tennis at the moment. Besides"—Teach rubs two fingers together—"This means getting paid. Wilson Sporting Goods will sponsor it."

Alice's head bobs at that. There's no prize money for winning amateur tournaments, even Wimbledon. Money is made through clinics, speaking engagements, sponsors, putting your name on clothing or equipment. Those types of things. A pro tour could go a long way toward Alice feeling like she's helping to share the load. Get paid. Play tennis. A win, win, right?

Teach echoes this sentiment as she says, "Why not earn a lump sum while you're playing some of your best tennis? Your horoscope today is all about timing. And here we are . . . the timing of the war is lousy, yet the timing of this tour may be just what you need."

Alice snorts. "For such a logical woman, it always gets me when you use my horoscope as a bargaining chip."

"It gets you?"

"It gets me amused. I don't know. Astrology feels like the opposite of a rational argument."

"My use of zodiacs, horoscopes, and astrology is perfectly rational. I'm a logical thinker. I objectively use all information available to me to develop a reasonable solution or a viable idea. The movement and positioning of the stars and planets is just that: informational. Why wouldn't I consider all the facts?"

"Fine. But what about your obsession with superstitions?"

"We all have our quirks, Alice."

Alice smells something burning. Teach's egg. She hides a smile. Teach no doubt pretends she doesn't notice, her hands going on her hips, her gaze intent on Alice. "Now, are we going to continue to discuss my psyche or the opportunity to make some money for yourself? For us?"

Oh, Teach definitely knows her bargaining chips. In this case, she knows full well Alice feels like a freeloader ninety percent of the time. Teach gives and gives. Alice takes and takes, with little contributions along the way, like designers paying Alice for her input. Mainly they want her name attached to the brand. And now Icely wants her name attached to the pro tour. But if she says yes to that, is she giving up on trying to help in the war? She hasn't yet tried the Red Cross. She may not be joining Helen Jacobs in the WAVES, but at least she'd be in uniform.

Alice twists her lips just as the telephone rings.

Teach lets out a low growl as she returns to the kitchen. She growls again, most likely a reaction to her burnt eggs. "If that's Icely for a second time today I'm going to ring his neck. I want you to do the tour as badly as he does, but does the man have no patience? I'm inclined to not answer," Teach says in her British accent, "because I can."

Alice rolls her eyes and answers the phone.

"Miss Marble," a man says on the other side of the line, "I hear you visited with a recruitment office today."

"Excuse me?"

The man's comment has caught her off guard. But also, his deep, upper-crust New York accent is unbelievably familiar. Alice tunes in nightly to the caller's fireside chats and hears this very voice come out of their radio.

"Mr. President?"

Knees suddenly weak, Alice drops onto the hotel bed. But is it impolite to be sitting while conversing with the president of the United States? Or do you only stand when the president walks into the room?

Teach is suddenly in front of her, dipping and weaving to move into Alice's line of sight. She swats at her coach to go away, then Alice scratches her brow, overwhelmed but aware the line of questioning that just ran through her head is ridiculous considering FDR can't see her right now. Unless . . . she leans to the side, peering around Teach and eyeing the apartment building across the street for any of the president's binoculared men keeping tabs on her. No, she's being ridiculous.

But—also—Alice is on the phone with Franklin D. Roosevelt, the thirty-second president of the United States. That's not something that happens every day. Or ever.

Sweat has built on her forehead.

"Miss Marble," he's saying, and she does her best to focus. "As I said, my office received a telephone call today from a recruitment office."

Alice's gaze darts around the room. "Which one?"

"You visited more than one?"

"I visited all of them," she admits hesitantly.

He guffaws, and she can't help but thinking the president is belly laughing on account of her. What a strange day.

"Now," he says, regaining composure, "I am even more interested in speaking with you. You see, I put a bug in the army's ear about keeping an eye out for a candidate for a program I'd like to green light. Imagine my delight when I hear you went knocking. Miss Marble, you're exactly the athlete I've been looking for to co-chair a physical fitness program for the Office of Civilian Defense. It'll be a great service to your country during these unique times. You'll speak to factory workers, college students, and women's groups about the value of exercise. I'd have you team with Jack Kelly. Being in the sport's world, I trust you've heard of him. You're our national treasure in tennis. Mr. Kelly holds the title in rowing. Anyway, what do you say? You'd be compensated, of course."

Are you even allowed to say no to the president? Is there some law against doing such a thing? Not that Alice would. He wants her to be part of the Office of Civilian Defense. It's not the WAVES or the Red Cross, but it feels like *something.* She lets out a long exhale, head bobbing, thankful for the opportunity. Then she asks a question she immediately regrets. "Is there a uniform?"

Alice slaps a hand to her forehead.

The president is silent a beat before saying, "A detail we can hash out later. But is it a yes, Miss Marble?"

"Yes, sir," she says, standing. Teach moves again as if they're dance partners. "I'd love that, sir."

"Wonderful. Look for a call from my secretary to get the ball rolling. Good day, Miss Marble."

Alice stammers out a good-bye, still stunned by the past thirty seconds of her life. Blindly she puts the phone back into the receiver.

Teach has a hand on her hip. "Do not tell me that you called Icely 'Mr. President.' Guaranteed that'll go straight to his—"

"That wasn't Icely. And sorry, Teach, but the tour will have to wait. Duty calls."

Chapter 9

"Before I forget. The president said something about your interest in a uniform?" Mrs. Abrams says.

Alice is following President Roosevelt's secretary down a long hallway. "Oh," she begins, cheeks heating, "it's fine. I'm fine. Unless you have something in white?" Alice adds as a joke.

But given the way Mrs. Abrams is looking at her, lips pursed, she may think Alice is serious. Alice is about to assure her of the quip when Mrs. Abrams stops in front of a door. "Here we are, Miss Marble. Good luck to you."

"Good luck?" When the president calls you personally, one would logically think you've already passed the test.

"We must make certain you have no deep, dark secrets," Mrs. Abrams says, face serious.

"Nothing shady in my past," Alice responds with a toothy smile. But isn't that what someone sketch would say? Alice is inside her own head too much. Typical tennis player, always overthinking, overanalyzing, and self-sabotaging.

She blows out a breath and crosses the threshold into a room where two men sit on a single side of a table. Their suits are identical. Their postures—hands folded on the table—are matching.

Their side parts mirror one another's.

"Hello," Alice says.

"Welcome to Washington," the one on the left says.

"This should be painless," the one on the right adds.

Alice settles into the lone chair on her side of the table and smooths out a wrinkle in her trousers. I should hope."

"We just need to ask you some questions," Left says.

"A routine check," Right adds.

"I'm an open book," Alice says, gesturing to a random jacketless hardcover on the table.

"Then as I said, this should be painless." At that, Left asks Alice about a trip to France she took in 1934.

"I came east and stayed at the Waldorf-Astoria until I left via the SS *Westernland* on May eighteenth."

"You went there to play tennis?"

"For tennis, yes. The trip took six days before we docked at Le Havre."

"Where'd you go next?"

"Paris."

"What mode of transportation?"

"Train. I stayed at the Ritz Hotel. Would you like to know who I bunked with?"

"Sure," Right said.

"Carolin Babcock and her mother."

"What'd you do next?"

"A plethora of things. The Louvre. Team practice at the State Roland Garros." Alice's stomach sours at the words.

"Are you all right, Miss Marble?" Left asks.

She licks her lips. "Yes, of course, just not a fan of what the State Roland Garros has become in these times of war."

Right nods solemnly, then asks, "This wasn't your only time

in Europe?"

"No, thankfully I returned in 1937 to play at Wimbledon, though it started off on a troubling foot with three days of rain."

She goes on to tell them of the tournament. Of her scores. Her opponents. Even specific strokes Alice did at specific moments.

Left and Right glance at each other a number of times.

"My second trip to Wimbledon was in 1938. This time I took the SS *Champlain*."

"Remind me of the ship you took to France in 1934."

"The *Westernland*," Alice answers, not skipping a beat.

Left's eyes drop to his notes. He nods discreetly.

"First time you played at Wimbledon, how many days of rain did you say there was?"

"Three."

"And who did you play in the quarterfinal round?"

"Which time? In 1937, I played Hilde Sperling. In 1938, I faced Simone Mathieu, the French champion. And in—"

Right clears his throat.

"Is there a problem?" Alice asks. "I'm trying to answer your questions to the best of my abilities."

"We can see that, Miss Marble. What gives us pause is that you're answering the questions too well."

"I wasn't aware that was a thing."

"Your recall of every trip you've taken is astounding. It sounds practiced," Left chimes in.

"Practiced? I didn't have a cheat sheet prior to walking in here."

"Yet you know every date, every stroke, every detail," Right points out.

Alice frowns while also giving a slight shake of her head. She reaches for the book on the table, flips to a random page, skims it, closes it, and folds her hands atop the table.

She recites, "'When you engage in actual fighting, if victory is long in coming, the men's weapons will grow dull and their ardor will be dampened. If you lay siege to a town, you will exhaust your strength, and if the campaign is protracted, the resources of the state will not be equal to the strain. Never forget: When your weapons are dulled, your ardor dampened, your strength exhausted, and your treasure spent, other chieftains will spring up to take advantage of your extremity. Then no man, however wise, will be able to avert the consequences that must ensue.'"

Left's forehead is a bed of wrinkles. "Are you a fan of *The Art of War* then?"

Alice shakes her head. "I've never read it before. And after that passage, I'm not sure I'll ever have an interest in doing so."

Right looks astonished. "You just recited it word for word."

It appears Alice has to spell it out for them. "I have a photographic memory. Eidetic. Whatever you'd like to call it."

She stifles a laugh when Left adds it to his notes—in all capital letters, misspelling *eidetic*.

"I think we're done here, Miss Marble," Right says.

"So you don't think I'm a spy or I'm up to something nefarious?"

Left smiles. "No. Not yet, anyway."

There is, in fact, a uniform. It is not white. It is quite drab. And green.

Still, when the cameras point at Alice during a publicity engagement in Washington for the president's new fitness program, she gives them her best smile. Jack Kelly is beside her. With him being a few inches above six feet and Alice at five seven, he towers over her, actually.

There's a renewed flashing of bulbs before a hand lightly grips Alice's arm. "This way, Miss Marble. I need a moment of your time."

"Of course," she says, blinking away the spots in front of her eyes.

A man not too different from Left or Right leads her to a quiet corner of the room, tucked behind the lights and backdrops. "I'll be curt," he starts.

She resists the quip of "Okay, I'll be Alice." He doesn't seem like the right audience.

The man continues, "In your new role, we also need you to attend parties and political functions. Your unique skill set will come in handy. Observe. Take mental notes. Then report back to us weekly."

"Report back what?"

"Anything or anyone unpatriotic."

"Oh," she says. "I can do whatever it takes."

"You can tell whoever asks that you've been invited to these functions on account of your involvement in the president's physical fitness program. You'll be given a typewriter with a Spanish keyboard to conceal your work from your roommate."

He must mean Teach. And Alice won't bother to ask him how they know she's been taking Spanish.

All she does is agree—a touch of exhilaration spiking her heart rate at the thought of being a spy for her country—and returns to her spotlight beside Jack Kelly.

Notes from FDR's Annual Message
January 16, 1941

Pay higher taxes: too many tight jaws to pinpoint anyone specific but not surprised!

Wartime sacrifices: no reactions??

America entering war: man (brown hair, mustache, brown suit, third row right side) scoffed. Heard called Erik?

Make more weapons for GB and more aid for GB: same man!! Played it off as a cough

Freedom of speech. Freedom of worship. Freedom from want. Freedom from fear: nothing of note

Man on the left side row 5 made suspicious eye contact with Erik.

Need to look into this Erik!

Alice is having fun.

Over the next few months, she attends event after event under the guise of being a guest of the Office of Civilian Defense. Afterward, she types up her notes in Spanish under the guise of completing coursework for her Spanish classes. Then Alice mails her intel to a PO Box. A real cloak-and-dagger operation. And she feels like a second-rate gossip columnist. She wouldn't mind being a bona fide one.

At a recent shindig, she was seated next to the great-great-grandson of Emma Willard. A revolutionary woman who was inducted into the Hall of Fame for Great Americans at the turn of the century and who has, to this day, a school named after her.

"She believed that women could master topics like mathematics and philosophy without being limited to the subjects taught at finishing schools."

"Hear, hear," Alice said, raising her glass to Emma's great-grandson. "She sounds like the type of woman more people should know about." And as Alice later sat at her typewriter, she imagined writing up the woman's remarkable story.

Maybe one day.

In the meantime, Alice continues attending events of the political and social nature, while also spearheading FDR's fitness program. The thing is, lots of the women, who Alice is flapping her gums at, work long hours on assembly lines before they go home to care for their families. Exercise is the last thing on their minds. Can't say Alice blames them.

Also can't say she's surprised when the plug is pulled on the program after only a few short months, which also puts an end to her clandestine activities.

"Done with your coursework?" Teach asks her one evening, not looking up from her book. "I trust you'll be able to understand what's said between coach and player if you ever encounter someone speaking Spanish now?"

"Most definitely," Alice says from a window seat, not taking her eyes off the snowflakes that dance through the illuminated beams of street lights. "Fitness program got the kibosh too."

"Lots of idle time on your hands now, huh?"

"Seems I do."

Teach licks her finger, turns a page. "Mm-hmm. Lots of time. No money coming in any longer either. A pity."

She knows her coach is being playful, but sometimes Alice's brain is her own worst enemy. She can't help thinking of her future and tennis and the debt she still feels like she owes Teach for all she's done for her. Again, Alice thinks how Teach gives and she takes. Alice twists her lips. "Think that offer from Icely still stands?"

Teach claps her book closed.

Chapter 10

It's as if Icely knew tennis would always surface to the top of Alice's life. The next day a tour schedule is proposed.

How convenient . . . she's opening in Madison Square Garden that *very* night.

All Alice has to do is sign on the dotted line, her signature earning Teach and her a whopping twenty-five thousand dollars. A Buick Roadmaster convertible sedan costs just shy of three grand. They could buy a slew of them. Not too shabby. Or with rent in Manhattan being fifty bucks a month, they could move from a hotel to an apartment and stay in New York much longer than anticipated.

A smile breaks on Alice's face as she enters the arena that evening and grows even larger at seeing an old friend, now her tour mate, Mary Hardwick.

"Mary!" she calls. "Glad to see you safely on this side of the pond."

They meet at the net, and knowing the cameras are on them, the women shake hands, prolonging the greeting while the press does what they've come here to do.

"Ah," Mary says in her thick British accent, her face dropping.

"The guilt at being here and not back home." But then she must remember the cameras and a smile finds Mary's face once more. "I've been helping with relief efforts at the very least. And now a portion of our tour proceeds are going toward war charities. This'll be good fun, Alice."

"When is tennis ever not fun? Especially with a sell-out crowd? And for a good cause?"

Alice gives Mary's hand a final squeeze and backpedals toward her baseline, tilting her head back to capture the full array of people who've come to see them play. She raises an arm, waving, and a roar fills the arena.

What fun, indeed.

There was a time Alice ached for the applause and to hear her name. Now it happens every time she steps foot onto a court. A true entertainer. She's won it all. Sometimes it makes Alice wonder what could be on the other side of tennis. If there's someone on the other side of tennis. What would that look like? A husband? A family? Coaching? Designing? Singing?

Honestly, it's all a bit overwhelming to ponder, and she settles onto the baseline. Once Mary and her get playing, Alice is quick to realize she's a bit rusty. She still found time to get on the court over the past few months, but the fitness program ate up much of her day. Now, her timing is off. She's catching the ball late. She's not able to get into any type of groove. Still, it's a bit startling when Mary takes the first game. Alice stares at the ground, a canvas sheet that's been laid down over the basketball court for them to play on, and tries to regroup in her head. In the many matches the women have played opposite each other over the years, Alice has never lost. It's a good reminder. Mary's strokes are firm, yes. Her defense is steadfast, yes. The problem is that Alice's attacks aren't landing the way she wants them to.

Mary also takes the next three games.

Teach once told Alice that if someone is going to beat her, she better make them actually beat her. Alice gets her feet moving. She gets to the net more quickly. She better anticipates Mary's shots. Alice plans her own. Her timing improves and, thank goodness, she begins winning games. Eventually the sets and the match.

Alice is sure the effort shows in the many beads on her forehead.

They do the whole "meet at the net and shake hands" thing again. "I'm coming for you next time, Alice," Mary says in a playful tone before walking off.

Icely takes Mary's spot. He talks under his breath, for only Alice to hear. "I love Mary's competitive spirit and I love how *you* made the game interesting."

"What do you mean by that?"

"We know you kept the game close to keep the game exciting. You're Teach's protégé, after all. Good business sense."

Alice bristles. "I did no such thing."

Mary is eighth in the world. Alice may've played badly, but Mary is *not* a picnic.

"Uh-huh," he says, like they're in on the same secret.

Alice has the urge to throw her racquet. Not something she's done in a while, nor something she'd do in front of a full arena. But you can bet your sweet patoot she's not going to have *that* exchange with Icely ever again.

She wins in Chicago.

She wins in Minneapolis.

She wins in Cincinnati.

All three convincingly, playing like the number one player Alice is supposed to be.

Alice and Mary, along with their male counterparts, Don Budge and Bill Tilden, continue to play arenas all over the country into the spring months. The newspapers proclaim how they're a box-office success, selling out upward twelve thousand seats at every match. It's lucrative for Teach too, who gives lectures and teaches clinics at each stop.

***

Before one match, when Alice is entering the changing room with an undeniable smile, Teach throws a towel in her direction. "Told you this would be good for us."

"It could be better for me," Mary says, intercepting the towel. She laughs. "I could be winning. Or I could be making what Don's making."

"Aren't we all making the same?" Alice asks, glancing at Teach.

Teach says, "You all should be."

Mary raises a brow. "You are if you're making seventy-five."

"Hundred?" Teach asks.

Though Alice doesn't think that's realistic. Not even for a second. No way he'd be offered that much less than what Teach got for her.

Mary snorts, confirming Alice's suspicion. "Not seventy-five hundred. Don got paid seventy-five *thousand* for this tour. Plus a percentage of the gate."

What? Alice doesn't say the word aloud, but her mouth moves as if she did. This time she does more than glance at Teach, who negotiated her contract for twenty-five thousand.

"That can't be right," Teach says.

"Well, I'm not just going to stand here speculating," Alice says. "I'm going to find out."

She storms onto the traveling court, head on a swivel for Icely. He's talking to some man. Alice doesn't care who he is. She taps

Icely firmly on the shoulder.

"Our star!" Icely says after he turns. "You'll have a mile-long line for autographs after this one. You're on in an hour. You ready?"

"Funny you should call me your star, with the disparity in what you're paying me and what you're paying Don."

Alice has faced prejudice before. Just the thought of what Myrick put her through releases a growl deep in Alice's throat, a reaction Icely must interpret is for him.

Perfect.

He makes a strangled noise as he uncomfortably eyes the man beside him. To the man: "If you'll just give us a moment." To Alice, as he distances them from the man: "What on earth are you going on about, Alice? Shouldn't you be getting ready?"

She puts a hand on her hip. "I know what you're paying Don. Seventy-five versus twenty-five, if I'm not mistaken."

Icely swallows hard. Guilty. Zero denial.

Alice charges on. "I don't care if he's a man and I'm a woman. Last time I checked, we're both human beings, deserving of the same opportunities. Both drawing in fans and selling out these arenas." She flaps her hand in the direction of the seats, some already filling.

"Alice, you have to understand—"

"I'm not playing," she says. Icely may be the president of the world's largest sporting goods company, but, frankly, this is bullshit. "I won't play unless you pay us the same. I fill as many seats as Don, if not more."

Icely nostrils are flaring. "You will play. Or we'll sue you."

"Go ahead!" Alice flaps a hand again for good measure. "Change my contract in the next hour or I'm not stepping foot back onto this court or the fifty, sixty, however many other courts you have planned in this tour. You'll have some explaining to do to that mile-long line of fans looking for my autograph."

Alice is seeing red when she storms back into the changing room. "How could you?" she snaps at Teach.

"How could I what?"

"It's true. You accepted a third less than what Don's making."

Teach's eyes close, and stay closed. It's clear she didn't know the disparity before today. Alice doesn't care. "It's your job to know these things, to negotiate, to make sure what I get paid is fair, yet all you did was make both of us," Alice says, gesturing between them, "look like fools."

Alice sits on the bench and begins to remove her tennis shoes.

"What are you doing?" Teach asks.

"I'm not playing. It's what I told Icely too. Not until he understands he can't pay me less on account of me having breasts."

"Good for you," Mary says.

"Aren't you mad?" Alice asks her.

She sighs. "Darling, my husband's the vice president under Icely. I've been taken care of."

Alice throws up a hand, stopping on the way down to point a finger at Teach. "Fool!"

Teach huffs. "I'll get you that new contract."

And she does. For the same amount as Don. The way it should've been from the beginning.

Chapter 11

After the tour wraps, all sixty-one stops, Alice feels adrift without the daily grind of travel and tennis. Without having a new goal to work toward. She sings a little at a night club. She helps Teach with this or that. She does a few table readings with a film producer. She dabbles with leisurewear designs for a label called Tom Boy when Straus, Royer, and Strass comes knocking. The whole time she wonders if any of it could be a replacement for tennis. Frankly, she's not sure.

Teach is watching her now as Alice pads through their kitchen. They've upgraded from a hotel to a roomy rental. Alice aimlessly opens a cabinet, the fridge. There's no chocolate in either. She wants chocolate. She pulls out a chair but doesn't sit. She opens the fridge again, expecting something dark, rich, and delicious to have suddenly appeared.

It did not.

"You need something to do," Teach says from the living room, Ethel Waters singing softly in the background on the radio. "Long term."

Alice finally sits. "I'm sure you already have something in mind that rhymes with *Dennis.*"

"You think you know me so well."

"Who's it with?"

"Bill, Don, and Mary again."

"Oh yeah? Who's getting paid the most this time?"

Teach scoffs. "The gig is exhibition matches at a bunch of military bases."

It's Alice's turn to scoff as she picks aimlessly at a loose thread on a placemat. "Those military guys want Marion Davies, not me."

"Not true." Teach motions toward Alice's dismantling of the placemat. "And stop ruining our stuff. Won't you give it a try? You wanted to help with the war, right? Oh, and didn't you say you wanted a white uniform? Consider your tennis whites just that."

"I'd been joking."

"Well, this is a real opportunity to give back to your country, Alice. The United States may not officially be in this war yet, but it sure seems like we're headed there. These men need you to keep their spirits up."

Alice shakes her head. "Laying it on a bit thick, wouldn't you say?"

Teach only shrugs, probably because she knows Alice is going to give in and do as she asks. If there's one thing that's been proven true time and time again, it's that Alice will choose tennis in the end. Before she can stop herself, Alice's mind begins to drift—to a choice years ago, to England, to a holiday in France, to a whirlwind, illicit romance Alice lost herself in. To him. To someone she once gave up for tennis.

***

The military men are not any less enthusiastic about having Alice and Mary stand before them than they would be for Marion Davies or Marlene Dietrich.

What a thrill. The amount of hooting, hollering, cheering, and celebrating Alice experiences as she travels up and down the East Coast throughout the fall and early winter months while playing for the servicemen is electric. Exhausting too.

In December, Teach and Alice rest their dogs at a friend of Teach's, a fancy film producer she's known for years named Arthur Loew. He also happens to be married to a rabid tennis fan who insisted they visit their estate, Pembroke, on Long Island.

"A bunk in a cold, draft barrack or a lavish suite, hmm," Alice first quips to Mr. Loew upon arrival.

"How did you ever choose?" Mr. Loew says. Then he snaps. "I think it's the indoor tennis court that really sold you."

Alice smiles. "Now you're speaking my language, Mr. Loew."

No matter how many famous people she's met, she'd never be so bold as to call them by their first name without an invitation. But he insists she call him Arthur. Very well. Besides, she's reminded once more about how there's something about being on a tennis court that levels the playing field. Soon she is playing doubles with the heir to Metro-Goldwyn-Mayer Studios and Loew's Theaters and two of his other guests, an Olympian skier and the under secretary of the navy. Their backgrounds and pedigree couldn't be any more different, yet they all understand what it means to hit a ball down the line, to serve an ace, to smash the ball.

It's good fun, and Alice and Paul Lehman, the under secretary, are leading 40–30.

They all turn as Arthur's butler hurries into the indoor pavilion. "Mr. Lehman, I have a phone call for you, sir."

"Who even knows I'm here?" the under secretary says with a sly smile.

"Well, whoever it is, hurry back," Alice says. "We have them on the ropes."

Paul winks at Alice as the butler adds, "It's urgent, sir."

"Oh?" is all Paul says, his pace quickening as he leaves the court.

"What do you think that's all about?" Alice asks Arthur.

"Something naval related, I'm sure. This truly is Paul's secret getaway. Only Knox knows his whereabouts."

"As in the Secretary?" Alice asks, skin beginning to prickle at the level of brass who is seeking out Paul.

Arthur nods grimly. "Knox has never called him here before, though."

More goose bumps erupt. "It must be a serious concern then if—"

"Mr. Loew," the butler says. This time he's not exactly hurrying. He's more scurrying. He looks as if he's seen a ghost. "Mr. Loew, the Japanese have attacked Pearl Harbor!"

In the tennis hall, a pin drop could be heard. Outside, Alice hears the sound of a small aircraft taking off, Paul no doubt inside and bound for the nation's capital.

San Francisco Gazette

Monday, December 8, 1941

America Declares War: Unprecedented Fury in Wake of Pearl Harbor Attack

SAN FRANCISCO, CALIF.–The United States of America has declared war on the Empire of Japan following a devastating surprise attack on the fleet known as Battleship Row at Pearl Harbor, Hawaii. This declaration, coming just hours after the catastrophic assault on the US naval base, marks a pivotal moment in world history and plunges the nation into a global conflict that will forever be remembered.

In an emotional address to the nation, President Franklin D. Roosevelt proclaimed December 7, 1941, as "a date which will live in infamy." He described the unprovoked attack on Pearl Harbor as an act of treachery and an assault on the principles of freedom and democracy for which the United States stands.

The devastating attack, carried out by Japanese aircraft, left the US Pacific Fleet in shambles. Multiple battleships, including the USS *Arizona*, were severely damaged or sunk, and the death toll is expected to be in the thousands. It is a day of immense loss and tragedy for the United States.

In the aftermath of this unprovoked aggression, the American people have rallied behind their leaders and are displaying a remarkable unity. The call for war has been met with widespread support from both the government and citizens across the nation. The United States will now join the Allied forces in their struggle against the Axis Powers, including Nazi Germany and Fascist Italy.

This sudden turn of events casts a shadow of uncertainty over the coming days, weeks, and months. As the nation prepares for mobilization, there is a determination that the attack on Pearl Harbor will not go unanswered.

If Alice felt emboldened to help with the war efforts before, that mindset is now doubled. No, tripled.

To think of the boys being shipped off who won't return . . .

And the wives who are left to mourn them. Quite a few of Alice's acquaintances and women she's met during the fitness program rushed into a marriage with their soldiers after only knowing them a short time—sometimes as short as twenty-four hours.

It's a story Alice hears more than once, and it turns her stomach every single time to think those women may be left heartbroken. War is something Alice can't understand. In tennis, there is a winner and a loser, but it's all in good fun. Save for an injury that will most likely heal, both sides walk off unscathed, a fire burning inside both players to get back on the court to either win again or redeem oneself.

In war, even after winning, so much is lost. There's no burning need to face war ever again. Alice sees that in Teach. Her coach has seen war before, and Alice thinks that's why it's not something Teach likes to focus on. But Alice can't help but fixate on it. In between playing at the bases, she begins visiting military hospitals. She sings. She plays cards with the men. She sits and talks with them. They trade stories. Often the tales turned macabre, as the mind seems to find its way to darkness during such troubling times.

At the bedside of man named Charlie, Alice shakes her head, a memory haunting her. "We can talk about puppies instead," Alice suggests.

"No," Charlie says. "Whatever it is, you've overcome it. Tell me about it."

Alice clears her throat and runs a hand through her short, blonde hair. Charlie locks eyes with her. "Well," she begins. "I was young at the time. Eleven. My best friend, Billy, and I did everything together: baseball, finding trouble, skating around town . . ." Alice smiles, a faraway expression coming over her face.

"We roller-skated a lot. Neither of us liked to move slow. We'd been skating that day. Racing, actually. I remember the sounds mostly. My skates, then Billy's clattering over the cracks in the road. Billy's laughter and his panting growing fainter as my lead increased. The rumbling of my wheels over the streetcar tracks. The sharp and sudden pinging noise of the car's warning bell. The screech of the streetcar's brakes. The horrified screams of those who witnessed Billy stumble on the tracks."

Alice needs to blow out a breath. Charlie reaches to squeeze her hand.

"It all happened in an instant. One moment that changed everything. The smell of it will forever be stuck in my head. A burnt odor. A sweet aroma from the candy store across the street. The ripe tobacco from my uncle's shirt after he arrived at the scene. He swooped me up and whisked me home."

Charlie licks his lips. "That's not easy.

Alice shakes her head.

"What happened next?" Charlie asks.

"You know, my brain protected me afterward, I guess. There's not much I can remember in the days that followed. It was all lost to me, until about a month later when I laced up my skates again for the first time. It was nice to do something I loved again. I didn't want to lose both Billy and skating."

Charlie is smiling now. "You persevered, Miss Marble. I like stories like that."

"I think of Billy still. It's not exactly the same—not like apples to apples—but when I'm playing on a clay court, it's slick. And sometimes when I'm sliding into a forehand, my brain flashes to those days with Billy. The sharp stop on a skate is similar to when I stop my momentum on the clay. Every time it happens, I smile."

"I obviously didn't know Billy," Charlie remarks, "but I think he'd be touched to know you remember him in this way. He may be gone, but it doesn't seem like you lost him after all."

"I guess not," Alice says, a wistfulness in her voice. "Hey, aren't I supposed to be cheering you up?"

"It can go both ways, Miss Marble." He taps his cheek playfully. "Especially with a kiss from the world's number one."

Why not? Alice tucks her hair behind her ears and delivers. It's the most action she's seen in years.

Chapter 12

The conversation with Charlie, though cathartic, weighs heavy on Alice afterward. After spending a long day volunteering at the hospital, she needs some tennis to feel more like herself, even if it's in the form of table tennis.

The Stage Door Canteen is just the place. It's a popular hangout for servicemen to unwind. The line for the table tennis is always a mile long.

The beauty of being Miss Alice Marble, however, is that she always gets ushered to the front of the line, where the men will gladly have her stay all evening long. Man after man steps up to challenge her. Man after man walks away in defeat, head wagging, hands clapping him on the back.

Alice beams. "Who's next?"

A naval man steps up to the table just as the opening chords to "Taking a Chance on Love" begin to be played on the piano.

"Oh!" Alice says, head perking up like one of the meerkats she'd recently seen in the Prospect Park Zoo. She pushes her paddle toward a man standing close by. "Take my place, will ya?"

At that, Alice hurries toward the music, leaning to speak into the pianist's ear. "Mind if I sing along?"

She's no Ethel Waters, but Alice can hold her own. The man smiles up at her, all the invitation Alice needs. She begins swaying before she adds a slow snap in rhythm with the music. Then she closes her eyes and sings.

Alice's eyes pop open at the sound of a rich baritone beside her. The man is tall, tall enough where Alice has to take a small step back to take him all in. She could add dark and handsome to her initial observation. A real Rudolph Valentino, after whom the idiom of "tall, dark, and handsome" was popularized during the Roaring Twenties. Valentino was considered the epitome of romance. The man beside Alice seems to have romance on the brain as well. His brown eyes are latched on Alice's.

It's not the first time a lonely serviceman has made eyes at her. She smiles politely and trains her eyes on the sheet music until her gaze betrays her, flicking back to the man. In between his verses, his mouth quirks into a provocative smile. Alice stumbles over a few words, her cheeks heating at her mistake—and at the intensity of this serviceman. With the dress blues and his insignia, Alice's guesses he's a captain in the army.

He runs a hand through his wavy brown hair, disheveling it in a way that makes Alice want to muss the strands further. What has gotten into her, besides the two cocktails she sipped on while playing table tennis?

The song is over too soon. Her heart's hammering in a way it hasn't done in a long time. Not since *him*, a man whose name she rarely lets herself think of or else the feelings will come rushing back. Alice tries to be casual now with this man beside her, but the question comes out way too quickly to accomplish aloofness as she asks, "Sing with me again?"

The man shakes his head.

"Your pick," Alice offers.

Still, he shakes his head. The pianist eyes them both, unsure how to proceed. Alice scratches her neck uncomfortably, thinking she must've imagined a shared attraction between herself and this army Valentino.

But then the man takes her hand and nods toward the tennis table. "If I beat you, Miss Marble, you'll have dinner with me."

She shouldn't be surprised he knows who she is. She comes to the Stage Door Canteen frequently and creates a scene at the table every time. Still, her pulse soars at him saying her name. At his confidence. Alice swallows roughly. "I haven't lost all night."

"I'm an excellent competitor."

"I'll be the judge of that," she says coyly as he leads her to the ping-pong table. The men make way for her, welcoming her back, stepping aside for her nameless captain to take the other side of the table.

He's good. But Alice has been playing with Dan since she could see overtop the board. She's better. Still, she's intrigued, and wouldn't mind a free dinner.

Alice lets him win. But she's not too obvious about it.

"I owe you a dinner," he says.

"You do," Alice says, already reaching for her coat. Her nameless captain truly was an excellent competitor. A fellow athlete, she surmises. Possibly golf with how smoothly he swings his arms. "Only, not tonight. It's late, Captain . . ."

"Crowley."

"Nice to have met you, Captain Crowley."

He all but pins her in place with his gaze. "Met me? This is it for now? Tell me it's not too late to walk you home?"

She likes this better, him pursuing her. "I suppose I'm going there anyway."

"Too late to come up for another drink?" Captain Crowley asks once they're outside Alice's apartment building.

"I suppose I'm having one anyway."

In actuality, Alice had no plans for a drink. She had no plans of meeting this man either. Teach will have a cow. She always does when anything or anyone takes Alice's focus from tennis. And in those times, it's tennis Alice has chosen. But these are unusual times. And Alice is certain this man will be gone in a blink, off on an assignment. Why not have a few moments of fun? Besides, Teach will be sound asleep at this hour. What she doesn't know won't hurt her.

"Why don't you have a seat," Alice whispers once they've entered her apartment.

"Nice place you've got—"

Alice shushes him. "My coach is sleeping." She removes a bottle of wine from a cabinet. "And I'd rather she not know you're here."

He raises a brow. "Oh, I'm to be a secret?"

Alice waits until she's beside him on the couch before she's answers. "It'll save me an earful. I'm just happy not to have a curfew any longer."

"Forgive me, but aren't you in your late tw—" He chooses not to finish the word.

Alice chuckles. "Late twenties, yes. But it took Teach quite some time to loosen the reins."

Captain Crowley takes the bottle and the wine opener. "Apparently not enough for us to speak at full volume." He follows his comment with a playful smirk.

Alice holds out their glasses for him to fill. "Nor enough for her to not balk at me for meeting a man." She remembers the day she arrived to live with Teach and, in her best British accent, she recounts, "'No boys. They're only a distraction. Tennis first. Always.'"

"And that's how it's been. Tennis first, always?"

The question flips her stomach and sparks a memory. Again, of *him*. She does her best to keep the emotion from her face and answers playfully, "Captain Crowley, I am not one to kiss and tell."

He laughs. "Fair enough. But, please, call me Joe."

Alice cocks her head. "I would've guessed Thomas. Or maybe Edward. John, James."

"Nope. Joseph."

She shrugs. "I suppose that's fine."

A smile erupts on his face. "You suppose?"

"Joseph Crowley." Alice sips. "Joseph James Crowley at least?"

Nope, he mouths.

"Arthur, Michael, Richard, Albert?"

Each one gets a head shake. He inches closer and quips, "You should take a sip with each wrong name."

Alice smiles. "Apparently I'd be whistled if we play that way. And I have practice early tomorrow."

"You're still practicing even with it all shut down?"

"There will always be tennis. Didn't we already establish that, Joseph William Crowley?"

"Nice try. I've followed your impressive career in the newspapers, you know."

Alice sips again, relishing the wine and the compliment. His leg is brushing against hers now. "I did *not* know that."

"You sure there's no room for romance in that life of yours?"

"Quite the forward question, Joseph Hen—"

He shakes his head.

"Drat." She swirls her wine. "The right time for romance hasn't presented itself yet."

Joseph grins mischievously. "Maybe we can change that, Alice Irene Marble."

Her mouth falls open. "How did you . . ."

He waggles a brow.

Captain Joseph Norman Crowley.

Alice eventually gives up and Joe tells her his full name. He also tells her how he's a small-town farm boy from Kansas. He put himself through school at Ohio State. He had plans to go into engineering, but the intelligence branch of the army felt differently after they discovered he had studied five languages. Now he flies for them.

Alice commits every word, every syllable he says to memory. And ever since their tête-à-tête in her living room, he has taken up residence in Alice's brain. He's forward. Presumptuous. Alice likes feeling wanted by him.

Teach knows something is going on, even while Alice dutifully continues her tour of military bases, but she can't place what exactly. Nor would she be pleased to know about Joe. The secretiveness of their budding relationship makes it that much more appealing. Enticing, even.

The only problem, at that very moment, is that Joe is likely boarding a plane, on his way overseas.

"I'm set to leave on assignment," he told her before a goodnight kiss the night before.

"But you still owe me a dinner."

"The very second I return," Joe promised.

Turns out, that's too many seconds to count, so many seconds where Alice alternates between swooning over their banter, his singing voice, and his handsomeness, and then a punching feeling of fear that Joe could be hurt overseas. She's heard too many stories of a uniformed soldier turning up at a wife's door with a yellow envelope. Inside is always a telegraph with the worst kind of news: her husband won't ever be coming home.

Finally, after three long months, the phone rings and she hears

Joe's tenor voice saying Alice's name and then identifying himself, as if his voice isn't engrained in her thoughts.

"Joe?" she says in jest, her heart beating a mile a minute. "I can't recall anyone of interest by that name."

"Are you trying to break a man's heart?"

Alice winds the cord around her finger. "I wouldn't dream. Where are you taking me for our long overdue dinner?"

Le Pavillon is fancy. The quiet corner table is very romantic.

Joe pulls out a chair, and Alice gives him a grin over her shoulder.

"So tell me," she says, spreading a napkin over her lap once seated, "how have you been?"

His gaze instantly casts down, and Alice quickly realizes her mistake. The United States isn't faring well in the war. The Japanese have taken Singapore, Java, and Rangoon, and Alice has heard terrible snippets about the Bataan Death March. There are also horrifying tales circulating about the Nazis, about gas chambers, about death camps. About so many telegrams being sent home to soon-to-be heartbroken wives and families.

Alice has been doing her darndest to distract herself and lift the morale of the servicemen every chance she got. And right now she wants nothing more than to make the soldier in front of her smile. She reaches for Joe's hand, wanting and needing to touch him. "It's good to have you back."

He's returned, unlike so many of the others. He's here, all in one piece. All hers.

"You are surely a sight for sore eyes, Alice."

Joe is thinner. Bags underline his eyes. "And you're as handsome as ever."

"I'm going to have to leave again."

Alice nods. "I know."

"This is sudden." A hand goes through his wavy hair. "But life can change in a blink over there. What if next time I go, you and I make it official first? We get on real swell, Alice. And just knowing you're waiting for me back here would make all the difference."

Her throat is suddenly twice its size. For a long time, Alice has ached for there to be room for romance in her life. She'd gotten close, once, and now, since meeting Joe, she's been giddy over the idea of him. Of late, she's begun to wonder if there could be something on the other side of tennis. Could that something be six feet tall, with dark hair, dark eyes, and charming as all get-out? But marriage? Not merely stolen kisses and butterflies, but a license declaring them man and wife and a shared life? That's what he's getting at, isn't it?

And so quickly after meeting. Though, Alice reminds herself, she isn't the first to receive this impassioned speech from a soldier. Most of the time it works.

"Joe . . ."

"It's sudden, like I said. I know that. But marry me, Alice." He palms overtop his heart. "What I'm feeling is real. You're funny. You're driven. Confident. Intelligent. Sexy as hell. We get on well, don't we?"

Alice nods. "Real well. It's just that . . ." She trails off. Alice doesn't want to say that she's not sure what's going to come next with tennis and she's not sure how Joe fits into that. Instead, she vocalizes a different concern, saying, "The thing is, I know of too many wives who live in fear. I don't know if I can be one of them."

"Are you saying you haven't worried about me while I've been gone?"

"No, I have," she's quick to say.

And he's made his point.

Still, Alice blows out a long breath and says, "Could we table this conversation for later?"

"Of course, love," he says. "Of course."

So they talk of family.

Joe's an only child. His ma's a schoolteacher. His dad works a farm.

Of funny moments.

One time Joe streaked through campus on a dare.

Of regrets.

He was once too late to say how he really felt. He's more straightforward now.

Of dreams.

Joe wants three kids.

Alice thinks she could want the same. She thinks, yes, there *can* be dreams beyond tennis. Or maybe concurrently with tennis, but at a less intense level. She's not in her early or even mid-twenties anymore. While she gets older, it feels like her competitors are getting younger and younger.

But . . . Wife. Mother. She tries the titles on for size and she likes how they fit. She likes how Joe's been able to make her think about herself as more than simply a tennis player.

After dinner, he walks her home. At her door, he leans in for a kiss. It's not their first of the night. Alice doesn't want it to be their last. "Teach is out of town. Come up?"

For precious seconds in her apartment, they laugh and banter. They're serious. They're goofy. When Alice's eyes betray her and begin to flutter closed, Joe carries her to bed.

"Stay," she says, not letting go. He cuddles beside her, holding Alice tight.

In the morning, the aroma of coffee awakens her. She pats the empty bed, an ache for Joe washing over her. She pads to the kitchen, finding him mid tune in Teach's apron, looking very at home.

She guffaws. "If Teach saw you in that . . ."

"Morning, love." He hands her a mug.

"I could get used to this."

"I could get down on one knee."

Alice gives him a warning look, made much less effective due to the smile she can't seem to suppress. The sound of a key rattling in the door's lock sees to that. Her lips move into an O shape. There's no time to warn Joe. Or hide him.

The door unlocks and Teach walks in.

Chapter 13

What is it about Teach that makes Alice feel like a teenaged kid instead of a twenty-eight-year-old woman? Perhaps it's the fact she still technically lives under Teach's roof. A roof that Teach just walked into two days earlier than expected. By the looks of her coach's face, things aren't quite what she expected either.

"Well, hello," Teach says, her gaze dropping to her apron on Joe. "Who do we have here?"

"This is Captain Joe Crowley," Alice offers. "He just stopped by."

"Did he now?" Teach questions. She checks her watch. "At this early hour."

It's not spoken as a question but an accusation.

"Hello, Ms. Tennant," Joe says, offering his hand. He's older than Alice—only by a year or two—but in that moment he may as well be prepubescent as well. "I was just coming by for coffee with Alice here." He takes what must be a scalding gulp. "But let me get out of your hair. You must be tired from your trip."

"Uh-huh," Teach deadpans.

Joe makes to leave, doing a stutter step before deciding to kiss Alice chastely on the cheek and whispering, "Lunch at the Stage

Door Canteen?"

Alice nods. Teach be damned, she's eager to see him again as soon as humanly possible. Bonus points for that happening away from the eagle eyes of her coach.

"Oh, and, Joe?" Teach says.

He turns on his heel.

"My apron."

Teach is not short on questions, beginning with, "Who was that?" and ending with, "He's not going to be a distraction, is he?"

A distraction . . . Teach's go-to when it comes to reasons for Alice not saying yes to love. But a distraction from what, exactly? Competitive tennis is still on pause. A distraction from the war? Hardly. Not when Joe is part of the fighting.

Alice sighs. There are many layers to that sigh. But she focuses on Teach's strong grip on her life.

She points out, "This is my life, Teach. If I want something beyond tennis, that is my choice."

"Is it now?" Teach says, arms crossed, luggage still at her feet.

Alice startles. "Yes. How is it *not* my prerogative? I may have given in before when you made me choose." She blows out a breath. "But I am not a child anymore. I'm in a different place in my career. I can love who I want, when I want."

Teach throws up a hand. "Tell me, is it love or is it lust? He's a captain in the army, Allie. Call this what it is, a one-night stand."

Alice's nostrils flare. Honestly, the fact Teach is making a stink only makes Alice want to lean harder into her relationship with Joe. She crosses her own arms. "That is *not* fair to say." And trust her, Alice could say a few unfair things of her own. Teach's history with love isn't the best. She was married before. A short-lived marriage that ended after Teach discovered the long-term affair her husband had been having. Teach swore off men after that.

"They'll all just hurt you," Teach had said to Alice years ago, wrapping up all men in that sentiment. "You'll let them in. You may even put your dreams on the back burner for them. For what? Them to change their minds and walk out on you, leaving you left with the pieces of your dreams to try to put back together? They're not worth it."

"I think Joe is worth it," Alice says now, knowing her coach is headed in that direction.

"Yeah? And what if he gets killed? How many times have we seen that happen? How many times have you felt bad for the women left behind? Do you want that to be you?"

"Of course I don't want that. But I think I want Joe. And if you'll excuse me, I have a lunch to get ready for."

Teach's next words chase Alice from the room. Alice doesn't listen; doesn't care what they are.

Lunch with Joe is grand. The week that follows is near perfection. Alice seldom lets Joe out of her sight while he's on leave. She postpones much of her obligations, which likely sparks Teach's ire. Not that Alice allows herself to notice. Every day Joe watches her practice, then they wander the streets of New York hand in hand. They lunch. They peruse museums and shops. They see *Tarzan's New York Adventure* and *Citizen Kane*. They pass on *One of Our Aircraft Is Missing*. That one hits too close to home. Every night they sleep in each other's arms.

"Tomorrow," Alice whispers to him in the dark.

"Tomorrow," Joe says solemnly.

In the morning, he ships out. Part of Alice goes with him. She's only loved one man before him.

It's how she knows it's love this time too.

During their exhibition games at the bases, Mary teases Alice about being lovesick. She can't even deny it. She longs for each crackly-sounding long-distance phone call from Joe.

"My friend Judy married her husband after only two dates," Mary says, hands squeezed together over her heart. "Think you'll say yes to Joe?"

Well, they've had more than two dates, so there's that.

But Alice only ever smiles in response, feeling like each time she sees Joe brings her closer to accepting his proposal. It's only been every few months that she's had the chance to slip her hand in his, put her arms around his neck, kiss his lips, daydream of the three kids he brings up again and again. Alice is happy to be in that position in this very moment. He's in New York during one of his leaves.

Forehead pressed against hers in bed, Joe says, "One day when we're forty, love, we'll look back and realize we have everything we've ever wanted."

There had been a time that'd only been tennis for Alice. But not anymore. "I'll marry you," she says back. His expression flickers to life and she's quick to put a finger over his lips to keep him quiet. "Teach is sleeping."

He lets out a muffled celebratory scream.

Alice chuckles. "I'm removing my hand now."

He grabs it, kisses her knuckles. "We mustn't poke the dragon, is that right?"

"It's best the dragon doesn't know at all. She'll get herself all worked up and smoke'll come out of her nose. I don't want the drama. I want the excitement. You're thrilled. I'm thrilled. We're doing this. That's what I want to focus on."

Joe leans back to better see Alice's face. His forehead scrunches. "Are you certain you want to keep this from Teach?"

"Yes. I want to keep this for myself."

Maybe it's true. Maybe it's also wanting the course of least resistance. Teach mostly pretends Joe doesn't exist. She likely believes

Alice will come to her senses, grow bored of him, or something will happen to break them up. And it's not that Teach dislikes Joe. Alice once caught her coach chuckling at one of Joe's jokes from across the room, even. Teach just doesn't like Joe's intrusion on her grand plan for Alice's tennis-centric life.

But if Teach doesn't know . . . not yet, anyway.

It's sound logic to Alice. And, hey, her coach is all about logical thinking.

Alice and Joe plan to marry the next day in secret aboard a ship docked in the Hudson.

"Small," Alice says.

"Small," Joe agrees.

Small is not what they get. The crew catches wind of their plans and a hundred sailors in dress whites insist on gathering on the deck for the ceremony. When Alice and Joe kiss, sealing the deal as husband and wife, a hundred caps are thrown in the air in celebration.

Belly laughing, Alice holds Joe's hand as they race toward a taxi afterward. "How long will it take for them to each find their own hat?"

Joe shakes his head, telling the taxi driver the name of their hotel. A honeymoon will have to wait. Joe is set to leave the very next day. "The questions that form in that pretty head of yours will forever amuse me."

Alice snorts. "I'm here to keep things interesting."

"Well, here's another question for you, Mrs. Crowley."

"Mrs. Crowley. I like the sound of that."

"How do you like the sound of us getting started on the first of our three kids?"

Her eyes go wide. "Now you're the one with the amusing questions." But maybe, just maybe, the answer to that one is yes.

Chapter 14

Then

Sunday, August 6, 1933
Easthampton, New York

Qualifications for the Wightman Cup had *not* gone as Alice and Teach had hoped it would. She was supposed to somehow successfully play the schedule Myrick dictated for her. She was supposed to prove herself and make the Wightman team. She was supposed to help her team beat the Brits. She was supposed to go on to Nationals at Forest Hill—and win there too.

But none of that happened. Instead, the final day of Myrick's ridiculous schedule consisted of four matches, eleven sets, one hundred and eight games. All in nine hours on the hottest day of the year. Alice was young; only twenty, but even youth hadn't been enough to keep her on her feet. Alice succumbed to the ridiculousness, losing consciousness right then and there on the court.

Alice woke sometime later at her host's house, a doctor hovering above her. He diagnosed Alice with sunstroke and mild anemia.

"Is that all?" Alice said, strength missing from her voice.

"I prescribe rest, Miss Marble. It'll be your best cure for the weakness and dizziness you're experiencing. When you're up to it, your coach has been calling. You've received a wire from your mother too. Lots of people have been worried about you. You can't be doing that to yourself again, you hear?"

"Technically it was Mr. Myrick who pulled that one on me."

The doctor chuckled. "He's getting his comeuppance, that's for sure. The press is having a field day." One eye scrunched as he thought. "I believe this morning's headline said something along the lines of 'Alice Marble Gets a Bad Deal.'"

Wasn't that the truth.

"When can I play again?"

The doctor frowned. "Miss Marble . . . Alice . . . I can do little more than stress that your body needs a break."

"How long of a break?"

"Months."

Alice's heart sank.

Dearest Allie,

I'm overjoyed to know you are back in California, but I am eager for you to be all the way home in a few more weeks. I need to see you with my own eyes. To witness that you're truly well and recovering. I know the iron injections can't feel good, but they will help. Do as you're told by the doctor and by Ms. Tennant. They both have your best interest in mind. I'd beg you to take more time off from tennis, but I know it'd fall on deaf ears, and while I'll always be your mother, you are no longer a child I can demand things of. I am at least relieved to know you have no tournaments scheduled in the immediate future. I believe Ms. Tennant found a wonderful solution to keep you active in the game while not being overly active, don't you? You'll do grand helping her with her lessons. And at Mr. Hearst's ranch, no less!

If someone would have told me that my daughter would be a resident tennis coach—a job I never fathomed even existed—teaching tennis to the rich and the famous at the home of a man who owns the largest newspaper in our country, I would have thought they'd lost their marbles. I'm proud of you, baby girl, and I know rubbing elbows with those movie stars will be a dream for you. Soak up every moment, so you can tell me every detail when you're home. You said you'll be there a month?

On our end, Dan has graduated from the police academy. No more laying floors. What a blessing for him to be doing something he is passionate about. George, however, is still pleased as punch to be with the flooring company. Please pray for your sister. Hazel and her husband are on very rocky ground. I'd be surprised if their marriage lasts the year. She's still at the telephone company. I'm glad she has that distraction. Nothing new on Timmy. We're still navigating his teenage years. He mostly ignores me, which is fine as he's keeping his nose out of trouble.

Please take care of yourself. I know it must be

frustrating to slow down and feel like you aren't in control. You get that from me. But your body will heal, in time. Give yourself grace until that happens.

I love you to the moon and back. God bless, angels keep, my baby girl.

Your loving mother

"Evening, Miss Tennant, Miss Marble," a guard said with a quick touch of his cap. "Mr. Hearst is expecting you." At that, the gate to a long winding drive opened.

Teach widened her eyes at Alice and pushed down on the accelerator. "Ready, Alice? Mr. Hearst's estate awaits."

Was she ready?

She wasn't even sure what she was getting herself into. A resident tennis coach? Living at the home of a millionaire to teach his wealthy and powerful friends tennis?

Alice thought she'd be training for the next big tournament. The Wightman Cup. Wimbledon. Those dreams still dangled in front of her, frustratingly out of reach. For now. While she healed.

And until then . . . Alice couldn't help her smirk. "I feel like I'm the actual Alice and we're about to chase a white rabbit down a hole."

They'd just turned off the Coast Highway and up the start of a mountain road. At the tippy top stood Hearst Castle. In theory. Alice couldn't see it yet through the trees and with all the switchbacks. Her knee bounced in anticipation. Mr. Hearst was known for hosting some of Hollywood's biggest and brightest stars. Alice had spent ten cents every chance she got to see folks like them on the silver screen. And there she was on her way to play tennis with them. How was this her life?

The road was dirt and narrow. They'd gone a few miles when Alice suddenly clutched Teach's arm. "Oh my gosh, are those zebras? Tell me Mr. Hearst doesn't have a menagerie on his property."

Teach laughed. "Zebras, not zeebras."

Alice shook her head. "You know you're American, right?"

Teach shrugged, a smirk on her face. Her parents were the British ones. Teach was born in California. Still, she'd picked up her parents' accent. "Anyway," she said, "I heard he has a game preserve."

"Wait," Alice said, "what animal is that?"

"You don't know? Isn't that something you're supposed to learn in grade school?" Teach broke her focus from the road to inspect the peculiar-looking creature grazing. Without a word, she returned her attention to the road.

A smile cracked Alice's face. "You don't know either, do you?"

"It's a . . ."

Alice laughed.

"Enough out of you," Teach said. "It's some sort of gazelle or elk or something."

"With markings like a cow?"

"Fine, I don't know what it is either."

"Thank you for admitting you don't know everything, Teach."

Her coach shot her a look.

Alice's shoulders shook with another laugh. "This all feels like a dream."

They were driving slowly, watching for animals. There were no fences or enclosures here. If the animals wanted, they could walk straight up to the car.

Of course, that was what happened when tall wobbly knees ambled toward them. Alice leaned out the window. "No way. You're going to need to pinch me pretty soon."

"What?" Teach asked, angling toward Alice for the same vantage point. This time neither of them needed assistance identifying the animal.

A herd of giraffes stopped immediately in front of their car.

"Shoo!" Teach said.

"Shoo? They're giraffes, not pigeons." Words Alice never thought she'd say.

"They're going to make us late." Teach beeped the horn. Little good it did them. Apparently giraffes didn't respond to intimidation. "How are we supposed to get them to move?"

Alice shrugged. "We wait? It's not like we get to hang out with giraffes every day." Or ever. "Besides, they can't stand there forever, can they?

They could stand there for at least five minutes, during which Teach beeped the horn at least ten more times. Alice had never seen such disinterested giraffes. In fact, she'd never seen a giraffe before. Period. Only a few zoos had them, yet Mr. Hearst not only had his own newspaper and media company but also his own collection of the majestic mammals.

"Look!" Alice pointed. "Someone is running this way."

"Finally."

A groundskeeper bent into Teach's window. "Hit some traffic, did you?"

"We're late," was all Teach said.

"Move on over," he instructed. "I'll get you through and take you up."

Teach shifted down the bench seat toward Alice. The man scooted in and, ever so slowly, started driving toward the herd. "They'll move," he said. "None of God's creatures want to get run over."

The giraffes sure waited until the last possible moment to

lethargically step out of the way, though.

"There we go," the groundskeeper said. "Not everyone gets to see the girls up close and personal like this. Only ever happened to Mr. Winston Churchill. They had him surrounded for over an hour. Lucky I heard you beeping long before then."

"Yeah, lucky us," Teach said.

"What other animals does Mr. Hearst have?" Alice asked.

The groundskeeper blew out a breath. "Too many to count, I'd say. But let's see, more than a hundred species, if I have to guess. Llamas, camels, kangaroos, zebras, tapirs." He turned the wheel sharply, making a turn, and nodded behind them. "Giraffes, as you know. The preserve is about two thousand acres of hillside and canyon. A tiny sliver of Mr. Hearst's 240,000 acres of land. Stretches all the way from the mountains to the sea."

"Wow. Lot more than my family has back in San Francisco."

Teach laughed. "More than anyone owns in the whole country, I reckon."

"Can't say for sure," said the groundskeeper. "The ranch takes up forty thousand acres of Mr. Hearst's land. You'll get your first view of La Cuesta Encantada around this bend."

Alice asked, "What's that mean?"

"The Enchanted Hill. You'll see why in a moment."

They crested a hill, and there was an honest-to-God drawbridge that stretched over a moat. Her mother's jaw would drop when she told her about this. Alice wouldn't be surprised if there were sharks beneath them as they crossed over the water. The courtyard on the other side was cobblestoned with no less than three fountains.

Then, of course, the castle. A white stone, red tiled roof, carillon bells, and two spires that stretched into the sky.

"Teach," Alice began in awe. "This is where we're meant to live for the next month?"

"On and off for the foreseeable future while you recover," Teach said, smiling. "How will we ever bear it?"

The groundskeeper chuckled, unfolding himself from the driver's seat. "You two enjoy yourselves now."

Outside the car, Alice spun in a circle. Mountains, castle, sea. Mountains, castle, sea. Extraordinary.

Laughing, Teach linked their arms and led them toward the massive front entrance. "How will we ever bear it, indeed."

Chapter 15

A butler gestured Alice and Teach into the largest room Alice had ever laid eyes on. An entire tennis court could've fit in the entry room alone. With space to spare.

How many times in one day could Alice be knocked over with awe? And to think, the evening was just getting started.

A hand touched her arm. Alice turned, looking into bright blue eyes that she hadn't known resembled the sky until that very moment. She'd only ever seen them in black and white on the movie screen. Alice was stunned speechless.

"You must be Alice," Marion Davies said.

Still, no words left Alice's mouth. Sorry, giraffes, but they didn't hold a candle to seeing Marion Davies in person. "I'm . . . I'm honored to meet you, Miss Davies," she finally managed to say.

"Oh, you will never call me that again. It's Marion. And the honor goes both ways. I lost track of how many titles you've won this past year. And I read in the papers what that wretched man put you though, playing all those matches like that."

The compliment went straight to Alice's head, filling her with a surge of adrenaline she hadn't felt in weeks. Her body was still recovering from that day and she'd somehow developed a cough she couldn't kick. She was thankful to be in southern California as the winter months set in. She was thankful to be here.

"And what a beautiful pin," Marion remarked.

Alice touched it with her fingertips. It was a tiny gold racquet with a pearl ball, studded with diamonds and rubies. "Teach gave it to me."

"I'd glue it to her body if I could," Teach joked. The pin had been mighty expensive. But the real value of the pin, for Alice at least, was in the meaning behind it.

Teach had gifted it to Alice after her collapse. "For good luck," Teach had said to her at the time. "And so you know, I'm mighty proud of you. I know what it feels like to feel inferior and to possess that dire need to prove myself."

"You do?"

"Of course I do. Believe it or not, not everyone finds me charming."

Alice hid a smile.

"When I was younger," her coach had gone on, "I had a hard time fitting in. I sounded funny, and the other kids sure let me know it. Remember how I told you I followed that woman with the racquet because she looked confident and strong? Well, I wanted to be like that too. I wanted to feel like I belonged. Tennis gave that to me. And when you wear this pin, I want you to *know* that you belong."

"Aw, you two," Marion said, a hand over her heart. Then she greeted Teach with a hug. "Shall we go say hello to the rest of tonight's guests? William has an open-door policy and everyone is welcome to stay as long as they wish. We're all one big happy family—that drinks too much and eats too much." She laughed. "Which is why we need you both. You'll whip us into shape on the courts." She gave a megawatt smile. "I just can't believe you're both finally here. I have to admit, I'm a bit starstruck."

By us? Alice thought. That was a first. But the fact of the matter was that tennis was the "in" sport with celebrities, Teach was the "in" coach after the press took a shining to her, and Alice was the "it" player, the stunt Myrick played actually making Alice more popular with tennis fans.

She touched her pin, a smile on her face, and with a pep in her step, Alice followed after Marion into a dining hall bursting with about fifty people. No, not people . . . film stars. She gasped and took hold of Teach's sleeve, tugging, once again gobsmacked.

Teach chuckled. "They're simply human beings like you and me, Alice."

Alice exhaled in awed exasperation. "Bite your tongue. I'm sweating." She tried to nod discreetly. "How is Charlie Chaplin in the same room as us right now?"

"Who?" But Teach couldn't feign ignorance without laughing. "Of course I know who he is." She touched her upper lip. "The ⊠stache gives him away."

"You know," Alice whispered, "he once won third prize in a look-a-like contest for himself."

"Of course you'd know that." Teach scanned the room, the thirty or so people standing in twos or threesomes. "The rest of them, though. No clue who they are."

"You live under a tennis-shaped rock." She nodded toward Carole Lombard. "She was wonderful in *No Man of Her Own* with Clark Cable. And, oh"—Alice head-pointed toward Marlene Dietrich—"She was just nominated for an Academy Award." She gasped. "Raoul Walsh. He's my favorite director."

Any one of them could sign up to play with Teach and her while visiting the ranch. Alice's mind whirled, wondering who she'd meet on the courts first.

"Stop staring like that. You're salivating. How do you know what a director looks like anyhow? He's not even on camera."

Alice blew out a long, slow, controlled breath. "This room is—"

"Alice! Eleanor!" Marion was back, pulling a man behind her. "Let me introduce the man of the hour."

"Hardly," he said in an unexpectedly high-pitched voice. He was on the shorter side and also the wider side, with the most welcoming smile Alice had ever seen. "I'm just the man who pays the bills. Man of the house, how about that?"

"Mr. Hearst," Teach said, shaking his hand. "We're delighted to be here. Thank you for the teaching residency invitation."

"Thank you for finally accepting. You too, Alice. Everyone here is so tickled to be meeting you."

Alice snorted. It couldn't have been the most appropriate response, but that was what came out. Mr. Hearst cocked his head, and Alice did her best to recover. "I'm sorry," she said, "this is all just more than I had been anticipating. You have a beautiful home, Mr. Hearst."

She'd been so enamored with the people in the room, she hadn't fully noticed the room itself. But it was spectacular. So much wood details, with silk banners hanging every few feet the length of the room; enormous tapestries acting as wall art; human-sized chandeliers. The dining room table with its large, red velvet chairs could've easily fit forty people. Fifty. Sixty. Alice wasn't sure. Every few feet down the table, candles flickered in ornate three-foot-high silver candlesticks.

"Thank you, my dear, and please," Mr. Hearst said, "call me William. If we're to be playing on the court together, it'll be much easier to say in a jiff."

"Very well," Alice said, not about to argue with a millionaire.

A waiter walked by with a tray, from which Marion plucked a

bell. She pushed her blonde hair behind her shoulder, then gave the bell a ring. "Everyone, take your seats. We'll be beginning dinner in just a moment." She took Alice's arm. "Let me show you where you'll be sitting and who your dinner partner will be." They walked until Marion tapped a man's shoulder. He turned. "George, please let me introduce tennis star Alice Marble."

How . . . how was Alice about to be seated next to George Bernard Shaw, the very man and playwright Alice had written her thesis on when applying to the University of California? "Mr. Shaw," Alice said, her head slightly shaking. "I've been following your work for years."

"Have you now? I'm likely to have written my first more than thirty years before you were even born."

Alice smiled, then quoted, "'The great secret, Eliza, is not having bad manners or good manners or any other particular sort of manners, but having the same manner for all human souls: in short, behaving as if you were in Heaven, where there are no third-class carriages, and one soul is as good as another.'"

His eyes went wide. "Impressive, Miss Marble."

George Bernard Shaw just called her impressive. She also just felt a sharp pain, turning to find Teach. "You said earlier to pinch you."

Dinner felt like an oxymoron: sophisticated yet unruly.

Alice and her fellow diners were served the most tender cuts of meat, turtle soup, escargot, truffles, and the most expensive wines, yet they draped paper napkins over their laps.

Alice was in the company of Hollywood's most elite, yet many guffawed, belched, and abandoned their manners.

They also played a game that completely delighted Alice. Mostly because she was the best at it.

"Okay, who am I?" Cary Grant said. "C. L. Those are my initials. I was discovered at the age of twelve while playing baseball in the streets. As such, I was cast as a tomboy in my first film, *A Perfect Crime*."

There was upward fifty people at the table and not a one of them seemed to know who he was talking about, except for Alice and, of course Carole Lombard, considering the clues were about her. She was smiling coyly to herself, her chin resting in her left hand. Mr. Grant winked in her direction, giving it all away.

Bebe Daniels called out, "It's Carole!"

The table laughed, clapped, and cheered. Ms. Lombard shushed them. "He would've fooled you all if it weren't for that subtle wink. Though I do think our friend Alice had figured it out."

Alice blushed even while relishing in the fact that she most certainly had.

William laughed heartily. "We cannot stump the girl. But can she stump us? Your turn, Alice. Who are you?"

Alice pressed her lips together, thinking. "Okay, I've got it. My initials are H.G."

"Howard," someone mused.

"Henry."

"Henrietta," another countered.

"Harley."

William waved his hand around. "Let the girl give another clue, will you?"

Alice ticked off three silent films the actor had been in. She was met with blank stares and guesses of first and last names that clearly did not begin with *H* or *G*.

Teach scratched her head. "Leave it to Alice, the human

encyclopedia, to stump us all."

William slapped down his hand. "We are not leaving until we figure this out. Though I was going to do a showing of Marion's film *Peg o' My Heart*, so perhaps we *should* hurry this along. Do we give up, friends?

The answer was unanimous.

Alice beamed, victorious. "I am Holbrook Glenn, the villain who tied girls to the railroad tracks."

Some groaned; others roared with laughter. William Hearst laughed so deeply that Alice feared for the three-hundred-year-old chair he leaned back in.

One thing was certain, however. Alice's first night at Hearst Castle was nothing short of spectacular. Never before had she had such a great time without a racquet in hand.

Chapter 16

Tennis lessons—and Alice—were a hit at Mr. Hearst's ranch.

In Alice's first match, she and William played Teach and Charlie Chaplin. Awaiting every serve, Mr. Chaplin leaned forward, twisting his lips, which had the effect of twitching his mustache in the most humorous of ways. It was enough for Alice to double fault, more times than she'd like to admit.

But playing was all in good fun. Slower paced. Less rigorous. More carefree. Alice had to admit, Teach's solution to keep her active but not too active was ingenious. And she ate up every star-soaked minute of it.

After each win, William gave Alice a bear hug and proclaimed she was the best partner he'd ever had. Though, without fail, his larger-than-life embraces set off a fit of coughing in her. She'd bang her chest with her fist while Teach looked on with concern.

Lots of concern.

And rules.

Alice was not allowed to swim; Teach feared it'd loosen Alice's tennis muscles too greatly.

She followed a strict diet, even stricter on account of her persistent cough.

Then there was the curfew. Always the curfew, even with Alice now twenty years old.

Sometimes Teach would slip in a morning or afternoon practice, but mostly Alice played with the many revolving guests. Her time at Mr. Hearst's ranch, however, was not a vacation, despite feeling as if she were on the set of something make-believe, with the estate's fourteen sitting rooms, thirty-eight bedrooms, rare paintings and tapestries, indoor Roman swimming pool, outdoor 104-foot-long pool, marble stairways, hidden passageways, and its gardens and fountains galore.

Not a bad place to work. Alice and Teach would stay for a month. Alice would visit her family. She'd return for another month, then go back to San Francisco. Before she knew it, winter had progressed to spring.

She loved playing against Hollywood's elite. Though there were quite a few who shouldn't quit their day job, something Alice joked about with Teach.

"Yeah, well, playing someone with a lesser and slower skill set is good practice for you. In future tournament play, I want you to set the pacing. Being able to change up the speed of play is crucial. It'll keep you in control."

"We like control," Alice said.

"Yes, we do. Our time at the ranch has been good for you. You're playing like the old Alice again. Perfect timing too."

Alice cocked her head.

Teach pulled a telegram from her pocket. "The tennis association has invited you to play a series of matches in France."

"France!?"

Teach held up a hand, a cheeky smile on her face. "Yes, in France, and then you'll go on to England to play in the Wightman Cup. No games from Myrick this time. You're on the team. Just like that."

Alice rolled onto her toes, a smile spreading across her face. "No qualifying?"

Teach tapped the telegram. "No qualifying. France, then England. We're on our way. How's that sound, Allie?"

"I don't have words," Alice said, cupping a hand over her mouth, her mind already thousands of miles away, aboard a steamship, in front of the Eiffel Tower, on the grass courts in England. With the other girls, not feeling like an outsider, but part of the team. Seen. Respected.

"You don't need words, only a racquet," Teach said, unable to help her own grin. "But I'd like us to go visit the wizard again first. Just to make sure he doesn't see something I've been missing as you've recovered."

Alice nodded. And just like that they were off to see the wizard, the wonderful wizard of Santa Barbara.

All started well with Whitey. He applauded her playing. But then, at the news of Alice making the Wightman team and going overseas, Whitey pressed his lips together hard.

"What is it?" Teach asked him.

They were sitting on his patio, the springtime air cool that particular evening. His wife brought out a tray of cocktails, her pace slowing at the look on Whitey's face. "Oh no," she observed. "He's got a bad feeling."

Alice wanted to stop this conversation right there and then. She knew her coach. She knew Whitey. She knew they were about to spout off some mumbo jumbo about something they saw in the stars.

Alice wasn't wrong.

Teach blanched, asking Whitey, "Did you see something in Alice's horoscope?"

He nodded.

"What is it?" Teach asked. "I haven't had time to look."

He started going on about her ruling planet, retrograde, the fact she was a Libra, her birth chart, him spotting a comet yesterday. A bad omen, he argued. Basically, "I don't think she should go," Whitey concluded.

"But I have to," Alice insisted.

Teach wrung her hands. "Your predictions have always been solid, Whitey."

"This is unbelievable," Alice said. "I'm on the team. On it. No song and dance this time. And we're going to let this opportunity slip us by because I'm a Libra?"

"What if you went with her, Eleanor?" Whitey suggested. "Keep a close eye on this."

"Fine. Yes. That," Alice said.

Teach shook her head. "We've had a profitable few months on the ranch, but someone has to pay to get Alice across the pond. I can't afford to take two months off from teaching."

"Everything will be fine," Alice said, leaning forward in her seat. "I promise, I won't do anything stupid. I won't be strong-armed into playing a schedule like before. I'll stick to the curfew. I won't even eat any chocolate. No chocolate soufflé, no nothing."

Alice could feel the internal battle inside Teach. Tension radiated from her. She sighed, the fight leaving her. "This opportunity is too good to pass up. I hope you're wrong about this one, Whitey."

He had the decency not to respond.

"So I'm going?" Alice said, so far on the edge of her seat she was about to topple off.

"The eighteenth of May," Teach said in a low voice, giving Whitey a less-than-enthusiastic look. "You'll board the SS *Westernland* from New York."

Alice squealed.

***

Alice arrived at the Waldorf-Astoria Hotel in Manhattan without a train derailment, mudslide, flash flood, hay fever, or any other incident that Whitey and Teach may have seen in the so-called stars. The next afternoon, without incident, she boarded the ship that'd bring her to Europe for the very first time.

Omens shomens.

She was feeling good. Mostly. There was her lingering cough and also a lingering doubt that she'd be able to compete at the level of competition she'd face in Europe. It'd only been a little less than a year since she'd collapsed on the court. And while she loved playing against Carole Lombard and Marion Davies, they were no Sylvia Henrotin, France's best.

In her state room bathroom, Alice smiled too big in the ship's small mirror.

It was meant to be a you've-got-this visual pep talk, yet the expression came off a bit deranged looking. She shook her head while she poked through her cosmetic bag for the gold pin Teach had given her. The little racquet with the pearl ball was nowhere to be found. Her lip quivered. Such a silly thing to upset her over a pin, but it was important to her.

Alice groaned loudly. Loudly enough to draw the attention of the stewardess who'd been helping to put away her belongings in her room.

"Is everything all right, Miss Marble?" a petite woman with a full head of dark hair said, stepping into the open doorway.

"Yes, sorry. It's only I can't find a pin I could have sworn I packed."

"I'd be happy to look for it," the stewardess said with a smile.

"Would you? I wouldn't be putting you out?"

"Of course not."

"I appreciate it, very much. Thank you . . ." Alice paused, not yet learned the stewardess's name.

"Miss Jessop. And you are most welcome."

Alice thanked her again, closed the door, and lifted the hem of her ball gown to use the toilet. She'd be joining her teammates Sarah Palfrey, Dorothy Bundy, and Josephine Cruickshank in the ballroom for a party with a slew of reporters, coaches, US Lawn Tennis Association members, and fellow travelers.

Alice flushed—or at least she thought she had, noticing too late she'd pushed the lever for the bidet as she stood. She held in a gasp, not wanting Miss Jessop to hear her, then let out a silent scream. Her dress dripped. By the time she changed, she was late for the party.

No bother, she told herself.

"I plan to win," she told a reporter.

"Feeling better than ever," she told another.

"Sure, I'll dance," she told a boy.

"Another, why not? I won't turn into a pumpkin."

"'*He loves and she loves and they love, so why can't you love and I love too?*'" she sang along with the music while dancing.

When the band took a break, Carolin Babcock cut in and took Alice's hand. "There's talk of a mind reader. She's predicting everyone's future. One of the reporters said you're to go next."

"Oh," Alice said. "I don't think that's necessary."

"Of course it is. It's all in good fun."

Alice opened her mouth to refuse, but Carolin was even more aggressive off the court than she was on it. In a heartbeat, the girl had dragged Alice through a cluster of spectators and stopped directly in front of the psychic. "Here she is! Miss Alice Marble."

She imagined Whitey's hard-pressed lips and Teach's anxious expression. Her own stomach was turning over.

The psychic was beautiful in her own way. Skin so pale she could've passed for albino, if it weren't for her pale blue eyes. Her hair was a white-blonde, long and wavy. The woman stretched out her arms, palms up. Alice felt she had no choice but to place her hands in the woman's.

She grasped firmly and said in a voice almost too soft to hear, "Look at me."

Hesitantly, Alice met her nearly translucent eyes. Alice instantly had the urge to pull back, to suggest that someone else be fodder for the reporter's article, but the mind reader held on tight.

Until she suddenly released Alice's hands as if she'd been burned. Still, their eyes remained locked. "You will rise like a rocket to the clouds," the psychic said, more strength in her voice than before.

The crowd gave an *ooh* sound. Many heads nodded. The trajectory made sense for young Alice. She'd proven her mettle. She'd recovered. She was raring to go.

The psychic's next words came out eerily quiet. "You'll rise. Then you'll fall."

Chapter 17

Now

SATURDAY, JUNE 17, 1944
MANHATTAN, NEW YORK

Alice is on cloud nine.

Despite the ongoing war, which now involves the United States. Despite the coolness between Teach and her, now that Alice put her foot down about wanting to be with Joe.

Though Teach still doesn't know about Alice getting married.

Not explicitly, at least.

Shortly after becoming Mrs. Joseph Crowley, Alice received a bouquet of flowers and a note from Marion Davies. How that woman found out about Alice's secret wedding is a mystery.

Happy you're happy

Teach saw the note.

Teach likely surmised about the marriage too.

But no words had been exchanged between athlete and coach in the days following Alice's nuptials. Nor in the many months that have since passed.

Partly because the marriage wasn't *supposed* to be talked about. Joe warned that a German spy could think to kidnap Alice as leverage against him, which felt like something out of a film. But the greater reason why Alice hasn't revealed this huge life milestone to Teach is because not much has changed in Alice's day-to-day. She still practices. Still plays at bases. Still volunteers at the military hospital. Still steals time with Joe whenever he's on leave, which isn't very often. They haven't yet honeymooned, nor have they made any progress in their clandestine baby-making operation, a dream Alice has wholly embraced. She'd would have to tell Teach after that mission is complete.

The one new thing going for Alice, however, came about rather unexpectedly. At her new office at 480 Lexington Avenue, Alice winds her pencil between each of her fingers, thinking back to the night she got the surprise gig. She'd been at a party and struck up a conversation with a man named Max Gaines.

"What do you do when you're not dressed as a penguin, Mr. Gaines?"

He had laughed good-naturedly. "I produce comics."

"And I whack a ball. It appears we both have childish interests."

Mr. Gaines chuckled again. "It appears so. But we have good fun, don't we?"

"That we do. Would I know any of your work?"

He smiled coyly. "*Green Lantern*, *Hawkman*, the new *Wonder Woman*, to name a few."

"Impressive," Alice said. "I do love the idea of having these heroes to look to."

"Inspired by real people, no less. William Marston, who writes *Wonder Woman*, has quite the interest in the suffrage movement. Margaret Sanger in particular. She's the inspiration there."

"Fascinating." Alice sipped her drink, contemplating. "Now . . ." She sipped again. "Wouldn't it be neat to have a similar comic where real-life wonder women are featured?"

"As in?"

"As in women who have made history."

"Such as?"

"Clara Barton, Florence Nightingale, Dolley Madison. I could go on."

"You could—and I'm embarrassed to admit it—but I likely wouldn't know those women either."

Alice clinked his glass. "The exact reason why this column is needed."

Mr. Gaines took a big pull of his drink, holding the liquid in his mouth before a large swallow. It'd given him time to contemplate. "What if you were to do some research, Miss Marble? Rough out some dialogue. Show me what these wonder women of history could look like in comic form."

Alice nearly spilled her drink from excitement. Hadn't she once thought having her own column could be a hoot? Hadn't she once sat beside the great-grandson of Emma Willard and thought everyone should know her story?

And thus she drafted, got the green light to go on, and, soon after, settled into her own desk on the nineth floor, home of the All-American Comics offices, as the new associate editor of the *Wonder Women of History* series.

So far she's written about Florence Nightingale, Clara Barton, Edith Cavell, Lillian D. Wald, Susan B. Anthony, Madame Chiang

Kai-Shek, Joan of Arc, Sister Elizabeth Kenny, and she is now tapping her pencil against her lip, contemplating how to begin the introduction to her ninth installment.

> Jane Addams of Hull House
> 1860–1935
>
> In a time when women lacked the right to vote, a remarkable woman reshaped the landscape of American society. This courageous, brilliant, and captivating figure was none other than Jane Addams, who fearlessly ~~stood up against~~

Alice crosses out stood up against, searching her brain for a stronger wording. *Confronted.*

> who fearlessly confronted the most influential politicians and business leaders in the nation to put an end to the scourge of child labor. And eradicate it, she did. Jane Addams, the passionate advocate for the marginalized, unquestionably stands as one of the most remarkable Wonder Women of History!

Alice smiles, happy with what she's written. And thank goodness for that. She checks the clock on her office wall. She has a few short hours before she's set to endure a battery of needles. The inoculations are necessary before leaving for a military base in Panama. Each jab will be worth it in the end. Alice is set to play at bases for a few weeks—and, in the final week, Joe will be coordinating his leave to meet her there. Finally, they'll be getting their honeymoon. And Alice won't allow herself to feel guilty that she's relieved Teach won't be making this trip, freeing Alice from her coach's eagle eye.

But for now . . . the comic. She draws a box where the illustrator will bring to life what she writes.

Jane was only six years old when she first glimpsed poverty with her own eyes.

Jane speech bubble: Father, are those homes abandoned? Or do people live there?

Father: Yes, people less fortunate than us.

A new box.

Jane speech bubble: When I grow up, I promise to help people who live in houses like those. I'll have a big house right in the middle with an open door.

Alice then writes a jump in time and leans on snappy dialogue to bring Jane's story to life. She begins with how Jane's memory of that day faded, along with her promise. She graduated from Rockford Seminary for Women with top honors. But to Jane's horror, those honors didn't equate to a degree, like they would have for a man.

Alice knows a little something about that . . . about having to hold her own to get the same opportunities as a man. And she did.

But back to Jane. She's determined to fight injustices, and in 1882, the seminary's name is changed to Rockford College. Jane is issued the very first degree. When a man named Rollin falls in love with her, she tells him she's not ready to be married. She has important things she wants to accomplish first, even if she's not certain what that entails yet. Maybe medicine, Jane ponders. Yes, she earns a degree in that too.

Only Jane suffers from poor health. Alice can sympathize with that all too well.

Jane's doctor suggests a trip to Europe. Fancy. No big surprise, but Jane's open to the idea, especially after she realizes she doesn't want to practice medicine after all. The trip will be her muse.

In London, Jane sees a large crowd of less fortunate people auctioning for half-rotten food. Jane is floored by what she witnesses, but also learns there's a hall that offers free food to the poor. She visits the public kitchen and is encouraged to find that the hall does more than feed the poor. There are classes and clubs. Jane is inspired to start something similar in America.

She calls it Hull House, and also realizes she's come full circle: keeping the promise she made when she was six years old.

Jane throws a grand Christmas party. She's shocked when the children don't want the candy she offers them. They claim they can't look at the stuff after working fourteen hours every day at a factory that makes the confections. Jane is appalled. Such long days. Making only four cents an hour. At their young ages. It's criminal, and come hell or high water, Jane will bring forth a law that puts a stop to it.

Of course she's met with resistance from the factory owners. But the conditions cannot be ignored, especially after seeing a child working with smallpox. It could lead to an epidemic. Still, Jane's proposed labor laws are rejected. Jane keeps fighting. It's not until 1899 she's victorious. Children under fourteen can no longer work for more than eight hours in a day.

Alice writes a conclusion, reinforcing Jane Addams of Hull House as a certified wonder woman. Then Alice signs her name.

That's always her favorite part.

Checking the clock, there's no time to edit or proofread. But her editor can help with that. She smiles, the same way she does every time she completes one of her comics. Women's stories need to be told.

Though, at the moment, this woman needs to get her butt to the hospital for her inoculations, even if she'd rather be confronting factory owners than getting jabbed. It'll be all worth it to see Joe.

Chapter 18

Alice's husband sure is lucky he's charming, handsome, and has *other* quality attributes. She reminds herself of that aplenty during the long fourteen days aboard a rocking ship, worsened by the nauseous aftereffects from the injections.

But finally she steps onto solid ground and onto the makeshift courts at Fort Gulick Military Reservation in Cristobal, Panama.

Mary Hardwick mops at her brow. "My goodness, Alice. It's hotter than a blister bug in a pepper patch."

"Come again?" Alice says, equal parts confounded and amused. Apparently her Brit friend has picked up some southern jargon while in the States. It's mind-boggling to think the war's been going on for nearing five years, Mary away from her beloved England all that time. How much longer could it last? Already it's longer than the world's first war against Germany.

All Alice wants is for the Germans to be defeated, for Joe to be back, and for their lives to move on. In the two and a half years they've been married, they haven't been together enough for anything to become commonplace. While it makes every moment together special and exciting, Alice aches for boring.

She raises her chin to Mary. "Shall we? We have some morale

to boost."

"Make the match quick, will ya? I'm already knackered."

"My pleasure."

Now to stay on her own two feet.

***

Next stop after the Fort Gulick Military Reservation in Alice's base tour is Coco Solo Naval Base. The ride is about fifty miles along a dirt road, driving in and out of valleys and around picturesque mountainsides. Mary got a jump on Alice earlier in the day because Alice overslept.

So it's just Alice and a boyish GI named Gilbert making the trek.

He looks at Alice in the rearview mirror and smiles. "Nice of you to dance with the fellas last night."

In truth, she doesn't do it for the soldiers. She does it for herself and for the women who love them, showing care for someone else's dark-haired "Joe." She returns Gilbert's smile, which is faltering now that he stretches his neck to better see the sky. "Heavy rains are going to get us."

"Oh?"

"I'll get us there safe, don't you worry. But I'm going to have to pick up the pace."

"If the storm will take away some of this humidity, I say let it rain."

The statement is all false bravado. Truth is, Alice loathes driving in the rain. The type of loathing that's laced with fear and bad memories on account of the fact her father's fatal car accident happened during a rainstorm.

But this young man doesn't need to know her fears, especially as he adds, "It's the flash floods that worry me. We get them in the mountains."

Gilbert accelerates, more than Alice is comfortable with. Dirt kicks up. A large single drop lands on the windshield.

Alice tenses. She wasn't in the car the day of her father's accident. But she was there in the hospital after. She was there when the doctor told them pneumonia had set in. She was there when the doctor shook his head and said he'd done all he could do.

Alice glances ahead at Gilbert. He's young, sure, but also confident. Two hands on the wheel, ten and two. He takes a sharp turn like a pro. And the next. Still, as they drive along a steep drop-off, Alice discreetly slides her hand from her lap to grip the door's handle.

Her fingertips barely find purchase before the truck skids atop the loose dirt. An expletive leaves Gilbert's lips, and Alice is suddenly seeing nothing but a valley a thousand feet below her. The truck bounces down the side of a mountain, not that Alice witnesses a second more of it. She tightly squeezes shut her eyes, popping them open again only after the impact of her body against the back of the front seat.

Her breath comes out fast. Blood pools on her lap from her nose. Gilbert's voice is ragged. "Miss Marble, Miss Marble. Are you all right?"

She stares at the truck's black flooring, tucked in a ball against the back of the driver's seat, her mind still playing catch-up. Then she makes the mistake of turning her head to get a better vantage point. All that stands between them and the remainder of a thousand-foot drop is the tree they hit while careening down the mountainside.

"Miss Marble—"

"I'm okay," she says, panic overtaking her. "But we need to get out."

Alice makes split-second decisions a million times over during a tennis match. Without waiting for instruction, she fumbles for the handle and shoulders open the door. The truck responds, shifting. Alice curses and begins crawling out, acutely aware of each placement of her hands and knees. Her nails dig into the soft earth when she's out.

Gilbert tumbles from the driver's seat, his own shirt stained with blood. A bump the size of an egg has already formed on his forehead. Alice gingerly touches her own head. Her fingertips come away red. Her vision is spotty. Her muscles feel drained, as if she's back at the courts having played one hundred and eight ridiculous games in one day.

The truck groans, shifting again. Small rocks and chunks of the mountain tumble.

"Move," Gilbert says. "Climb."

His hand wraps around her ankle, all he can reach, and he pushes her.

The truck groans again, this time gravity having its way with the heavy metal. Slowly, then all at once, the truck lists to one side—and then is gone, uprooting the tree in the process.

Gilbert mumbles. "Holy mother of . . ."

The truck plummets, a flash of army green growing smaller, until a bang and an explosion of fire. Within seconds, a plume of thick black smoke rises.

Alice drops her forehead into her hands, fighting with herself to slow her rapidly beating heart, to conquer the fear of unraveling from the child-like pose she's in, and begins again to try to save her life.

"Climb," Alice demands of herself. "Climb."

Then suddenly Teach is in her head, her stern, deadpan voice telling her to get her butt moving. "It's do or die time, Alice," she'd say during a match. Never before had her coach's words been more literal.

She stretches out an arm, again digging her nails into the earth, and she claws up the bank.

One feet, then two.

Alice hears Gilbert close behind her.

At her movement, loose earth and stone fall away beneath her hands and feet. A foot slips. Alice slips. She collides with Gilbert, who cries out as he fights to keep his own grip on the mountain.

They hold.

Alice doesn't apologize. She'll do it after he does, after they get out of this mess. The rain comes then. Funny, she'd forgotten about that single large drop. Each droplet now is a dark speck on the dirt, the number of specks growing and growing.

Alice quickens her pace, never feeling like there's enough air to fill her lungs.

Ten feet, fifteen feet, she climbs.

Almost there.

Then she's at the top. Caked in mud. Covered in blood. Alice rolls to her back, completely depleted, and lets the rain wash over her.

"I'll tell ya," Mary Hardwick says from a chair at Alice's bedside, "what some people won't do to miss a match. Afraid I'd win for once?"

Mary glances at Alice's hands, not that she can see the missing fingernails or scraped-off skin. Alice's mess of hands are wrapped up tight in bandages.

Alice scoffs. "I'm sure you wish my hands were rendered useless five hundred bases ago."

"You kid," Mary says, lines marring her forehead, "but how are you really?"

Alice twists her lips. Even that hurts from a gash. If she thinks too hard about what happened and how she could've died, she'll burst into tears. It's already happened twice. "I'm in pain."

"All that's over now, and you'll heal. You'll be back to beating me on the court in no time." She tries for a smile. "And think, Joe will be here soon."

"In two weeks."

Two achingly slow weeks, during which Alice can't do so much as lift a pen to write her mother. Then, at the exact moment the doctor unravels the gauze, Alice getting a first look at her shiny, too-red skin, Joe barrels into her hospital room. He stops in his tracks, his chest rising. He holds the breath, his body tense, until he lets it out, then goes the final distance to Alice in three quick strides.

What he says Alice can't exactly decipher at first. But he's worried. He's thankful. The last part she hears: He's going to see that the young GI is on latrine duty for a week.

"Stop that," Alice says, tears in her eyes, so overwhelmed by Joe finally being here and by his show of love for her. "He didn't mean to drive us off a cliff."

Joe's face pales. "How can you be so cavalier?"

"I have to be or else I'll fall apart. My dad, Joe. My dad—"

"I know, my love. I know." He's holding her then, carefully, gingerly. "I'll always be here to keep you together."

"Promise?"

"Always."

***

Originally Alice thought she and Joe would spend their honeymoon hiking and sunbathing and making love.

There is no hiking. There is no sunbathing, as Alice cannot leave the bed in their private barracks on account of a concussion. But considering Alice cannot leave the bed, there is an enormous amount of tender lovemaking.

It's not the worst honeymoon. They're together, experiencing the simple pleasures of it being just the two of them, waking up together, sharing the newspaper, engaging in playful pillow talk.

There is no talking of the accident.

There is no talking of whatever dark mission Joe is off to next. Or when he'll go.

But it is soon, always too soon.

Joe's head rests on Alice's stomach. She runs her hand through his wavy hair. She could do it forever and never grow tired of the feel of the strands passing through her fingers. He rolls over, propping up his head. "Will you be more careful?"

"As careful as I can be." She could point out that she wasn't the one driving, but Joe knows that. He needs to say it, though. "You're the one I worry about." Her hand falls on the bed, and Joe intertwines their fingers.

He asks, "Will you tell Teach soon?"

He asks because Alice doesn't wear his ring. It's stowed away in her jewelry box for safekeeping. Secret keeping, actually.

"Yes. I will. As soon as I'm back in New York."

Joe feigns surprise. "Are you saying you'll choose me over tennis?"

She grins. "There was never a contest." But then in a more serious tone she adds, "I could've died—"

"Shh," Joe says.

"It's true, Joe. But it's over, in the past. What's not over is my relationship with Teach. I need to make that right. And you and I need to start living our marriage, out in the open, for all to see."

"Well, maybe not *all*. We still can't go parading it around until this war is over."

"Stupid Nazis." Specifically any spies in the States who'd want to use Alice against Joe.

"We're getting close, love. I'm doing all I can."

She kisses him. That's what worries her.

Chapter 19

Alice flushes the toilet and quickly stands, wiping a hand across her mouth. Spots erupt before her eyes. She just heard Teach come into their New York apartment. She soldiers herself, fingertips steepened against the vanity countertop, looking at herself in the bathroom mirror.

Currently she's experiencing two emotions. She touches her belly, giddy. That's the first emotion, all on account of the Joe Junior she's baking in there. She found out shortly after returning from Panama. Add it to what she has to tell Teach, which is the reason for the second emotion: anxiety.

She squares her shoulder, unsure how Teach will react. Dropping an "I'm married" bomb would've been hard enough. Alice did always like to go big, though.

She takes in a gulp of air and joins Teach in the living room. Teach is scurrying around, overturning pillows, then on her knees, peering under the couch.

"What'd you lose?" Alice asks her.

"My mind apparently." She growls low in her throat. "My reading glasses."

Alice bites back a laugh. "The ones currently atop your head?"

Teach pats there. "It's been a day. But I should've expected it to be. Mercury is in retrograde."

"Oh," Alice says, thinking maybe it's not the best time to spill the beans. But, of course, Teach can read Alice like a book.

"What is it? You have something to tell me."

Alice sits. Teach will likely need to as well. "Well, I'm just going to say it."

"Then say it."

"I'm trying."

"Try harder."

"Teach." Alice frowns. "I'm pregnant."

Teach sits.

Alice's knee bounces. "Did you hear me?"

"Of course I did. I was just taking a moment to silently curse Mercury. Do you know who the father is?"

That narrows Alice's eyes.

"Fine," Teach says, rightfully looking abashed by the out-of-bounds barb. "It's Joe. Should've figured this would be coming after that secret wedding of yours."

Alice knew she knew. Still, her cheeks heat. "I'm sorry."

"You should be."

"Not for getting married. I love Joe. But for not telling you or including you. I knew you'd make a stink about tennis."

"Yeah, well, what about tennis?"

It's always about tennis with this woman. A defense mechanism, perhaps. Many people in the industry suspect that Teach and Alice have a mother/daughter type relationship. They live together, after all. Though they aren't the only coach/athlete who have that arrangement. But Alice wouldn't call Teach motherly. It's just that sometimes Teach blurs the boundaries of what is tennis and what isn't.

Alice relaxes her shoulders, but only a little. She's not seventeen anymore, letting Teach call all the shots in all areas of her life. "The doctor says I can still play for another six or seven months. Then we'll take it from there. But being a wife and mother is part of my career now. We both need to embrace that."

"But there will still be tennis."

"You are incorrigible."

"I'm your coach, Alice."

This is true. "There will always be tennis. We'll just have to figure out at what capacity"—Teach opens her mouth, but Alice doesn't let her speak—"When the time comes. And hey, Josephine Collins has a little girl. She's still playing. Top ranked, even."

"Mm-hmm." Teach snatches the reading glasses from her head, the nose pads snagging on her hair, and shoves them on her face as she picks up a book from the coffee table. The conversation is over. Teach will pretend to read while she licks her wounds. But that is fine. Alice has said what she needed to say. Mother, wife, tennis pro, comic writer—Oh, Juliette Gordon Low, the mother of the Girl Scouts, could be the perfect next Wonder Woman for this soon-to-be-mama to tackle. But yes, all of those things. Maybe not always in that order. But all of them. All at once.

"One day when we're forty, love, we'll look back and realize we have everything we've ever wanted."

Joe had said that after they'd first met. Turns out, thirty is the new forty. Alice always did like being an overachiever.

[Wonder Women of History logo]
[Introduction]
Juliette Gordon Low
1861–1927
Juliette Gordon Low, a woman of grace, wit, and unyield-

ing determination, is best known as the mother of the Girl Scouts of America. The concept of girl scouting was a seed Juliette, affectionately known as "Daisy" by her friends, brought back from England. What began as an intimate tea party in 1912—with just eight girls—blossomed into a million members. Her tireless efforts knew no bounds in her quest to empower and uplift young women all around the world, all bound by a creed to serve God and country and to help people at all times.

[Box 1]

[Description: 3-year-old Juliette/Daisy is startled awake in bed by singing soldiers outside their home]

Narration: In 1864, war raged between the north and the south.

Juliette: War sound so sad, Mama!

Men outside singing: Weeping, sad and lonely, Hopes and fears how vain! Yet praying, When the cruel war is over, Praying that we meet again!

[Box 2]

[Description: 3-year-old Juliette/Daisy comforted by her mother]

Mama: It is sad, Daisy.

Juliette: I wish it would stop. I don't want anyone else to be hurt.

[Box 3 - Narration box]

As Juliette aged, her compassionate heart grew with her. She began the Helpful Hands Sewing Club.

[Box 4]

[Description: Juliette in a sewing circle with friends]

Daisy: If only we had four hands each!

Friend 1: We could help even more people.

Friend 2: At least we're doing something!

Friend 3 [pricks herself]: Ouch!

[Box 5]
Narration: In 1886, Juliette married an Englishman named William Low.
[Description: Juliette/William leaving the ceremony as rice is thrown]
Juliette: Ow!
William: Daisy, are you all right?
Juliette: I will be!
[Box 6]
Narration: But Juliette wasn't the same ever again. A grain of rice caused an abscess in Juliette's ear that left her partially deaf. Still, she didn't let that stop her from trying to help anyone in her path.
[Box 7]
Narration: During the Spanish-American War, Juliette helped as a nurse during a typhoid epidemic.
[Description: Juliette corralling a group of women in a room full of sick men]
Juliette [cupping her good ear to direct sound there]: Okay, ladies, we have to work together in an organized fashion.
Nurse 1: I'll fetch the leeches.
Nurse 2: I'll boil clean water.
Nurse 3: I'll prepare doses of opium.
[Box 8]
Narration: During a trip to England, Juliette attended a party where she met Lord Baden-Powell.
[Description: socializing]
Juliette: The Boy Scouts? Do tell. Does such a group exist for girls?
Lord Baden-Powell: Indeed, the Girl Guides.
Juliette: Oh!
[Box 9]
Narration: In 1812, Juliette had the grand idea to introduce

Girl Guides in Savannah, Georgia.
[Description: 8 young girls and Juliette at a tea party]
Juliette: We'll spend time outdoors, help others in need, and earn badges.
Girl 1: I'd like to join!
Girl 2: My cousin in Atlanta would love something like this.
Juliette: Why stop in Savannah? Or Atlanta? I'll organize troops all over the United States!
Girl 3: The world!
[Box 10]
And they did, despite Juliette's failing health. During the Great War, the Girl Scouts were awarded a medal by the US government for patriotic service.
[Description: sick Juliette sitting by a fire with a friend]
Juliette: We've accomplished so much, but there's still one thing I dream of.
Friend: World peace?
Juliette: Yes! But also a camp for all the Girl Scouts around the globe to come together.
Friend: Austria, China, South Africa! It'd be an undertaking.
[Box 11]
Narration: But like they did with so many other challenges, the Girl Scouts' organization worked tirelessly, before Juliette's health could worsen. The next year, in 1926, a world camp was held. The following winter, Juliette passed away.
[Description: Juliette in bed, nurse nearby]
Juliette: What a life I've lived.
Nurse: You've helped so many and started something that'll live on for years to come.
[Box 12]
Narration: Honesty and fairness, friendliness and help-

fulness, consideration and thoughtfulness, courageousness and strength are what every young girl can attain by following in the footsteps of this intrepid Wonder Woman and world leader.
[Alice Marble signature]

At five months pregnant, most people are none the wiser to her condition. Of course, Alice told Joe during one of their static-filled phone calls. He's over the moon, already planning numbers two and three when this first one isn't even out yet.

In fact, the first one isn't even showing yet, especially in the drop-waisted frock Alice chose for that evening's party. There always seems to be a party to celebrate one thing or another.

And this one is turning into a late night.

Alice hides a yawn and forces a smile, no longer in the mood for small talk. She discreetly touches her belly, not sure if it's gas or if the baby is quickening. She tells herself it's the baby. *The baby. The baby. The baby.* All her thoughts lately have revolved around him or her, and Alice couldn't be happier. It's comical to her, really, that such a small thing has taken such a great hold on her and her future.

Alice says her goodbyes and starts the long drive back to the city from Long Island. She barely has time to register the oncoming driver swerve into her lane. She tightens her grip. She yanks hard on the wheel.

But it's too late.

Chapter 20

This isn't the first—and it likely won't be the last—time Alice returns to herself, blinking, a sterile room, blanched faces slowly coming into focus.

There's a tightening on Alice's hand. Slowly her eyes trail to the source. Teach.

"Shh," Teach says, gaze jumping to a nurse. "Save your strength."

Alice isn't sure she's ever seen tears in her coach's eyes.

"There was an accident," Teach goes on.

An accident? The details are fuzzy. At first she only recalls the crash from a few months ago, the one so similar to her father's. But then last night hits her like a brick and Alice fights the sickening feeling climbing up her throat.

The nurse squeezes Teach's arm before she slips from the room. Teach clears her throat, growl-like. "The fool was drunk. I could kill him. You need to stop scaring the bejesus out of me. But you're going to be okay."

"Be okay," Alice mutters. Then she remembers the greatest thing of all.

So does Teach. "The baby. I know, Alice, I know. But Joe and you are just starting out. You can try again. You can have a whole slew of babies."

She's groggy, the anesthesia still wearing off, but Alice touches her barely there stomach. It feels the same. But her coach's words . . . they're breaking through the fog. They're breaking her heart. Loss swoops in and is like a hand around her neck. She struggles for breath and for the strength to ask, "Our baby's gone?"

Teach forces a swallow, then a nod. "No broken bones, Allie. Only a minor concussion this time. Nothing stopping you from trying again once Joe is on leave. I already asked the doctor and that's what he said."

Alice closes her eyes. Maybe she won't ever open them again. That'd be just fine. Gone. Her baby. Her baby with Joe.

"Joe," she says, staring into the nothingness behind her lids, her limbs feeling rooted to the hospital bed.

She hears Teach say, "He'll be back on New Year's Day. Right as planned in a few short weeks."

Alice decides to stay in the darkness. It's where she'll live now, until Joe rescues her. It'll be better then. Her voice is gravelly. "Don't tell him."

There's silence. Finally: "I can write him for you."

"No."

"You'll tell him when he's back?"

If Alice isn't mistaken, there's relief in the question.

But yes, she'll tell him. He won't hear about the accident overseas, on the front line, at a base, wherever he is. But when he's back, they'll mourn the loss together as husband and wife. For now, she wants to do nothing but lie there and exist in the darkness.

***

Teach has never before been more festive and animated.

There are decorations, a Christmas tree. "Have Yourself a Merry Little Christmas" is playing on the gramophone.

And did she bake? It smells that way. It also doesn't smell successful.

Teach is doing it all for Alice, she recognizes that. She's been out of the hospital about a week. Or more. Alice isn't sure. The emotions of losing her child ended up finding her in the darkness. It'd been a battering that Alice fought through. She wouldn't say she won. She survived.

When Teach asked if a party would help cheer her up after all she'd been through, and now that a trip west to be with her family would be too taxing on her, Alice said, "No, but it could be a distraction."

"Yes, okay," Teach suggested. "Something intimate. We'll sing and dance. Drink and eat."

Teach threw herself into the preparations straightaway. Now it is Christmas Eve. Mary Hardwick, Mary's husband, Charles, Don Budge, and Don's wife, Deirdre, will be arriving within the hour. Alice sits by the window, watching people walk by below, holding packages, breath visible, cheeks rosy, holiday spirit oozing from them.

She spots Teach heading into their building and glances toward the kitchen where she thought her coach had been all this time. It explains the burning smell.

Slowly, as if Alice now owns the bones of a ninety-year-old, she pushes off from the couch. Teach somehow still beats her, holding a package she picked up from the doorman on her way in.

"For you," Teach says.

"From Hazel? Dan?"

"Nope."

Alice takes the small parcel, her insides warming at the sight of the return address. Teach is smiling. "Suddenly you are a fan of my husband?"

"I'm president of the Alice Marble fan club."

"Are not," Alice says with the shake of her head. "You only want me back on my feet."

"I do. But I am also your biggest fan, and have been since I took a chance on you in your mum's living room. I only want to see you win, Alice, in all you do."

"Well," Alice begins, picking at a tear in the packaging, "thank you."

"What is that smell?" Teach's eyes shoot open. "The oven."

She scurries off, Alice chuckling softly, the first time she has in weeks. She carries the package like a baby bird toward her bedroom.

Inside, a letter sits on top a smaller box.

My love,

For you,
To make this day sweeter.
Your loving husband

Tears spring to her eyes. The thoughtfulness of this gift found beneath the letter clogs her throat. Not only is the perfume Marlene Dietrich's favorite—and he knows she'd love it for that reason alone—but the reference to making the day sweeter has nothing to do with the perfume's scent. She's smelled Bandit before. It's the enfant terrible of the Piguet fragrance collection. There are dark notes of leather, moss, and smoke, with only subtle hints of galbanum and orange blossom. It's a daring blend, not sweet at all. Joe referenced making the day sweeter because he knows Christmas Eve—the day she lost her father—is a hard day for Alice.

She wipes beneath her nose, then falls back on her bed, clutching the bottle. Beside her on the bedside table is a stack of letters from her sister and brothers. She's loved. She'll be okay. Still, Alice stays just as she is, the perfume bottle to her chest, until the doorbell announces the arrival of their first guest.

Alice has the most ridiculous of friends. They're all sloshed, including Teach. She's one drink away from getting on the table. To see her coach actually lose control, now that'll be something. A first, really.

She sits back, watching, laughing, milking a too-strong cocktail, missing Joe. One more week, she tells herself. Then he'll be back in New York. A full seven days on leave. Then the empty pit in her stomach will begin to heal.

She's been living on *thens*.

Then they'll lose themselves in each other.

Then they'll try again.

Then their dreams will continue.

Then she'll hold on as long as possible before he boards the ship.

But then they'll be one day closer to this godforsaken war being over.

From what Alice has heard, there's an ongoing battle along the Western Front. It's nerve-wracking to think Joe could be involved. It's reassuring to know he'll be far, far away soon enough.

What if it's all over before he's set to return? It's enough to make a girl giddy, and a welcomed change from wallowing on how the past month has been absurdly unfair and unkind.

A knock sounds on the door.

"I'll get it," Teach sings, already on her feet. The woman sashays across the living room. "Hello," she bellows, throwing open the door.

"Who is it?" Alice calls. "Could Tilden make it after all?"

How dare people wish to spend Christmas Eve with their families.

Teach doesn't answer. She's blocking the view of the new partygoer.

"We're not expecting anyone else, are we?" Alice asks the room.

Mary has a better vantage point. She palms her mouth. Looks between Alice and whoever is at the door.

Alice rubs along her collarbone and asks, "What? Who is it?"

Blindly, Teach tries to set her glass on the table where they stash keys and whatever else is randomly found in their pockets. Tennis balls. Receipts. Lozenges.

Teach misses the table. The glass shatters, a golden liquid splashing on the walls and Teach's cream-colored trousers.

Alice's heart is beating wildly now.

She no longer wants to know who's at the door. Leave her ignorant. Leave her for a few beats more in denial.

Then Teach reaches for something. A yellow envelope. A telegram.

Then Teach steps aside. A man in uniform stands in the doorway.

For the rest of her life, Alice will forever remember his somber expression as it locks on her.

Then he tells her.

Chapter 21

Then

May 31, 1934
The American Hospital at Neuilly, France

It was crazy how life could be altered in an instant.

It had all started when Alice boarded the SS *Westernland* set for France to play in a series of matches before going on to England to play in the Wightman Cup. It was on the ship, across the table from the icy-eyed psychic, that Alice received that chill-inducing omen.

"You'll rise. Then you'll fall."

From there she had docked, caught a train to Paris, ogled the Eiffel Tower, was swept up in the awe of being overseas for the first time, and arrived at the Ritz Hotel.

However, none of those things did the altering. Sure, after the long journey, Alice's skin no longer held her usual olive coloring.

And yes, dark circles had accumulated under her eyes. But no, not life-altering. Not yet.

Nor did her life change on account of the conditions of the stadium in Paris, which was as airless as a shoebox and hot as a steam bath. Or because Alice's game seemed to be off in each match and that persistent cough of hers labored her breathing.

Usually something life-changing happens in a moment. A phone call. A telegram. A death. An accident.

In Alice's case, it was a declaration.

"You'll never play again."

That was what Dr. Dax had just said to her, with the bedside manner of a boulder.

She was in the hospital. Again. She had collapsed. Again. She'd been playing Sylvia Henrotin in a match. A match that meant nothing in the grand scheme of things. Just one of the friendly matches the tennis association set up for Alice and her teammates to play in before they went to England to play in the Wightman Cup.

But while playing against Henrotin, Alice's vision had begun to wane. She tried to keep the Frenchwoman's face in focus, to breathe, to keep her feet moving. But she couldn't. Henrotin swum before her eyes, then Alice went down.

Sunstroke and mild anemia were what she'd been diagnosed with after her collapse from Myrick's shenanigans, but she'd been able to come back from that. Even an article in the Parisian papers that very morning—with the most embarrassingly horrid photo of two men carrying her from the court, Henrotin looking on with concern—had high hopes Alice would recover just fine. So what on earth was this doctor saying now?

"You'll never play again."

She wrinkled her brows with confusion and anger. Just that slight movement made her body ache.

Dr. Dax pointed to an X-ray of her lungs and cut straight to the point. "You have tuberculosis," he said. "I regret to say you'll never again have the strength to play."

What was he getting on about? He'd said it twice now, in two different ways, but she still couldn't accept any of it as reality.

"For some people," he said, "tuberculosis bacteria can be inactive for a lifetime. For others, especially those with a compromised immune system, the bacteria becomes active, multiplies, and causes the disease. You've likely had the bacteria for a while now, and your health in the past year has most certainly been compromised. You've had a cough all that time, you say?"

She raised a hand, waved it. This wasn't happening. The rest of her Wightman team had left only hours ago to go on to London. Even though Alice understood their necessity to leave, to keep the team's schedule, it was horrible to be left behind. At the time she told herself she'd follow after them in only a matter of days. She was not going to miss out on playing in the cup, not after all she'd been through to earn her spot on the team. Wightman Cup. National Championships. Wimbledon. Those were her and Teach's goals. Now this quack was telling her she'd never be able to play again. "There has to be a mistake."

Dr. Dax shook his head. "I'm afraid not."

Alice's neck pricked with unease. Dread, actually. Like the rug had been pulled out from under her. Or as if she were trapped, desperately searching for a way out. "Okay," she said, trying to calm her racing thoughts, "how do we treat it?"

"Rest, isolation, fresh air, exercise, and good nutrition."

"Exercise?" Alice didn't care a lick her tone was impudent. "You just said I couldn't play tennis."

"Not at the level you are accustomed to, Miss Marble."

Tears stung her eyes. The feeling of entrapment was intensifying, the walls closing in on her. "I want to go home. I don't want to be here any longer."

Quite frankly, she didn't want to be alive. It felt as if everything had been taken from her in Dr. Dax's deadpanned four words.

"You'll never play again."

Or maybe the instant everything changed had been from another set of ominous words.

"You'll rise. Then you'll fall."

It took six weeks for arrangements to be made and for Alice to return to the States. Teach had made the drive from California to New York. She stood at the end of the gangplank, arms stiff at her sides. Alice couldn't believe she was there. Couldn't even make eye contact.

Teach was a tennis coach, yet Alice was no longer a tennis player. She'd let Teach down. Herself down. Her brother, who sacrificed so much. Her mother, who supported her endlessly, writing a letter every single day Alice was apart from her. Hell, she even felt like she let that jerk Myrick down. Back in France, the nurses spoke under their breath about what they overheard Myrick saying: how he never should have given in and let her on the Wightman team. Alice told Teach, who was ready to dance on his eventual grave, blaming him for Alice's illness. When Teach called Myrick on it, he, of course, took no responsibility, and even went so far as to say that Alice was a liability. A bad investment. Now that she'd never play again, there would be no gate receipts to make up for the medical expenses she'd incurred him.

A sob bubbled up Alice's throat as she was wheeled toward her former coach.

Teach wrapped her in an awkward hug that pinned Alice's arm against the wheelchair. "I'm so sorry . . . If I had gone . . . Whitey said . . ." Then Teach pinched her nose, quite effectively also pinching off her emotions. She tried for a smile. "Let's get out of here, huh?"

To do what?

Twenty years old. No college education. Very little job experiences. Alice had never thought beyond tennis.

Alice *was* tennis.

She shivered at the breeze coming off the water, her body not getting the memo it was a balmy summer day.

Alice said nothing. She just allowed herself to be taken away.

Big Apple Tattler

Sunday, July 15, 1934

It's the End for Tennis Great Alice Marble

NEW YORK, N.Y. - The tennis career of Alice Marble, a Californian who traded in baseball to emerge as a marvel on the tennis courts, ended abruptly weeks ago during an exhibition match at Roland Garros Stadium in Paris. Miss Marble, a student of Eleanor "Teach" Tennant, is only twenty years old.

Miss Marble, who previously suffered from anemia and sunstroke, according to her team doctor, was admitted to the American Hospital at Neuilly after collapsing on the court while playing France's No. 2, Miss Sylvia Henrotin. United States Lawn Tennis Association president Julian S. Myrick gave no comment.

To achieve her stature as the golden-haired princess of women's tennis, Miss Marble overcame many obstacles. Born on Sept. 28, 1913, in the lumber town of Beckwourth in the Sierra Nevada, she relocated to San Francisco with her parents and older siblings at the age of five. In 1920, Marble's father died after complications from an automobile accident. The family was thrust into poverty.

Miss Marble was a chubby girl athlete, adept at boxing, baseball, and basketball. Her athletic skills turned to tennis at the age of fifteen, quickly accumulating many wins in junior tournaments all over California and catching the attention of tennis instructors Eleanor "Teach" Tennant and Harwood "Whitey" White. The world held high hopes for this tennis prodigy, whose progress was tested in 1933 by a case of sunstroke after Marble played 108 games of tennis in one day in Easthampton, Long Island.

How sad for Marble to fight back, rising to the World Top 10, only to fall victim to poor health once again. We wish this young tennis star had the opportunity to reach her full potential.

DEAREST ALICE STOP
YOU ARE ALWAYS WELCOME AT THE RANCH STOP
WITH LOVE STOP
MARION AND WILLIAM

"Wait?" Alice said. "Where are we going?"

This wasn't Beverly Hills with its tree-lined streets and perfectly maintained lawns.

Teach kept her eyes on the road. "We're not going to my house."

"Then where are we going?"

Teach didn't respond, and it felt like a fist was closing around Alice's insides. First they'd gone to San Francisco. The whole way from New York to her ma's house, Alice's guilt flared like a disease of its own. How would her family pay for her ongoing medical expenses? It really wasn't a question. They couldn't.

As soon as Teach parked along the curb, her brothers had rushed outside. Alice's mother was on their heels. Not a single one of them hadn't been crying.

"Enough," Teach had said as Alice's brothers carried her inside. "This isn't a wake. I personally don't care that Alice's tennis career is over."

Lies, Alice had wanted to scream.

Even some second-rate gossip rag had written about the end of her career like it was an obituary. Teach had insisted Alice not read anymore newspapers after that. The fact her former coach was being so supportive actually made Alice feel worse—and for the tears to fall harder.

How easy it'd been to feel sorry for herself. She was settled in her old bedroom she used to share with Hazel. It felt smaller, different. Despite it being summertime, the house felt drafty and cold. Her mood felt just as bleak.

Seemingly a million times a day, her mother climbed the steps to palm Alice's cheek, smooth the wrinkles from her bed, bring her books, try to encourage Alice to eat.

The image Alice had always had of her mother was short yet heavyset. But as Alice watched her mother flit about the room, she recognized exhaustion behind her eyes, a thinning waistline, and a perpetual strain on her face. It wouldn't do. Alice had been a burden in too many ways, and Alice decided to write to Teach, not as her student, but hopefully as a friend.

To Alice's complete surprise, Teach came for her with the recommendation that Alice would recuperate more quickly in a drier climate. Specifically, with her and her sister, Gwen, in Beverly Hills.

Alice's mother objected; she could care for Alice just fine, thank you very much. But Alice saw the fatigue on her mother. In the end, her ma agreed to Beverly Hills.

But that wasn't where they were currently headed. Teach had just said as much.

"Then where are we going?" Alice asked again.

"Monrovia."

It still wasn't an answer. They drove through a very suburban-feeling town surrounded by rolling hills and mountains. At the mouth of a canyon stood a gigantic, three-story, white building.

"There," Teach said matter of factly.

They approached a gate with words etched into the ironwork. POTTENGER SANATORIUM.

Alice's head whipped toward Teach, the fastest she'd moved in weeks. "You're having me committed?"

Alice didn't think she could fall any further. She'd been wrong.

Chapter 22

"I'm not having you committed, Alice. It's a sanatorium, not an asylum. You're here to rest."

"My mother agreed to this?"

"Your mum will be just fine."

Alice balked; her mother didn't even know this was happening. Bet Dan didn't either. But the real concern was money. "Who's paying for this?"

"I am," Teach said.

Alice could only gawk at her.

"What? You called me for help, didn't you?"

"For advice."

Teach raised a brow. "Well, my advice is that you recuperate in a warm, dry climate that's quiet and where there's a doctor who can look after you. It's the best place for you. I'll write your mum. She'll understand."

"But . . ." Alice was nothing more than a pawn being moved around a chessboard. So little of her life felt like it was in her own control. The thing was, in the past, Teach usually did this kind of thing for her own gain. Alice scratched along her brow, confused. "But you're not my coach anymore."

Teach snorted. "Who says?"

Alice wanted to scream. Maybe the doctor who said she wasn't a tennis player anymore? And if she wasn't a tennis player anymore, there'd be no way for Alice to pay Teach back for this.

She opened her mouth to object when Teach shushed her. "Just get better, okay?"

"How long am I going to be here?"

"Six weeks."

"And then what?"

Teach parked in front of the grand-looking white building and beeped her horn. "Bollocks if I know."

Alice's bottom lip quivered and tears pooled in her eyes as a woman in a white nurse's uniform appeared from the entrance to the Pottenger Sanatorium.

The Pottenger Sanatorium for Diseases of the Chest Is Here for Your Loved One with a Hygienic, Dietetic, Open-Air Regimen

1. THE ISOLATION OF THE PATIENT. He will be removed from the distractions and influences of business and domestic responsibilities and be placed in attractive subtropical surroundings and an open-air environment.
2. A CAREFULLY CONTROLLED EXISTENCE. Your loved one is under close medical supervision to promote healing in our favorable all-year-round climate that is peculiarly free from storms.
3. SUITABLE DIET. Your loved one will be given only wholesome foods designed to improve his condition.
4. HYGENIC LIVING. He will heal in a clean, pure-air environment.

5. INACTIVE BEDREST. Exercise can be extremely dangerous, and no other factor so strongly militates against cure. As such, he will be treated with inactivity and bedrest until exercise is no longer harmful.

The Sierra Madre Mountains to the north. Unrestricted view of the San Gabriel Valley to the south. The ocean off in the distance. A natural ravine running through the grounds. Gardens perpetually in bloom. Benches and swings. Sprawling native live oak trees. Winding paths. Private bungalows—with running hot and cold water, lavatories, a massive closet, and three sides of the tiny buildings made up of screens to maximize open air and sunlight.

It was all picturesque, state of the art, and the perfect environment to do nothing but rest.

Alice hated every inch of it.

She didn't want to be inactive. She wanted sweat in her eyes, muscles aching from three-hour workouts, blisters and sores. She missed the butterflies smacking at her insides before a big match, the roar of the crowd, the burst of life inside of her when she served an ace.

In the corner of her bungalow, Alice's tennis racquet leaned against the wall. From her bed, in which she was rarely allowed to leave—she even ate all her meals there—she glared at the racquet like it was mocking her.

"Stop it," she spat at the inanimate object.

And now she was losing her mind.

It'd only been a week.

She had five more to go.

Teach came daily. Sometimes Teach's sister, Gwen, came too. A fifty-mile round trip.

"You shouldn't," Alice told Teach. She wasn't only protesting

Teach's visits every twenty-four hours. It was also the fact she knew Teach was giving twice the number of lessons to pay for Alice's stay there.

"You said that yesterday," Teach said. "Yet here I am. You might as well save your breath."

"What else am I supposed to use it for?" Alice said glumly.

"You could sing."

Alice rolled her eyes, glancing at the radio. Her only companionship was food, endless amounts, it seemed, and the soap operas, mysteries, talk shows, and news that played endlessly throughout the day in her tiny, private, modern, open-air bungalow. Sure, the doctor came twice a day, and the nurse poked her head in on an annoyingly regular basis, but Alice had never felt more alone. She had no desire to sing.

"Brought more letters from your mum," Teach said. She began digging them out of her bag. "Oh, and something else I think you may appreciate."

"Yeah?" Alice said, exhaustion in her voice. Never before had she felt so drained.

Teach held out her palm, a small object resting there.

Alice gasped. It was her pin, the one she thought she lost before her ill-fated trip to Europe. "Where did you find it?" Alice took it and rubbed a thumb over the racquet, pearl, diamonds, and rubies.

"It was caught up in the lining of a pocket in one of your tennis shorts. Found it when I was unpacking the clothes you took with you to . . ." She trailed off. They both knew where Alice had been and how she never got to play in the cup after all.

The excitement that initially surged in Alice melted away. The pin was her lucky pin. That Teach gave to her when she'd said she was proud of her. Her lucky pin she wore while playing tennis. Something she didn't do anymore.

She glanced at her racquet in the corner. Then she put the pin aside. She had no need for either of them anymore.

When Alice was younger, she was what folks called chubby. After taking up tennis, the excess fell away. It was replaced with hard, thick, game-winning muscle.

After only a few weeks in bed, Alice stared down at her slack legs. A tear leaked out. Quite frankly, Alice was shocked her tear ducts had any left. Disheartened, she flicked her thigh. The skin jiggled like gelatin. Bedrest plus emotional eating was not a winning combination. Much of the toning, firmness, and muscle had atrophied from only leaving her bed to use the lavatory. Her arms too. She'd lost the definition there. Her biceps quivered when she lifted anything heavier than a book.

Have mercy, she was tired of books and magazines. For the life of her, she couldn't retain a lick of what she read. That was saying something for someone with an eidetic memory . . .

She sniffed, disgusted with herself. How had she become *this* version of herself? Twenty-one years old—because, yes, she'd celebrated her birthday lying down, Dan and Hazel making the long seven-hour bus ride for a rare visit—and she was already feeling completely washed up.

Teach walked in, a pep in her step, and Alice quickly wiped away her tears.

"Week six, baby," Teach said, her voice as upbeat as her strut. "You ready to fly this chicken coop?"

Despite herself, Alice chuckled at Teach's enthusiasm. She owed her a lot, more than the cost of Alice being here for six long, excruciating, motionless weeks.

And Alice *was* ready. She wanted out of this slice of hell she'd been existing in. But, if she was being honest with herself, she wasn't sure if she felt better or not. Only walking to and from the bathroom wasn't much of a barometer of her body's recovery. Mentally she was also a bit scared. What was waiting for her after she left?

The question was premature.

The question festered for another six weeks, the doctor insisting Alice extend her treatment.

The question took on a life of its own, burrowing deep in Alice's darkest thoughts that she'd never get better.

The question became her worst enemy when, again, the doctor tacked on another six weeks to her stay.

The question ate away at her when she spent Christmas Eve in the sanatorium and not with her family, the first time she hadn't been with them since her father's death.

The question mocked her when she spent the new year feeling like a prisoner.

She let the letters from her mother pile up on her bedside table. But there was one that Teach kept moving to the top.

"You should read all of them. But this one . . . you should really read that one," Teach would say, tapping it.

"Go on, read it," Teach would suggest another day.

"Why's it matter?" Alice said. "What's any of it matter? Dan's doing great on the force. Hazel is thinking about dating again. George is doing just fine. Tim is as persnickety as ever. Nothing ever changes."

"Just read this one," Teach said, tossing it onto Alice's lap. "Do it for me."

"Fine," she said with a sigh. "I'll read it."

Chapter 23

Alice eyed the envelope in her lap, wary of reading about how other peoples' lives were progressing when hers was painfully static.

Teach backpedaled toward the bungalow's exit, smiling ear to ear. What was she getting on about with that grin?

Then Alice saw the return address.

Carole Lombard.

Alice's mouth fell open and her eyes flicked to Teach, who saluted her like a general in the army.

Alice tore open the envelope and had the letter out before the screen door banged closed.

She'd become friendly with Carole at the ranch, all but embarrassing herself with the facts she rattled off about one of her favorite film stars.

Carole was born in Indiana. Her real name was Jane, a film company suggesting she change it. She chose Carole after a girl she played tennis with. In the 1920s, she starred in more than twenty silent films. "And you're in the midst of a seven-year contract with Paramount," Alice had recited. She'd read all about Carole in interviews.

Carole had laughed, when, really, she could have run in the other direction. And now Alice was holding a letter from her.

Slower than she'd ripped open the envelope, she carefully unfolded the paper.

Dear Alice,

I sincerely hope it's all right that Teach told me about your plight. It was done so with your best interest in mind, I can assure you. You see, I have a story of my own I'd like to share with you, one you miraculously did not comment upon when we first met. I can only assume you don't know about this moment in my life. Not surprising, as my film company at the time largely kept it out of the press and interviews. I'd done three films with them, with Fox, in 1925. I had a tremendous gap between my first film in 1921—remember the one where I'd been casted after they caught me playing baseball with the boys—and these back-to-back films. I believed my star was on the rise and I'd keep making film after film after film.

But then I was in a horrific automobile accident. My face sustained much of the damage. I required one hundred stitches and hours of surgery, devoid of any pain medication. I shiver at the memory even now. For six months, I lay on a hospital bed, much like you are today. Four months of that time I wasn't allowed to move an inch for fear of undoing all the doctors had done to make me look human again. To make matters worse, Fox cancelled my contract.

They didn't think I'd have a face for film any longer. The doctors said as much too. They told me I'd have scars—and I still do, to this day, on my left cheek, across my upper lip, and through my eyebrow.

I wanted to die. To vanish. I felt lost. I wasn't sure who I'd be anymore. I mourned a career that felt cut off at the knees. I cried, a lot. You may feel similar, Alice.

Then I began to think that I had nothing to lose by trying. So I began to fight. I became cognizant of things such as lighting, the nuances of cinematography, and well-placed props. Have you noticed during close-ups that I often rest my cheek on my hand? Or that the right side of my face is shown instead of my left? The other scars are easily concealed with lipstick and brow makeup. By being stubborn and not taking no for an answer, I found ways to exist in my chosen path. Two years after the accident I made my way back onto the screen and appeared in thirteen short films that year alone. I didn't give up my dreams. Nor should you.

You'll have to fight for it, maybe really hard. But the young woman I remember at the ranch is a fighter.

You have my full
support and my love,

Carole Lombard

Alice held the letter atop her chest. Then she reread Carole's words again. And again.

It was no secret Alice revered film stars. Many came from humble beginnings. Many were turned down a hundred times before hearing their first yes. As they acted, they were so much more than pretty faces. They were transportive. Carole's flicks had taken Alice to horse races, train robberies, mining fields. They made her laugh, cry, and kept her on the edge of her seat.

Alice marveled again how life could be altered in an instant. It happened during Carole's accident. It happened when the doctor said Alice would never play again.

But it also happened when Carole decided to fight.

Alice wanted to fight too.

***

"Rise and shine," Teach said after a quick *knock, knock* on the door's wood frame.

Only two steps into Alice's bungalow she stopped in her tracks. Her face lit up with surprise, confusion, and a hint of delight.

"Going somewhere?" she asked Alice, who sat on the edge of her bed.

At Alice's feet were her suitcases and her racquet. "Didn't you say we were flying this coop?"

One side of Teach's lip curled into a smile. "Yes, but that was quite a few months ago."

"Exactly."

"Did I miss something? Did the doctors clear you to leave?"

"Not exactly."

"Are you feeling better?"

Alice threw up her hands. "Who knows? It's hard to tell if I'm improving or not when I'm not allowed to leave this bed."

"The doctors do tests weekly."

"I haven't seen the results, have you? All they do is keep adding on more time. You keep paying the bill. Feels like we could do this forever. I'm never going to get well here."

"So you packed your bags?"

"Your eyes work."

"And apparently your wit works again, Allie."

Alice smiled. She didn't know her lips could even move that way anymore. "I've decided to fight."

"Did you now," Teach said, the words quiet. She clucked. She rubbed her lips together. She clicked her tongue a final time. "I'll make you a deal. If you can make it to the car, we'll leave today. Right now."

Alice nodded. Her coat was already on. She bent to pick up her bags, but Teach slapped her hand away. "I've got those."

And what a feeling it was to know Teach still had her back. But when Teach tried to support Alice's elbow, Alice shook her off. "I can do this."

At that, Alice squared her shoulders and took her first steps toward the door. She shuffled as quickly as her weak body could go. "I feel like Carole Lombard when she played a secret agent."

Teach laughed loudly.

"Shh," Alice said, already short of breath. At any moment, she expected one of the nurses to stop them from their escape. "Where's the car?"

"Around the bend."

A bend had never felt so long. Alice's breath was no longer short but completely labored. Her vision began to blur.

"Oh no you don't," Teach said as Alice began to buckle. "Let me help you fight."

Teach guided Alice the final steps, propping her against the car's side while she opened the passenger door. "In you go," she said.

Alice fell inside. Teach's coat appeared on her lap.

Behind the wheel, Teach fumbled with her keys. "Am I allowed to laugh yet? I feel like I'm breaking the law by busting you out of here."

Shivering now, her body depleted, Alice motioned for Teach to have at it. Teach did just that, bellowing out a nervous laugh as she navigated them down the winding roads, pass the beautiful gardens, away from the mountains and the sea. Alice closed her eyes, feeling hopeful for the first time in many months.

Chapter 24

Alice stepped off the scale. Her gaze flicked around the bathroom at Teach's Beverly Hills home, too overwhelmed to focus. She'd lost nearly all her muscle yet gained forty-five pounds at the sanatorium. How was that possible?

She steadied her gaze, now staring at a chipped tile. And stared and stared. Could she do this? She could do this. She just had to keep going. Nothing worth fighting for was easy. Wasn't that what they said? Though Alice wasn't sure who "they" were.

Successful people, she imagined. People who set and met their goals. Who fought to be their best selves.

For Alice, that was a tennis player. The *best* tennis player. She remembered what Mary K. Browne said to her a few years ago, that there were words above the entrance to the courts at Wimbledon that she wanted Alice to take notice of.

Alice had sat straighter and asked, "What do they say?"

Mary had leaned into Alice like they were old friends even though they had just met. "You'll see for yourself."

Alice *really* wanted to see for herself. She inhaled deeply, knowing it was up to her to make that happen. "Teach!" she yelled as she left the bathroom.

"Not home!" Alice heard Gwen call from somewhere in the house.

Even better. Teach wouldn't be privy to what Alice was about to try: walking around the block.

Just that. A simple walk.

A walk that'd push Alice to the limits.

But it'd be a start. Alice would even show herself some grace. If she needed to stop, she would. But she'd go the entire way, even if it took her all night.

Though Teach would be mad if she was late for dinner. Couldn't let Alice's rare steak and steamed carrots get cold. Her diet came doctor recommended. Teach had consulted with a new one—Dr. Commons—just the day before, done with the doctors who said Alice would never step foot on a tennis court again.

This one had run the same X-rays and exams, spoke about the scarring on Alice's lungs, but in the end he'd come to a very different conclusion.

Severe pleurisy and secondary anemia.

"Dumb it down for me, Doctor," Alice had said, standing in front of a fluoroscope.

Dr. Commons moved a slide up and down, studying the screen. He smiled kindly. "Severe inflammation of the lining of your lungs."

"But not tuberculosis."

"If it was, it's not any longer."

"So I can play tennis again?" Alice had asked, almost too afraid to say the words.

"You can certainly try after you've regained your strength. Estimate two and a half weeks of recovery for every week you spent on bedrest."

That meant nearly a year.

She was determined to do it in half the time. The road in front of Alice would be long either way.

The literal road in front of her felt comically long. Was this a city block or an airport runway? "They" also said one foot in front of the other.

Alice did just that. She was panting by the time she reached the corner. God must've put a light pole in that very spot for her to lean against and collect her breath. Across the way, two little girls were sitting on a stoop watching her—*doing what*—dog it?

That wouldn't do. She pushed off, focusing on the next corner. She made it. Two more to go. Sweat poured into her eyes, Alice's body not having worked this hard in ages.

On the final stretch, a mother with a stroller passed her. *Her.* The girl who used to hustle for three sets and still have energy to go. But that was okay. It'd take time, she reminded herself.

One step after another, until she'd done it, she made it back to the house. She made it up the front steps. She made it through the house, past Gwen sewing at the kitchen table, and out the back patio door. Stripping off her clothes down to her underthings, she made it across the cement deck and into a small swimming pool until the water lapped at her chin.

She'd made it.

***

Hope was a type of drug, perhaps the most addicting kind.

Alice walked every day. The walk turned into a jog. She began skipping rope. Not well, the markings on her shin clearly showed, but her muscles were growing stronger.

Strong enough to pick up a racquet again? She hadn't yet done that. Fear held her back, battling with the hope that she'd actually be able to play an entire match. If she could, that opened the door to a new level of fear: Could she actually play competitively again? Could she still go after her dreams?

"Just come to the ranch with me," Teach urged. "It was good for you last time."

"I still feel like a cow."

It'd only been a few weeks.

"You're scared," Teach said. "I get that. But we need to get you around tennis again. Come to Marion's court tomorrow. Carole's been asking after you."

Carole, the very reason Alice wasn't doing another six weeks in the joint. Or at least the sanatorium had felt like prison.

"All right," Alice agreed.

Carole Lombard greeted her with a bear hug and a knowing smile. "Nice to see you on the other side."

Alice laughed. "It's nice to be here. Thank you for your letter."

"Us ladies have to help each other out, don't we?"

"Yeah, yeah," Teach said and tapped her watch. Carole backpedaled to her side of the court, mouthing to Alice, "She's so bossy."

Wasn't that the truth?

"Alice," Teach said. "You're on ball duty. Got it?"

Ball duty? She should be hitting the balls, not shagging them. That stung. She wanted to say no for that reason alone, but also because it wouldn't be easy. Alice had done lessons with her many times. She knew Teach used *many* balls.

After Carole's lesson, she now knew that Teach used over five hundred. Her back ached, her thighs burned, her lungs protested.

She did it all again the next day. And the next. Teach coached a whole hoard of influential women.

Pauline Gallagher, wife of comedian Skeets Gallagher; Diana, wife of musical director George Fitzmaurice; Beth, wife of Al Newman; Frances O'Neill, wife of Edwin Justus Mayer; Dorothy

Fields, the famous lyrics writer; and actresses Leila Hyams, Enid Storey, Norma Talmadge, and, of course, Carole.

Alice couldn't have asked to be around a more lovely group of women. She began helping Teach schedule their lessons, she kept track of their match results, and she continued picking up the seemingly endless number of balls.

She lived and breathed tennis.

Only, it wasn't *her* tennis.

Every day Teach brought Alice's racquet bag. Alice eyed it. She felt the tug toward it. That desire to unzip the bag, take out her racquet, and hold it. Use it. Fear had held her back.

Until now, no longer content to be an ancillary player in her own life. She met Teach's gaze.

Teach smiled. "About damn time."

Chapter 25

Teach would officially be Alice's coach again—if she could just toss the ball into the air and hit it over the net.

Such a simple thing she'd done a million times before.

She had Teach's enthusiasm.

She had Dr. Common's green light.

She possessed the desire to smash the gosh darn ball.

But her hands trembled as she bounced the ball again and again and again.

"You can do it, Allie," Carole called from the other side of the court.

That woman, endlessly supportive.

"Stop that," Teach said to Carole. "She's our opponent." But then to Alice, she shouted, "Just like riding a bike. Or in your case, Alice, just like lacing up your roller skates again."

Billy burst into her head. She liked that she could think of him and smile. If he could see her now, he'd be smiling too. She glanced at her doubles partner, Louise Macy, a fashion journalist. Louise gave her an encouraging nod.

Alice licked her lips. Why was this so hard? But she knew the answer to that. What if it was too soon and her health relapsed?

How any times could a person begin again and still be taken seriously? Did she dare hope? What if she couldn't get back into tournament shape? Playing doubles with celebs was one thing. Competing at Forest Hill or Wimbledon was an entirely different ballgame. What if she was nothing more than a social player from here on out?

"Alice," Teach said in a low voice, drawing out her name, saying so much even though she'd said so little.

Alice had to try. It was now or never. She stopped bouncing the ball and tossed it above her head. It wasn't her strongest serve, not even close. She was testing the waters. Apparently Teach was too. The return was a plum. Soft, slow, a three-year-old could have handled it. A chuckle bubbled up Alice's throat as she smacked a sizzler down the line between Teach and Carole.

The expression on Teach's face let loose the remainder of Alice's laugh. That felt good. Damn good.

Sick? Not Alice.

That was what she told herself. That was what she chose to believe. New York and France were in her rear-view mirror. Ahead of her: the US Championships and Wimbledon.

Alice had once been number three in the country—and she wanted it back. No, she wanted number one.

"Smokes, you still got it," Teach said in a fiery voice, the excitement in her eyes reminiscent of a kid at Christmas and not a thirty-something woman. "Now we need to build your stamina. Slowly. No more than three games a day for now. Dr. Commons needs your blood count higher before you do more than that."

In France, Alice's hemoglobin level had been fifty. Even the thought of it sent a chill through her body. Dr. Commons wanted her numbers double what they'd been, to at least a hundred, the threshold for anemia.

So she took it slow, despite now feeling raring to go. Soon one set of tennis a day became two. Playing doubles. Not singles yet. But it was progress. It was long days of sunshine, tennis, and helping Teach with her coaching.

"You're going to be the world's best, Alice," Teach said after every grueling set. "And I have an idea that could help."

"Let's hear it," Alice said, exhausted yet feeling rejuvenated from her coach's enthusiasm.

"Cabbage?"

"Excuse me?"

"The good doctor shared a tip with me. Laborers who work in the desert put cabbage leaves under their hats. Apparently the cabbage gets hot but the head stays cool. Helps with sunstroke. Want to try it?"

After her accident, Carole Lombard found her way with things like props and lighting. Cabbage wasn't quite as Hollywood, but, hey, "I'll do anything."

Alice was a newly minted twenty-two-year-old. She'd been sidelined for nearly two years from competitive tennis. With cabbage atop her head and fire in her heart, she was ready for her first real contest. Dr. Commons had estimated her recovery would take upward a year. She simply couldn't wait that long. She wanted to be on the court again in half that time. But her body demanded nine months. At least she was back.

The other entrants at the Racquet Club end-of-season

tournament were some of southern California's best: Dorothy Bundy, Carolin Babcock, Dorothy Workman, and Gracyn Wheeler.

The last she saw Carolin was a goodbye from a French hospital. "You look wonderful, Alice. Truly," she said now.

Alice felt wonderful.

She played wonderfully too, advancing to the finals lickety-split.

Carolin shook her head, though not unkindly. "Why am I not surprised to see you here?"

Alice shook her old teammate's hand over the net. "I plan to make it hard on you."

Actually, she planned to win, the crowded stadium already chanting Alice's name. It bought tears to her eyes. Such a little thing that meant so much to her as she was starting out. And now she was starting out again.

Saying she planned to win definitely felt brazen. Not only was her full strength lacking, but so was her confidence.

But winning. That was the only cure when you'd lost your confidence.

Beating Carolin 6–2, 6–2 was a giant leap in the right direction. So was the standing ovation she received. Bonus: It was ridiculously comical how the stench of cabbage trailed her off the court, the officials' noses scrunching but the men not knowing the source. She was tempted to tip her hat and ask them if they had any corned beef handy.

"That smile," Teach said, pushing through the bodies and climbing down from the stands. "You're back, Allie. You're back."

"You never gave up on me," Alice said.

"Never going to, kid. But we still have lots to go." She wagged a brow. "You ready for more?"

***

"I am. I know I'm ready," Alice told Dr. Commons. It was only a tiny lie. The Racquet Club tournament had been everything Alice had hoped it'd be. It also left her muscles fatigued and her lungs achy. In his office, she sat straighter and urged the words from him: *Yes, Alice, you can go east for the season and the US Championships.*

But that's not what he said. "I'm not convinced. I'd prefer you wait another year."

But Alice didn't have a year to wait.

Margaret Osborne was seventeen.

Dorothy Bundy was nineteen.

Gracyn Wheeler was twenty-one.

Alice was the oldest at twenty-two.

She needed to be competitive *years* ago. Not a year from now.

Dr. Commons ran a hand through his jet-black hair, then tapped her thick medical folder rhythmically. "You say you need conditioning and not rest?"

"Yes, sir."

Again, maybe a tiny lie.

"I'll make you a deal, then. Play another tournament. If your counts remain steady and you're not depleted after, then I'll pack your bags myself."

She smiled. "You really must care for me, Doc, if you're willing to pack my underthings."

"One more tournament," he said, fighting for professionalism while the curl of his lips said otherwise.

***

San Francisco. Home. Her tiny, white-framed house atop a hill. Her brothers. Her sister.

Alice beamed, standing at the bottom of the worn cement

stairway.

"Well, don't just stand there," her mother called from the doorway.

Alice took the steps two at a time, just as she'd done as a child.

At the top, her mother was waiting with open arms. "I may lock you up and throw away the key," she said into Alice's hair.

"Can't do that," Alice said, putting space between them so she could see her mother's face. She had aged in the past year, her cheeks sunken, the lines on her forehead more pronounced. Enough so that Alice lost her train of thought.

"I know, I know," her mother said. "You've got a tournament to play. I'm just happy it brought you home for a visit."

The original plan of alternating between Teach and home went out the window while Alice fought to get back on track with tennis. Not being home in so long was a sacrifice. A big one. She studied her mother more. Thinner. Fatigued. "Ma—"

"Let's get you inside." She grabbed Alice's elbow, certainly not void of strength in her grip. "I made your favorite. Your room's all ready. Hazel even cleaned up her side. Don't mention George's thinning hair. He's sensitive. Oh, Dan will have to tell you about the handball tournament he played in. He got second, but act surprised. Timmy—"

"Ma." Alice stopped them. "You've lost so much weight. Have you seen a doctor?"

Alice's mother snorted. "I'm certainly not going to complain about losing weight." She dismissed her daughter's concern with a wave of her hand. "Timmy snuck out again. Maybe you could talk to him."

"Sure, Ma, I can do that."

Her mother palmed Alice's cheek, moisture in her eyes. "I'm just so happy to have you all under one roof, even if it's just for a short time. Now let's get you settled. You've got a tournament to win." Her mother thrust a fist, her enthusiasm for Alice so touching that her own eyes filled with tears. It was good to be home.

San Francisco Gazette

Saturday, June 27, 1936

San Francisco's Prodigal Daughter Has Returned to the Tennis Courts

SAN FRANCISCO, CALIF. - For the past seven days, one name has been on everyone's lips during the California State Championships at the Berkeley Club: Alice Marble. She's back with a bang, after a two-year hiatus from tennis—and an even longer departure from San Francisco's tennis scene after going under the tutelage of Eleanor "Teach" Tennant. Marble's return hasn't been met with the warmest of welcomes. It seems some players are holding a grudge, grumbling about Marble leaving our fine city for Los Angeles four years ago. Others are criticizing her game, claiming Marble has been playing like a man in an aggressive net-rushing style. However she's playing, it's working. Marble breezed through the preliminaries and is set to face Miss Margaret Osborne in the finals tomorrow.

Margaret Osborne is not only ranked as the top player in northern California, she's also been the darling of San Francisco since Marble's exodus. Marble (22) and Osborne (17) both grew up playing on the same courts at Golden State Park. Both strong, quick, and daring players, tomorrow's match will be one to watch.

Chapter 26

Alice linked her arm through her sister's as they entered the Berkeley Club's main entrance. Alice's grip on her tennis bag was tight, her knuckles white. She admitted through a whisper, "I'm nervous, Hazel."

"Nonsense, Allie. You're spectacular."

"Nobody likes me anymore."

Hazel shrugged, her auburn curls bouncing. Alice snorted. "No positive words of advice for that one?"

The women turn the corner, headed toward the dressing rooms, Alice avoiding eye contact with anyone they passed.

"You're just going to have to win them over."

Easier said than done. No one had flat out booed her, but she also didn't get the standing ovation she'd gotten in southern California.

Hazel squeezed her hand. "I'm going to go claim my spot in the stands. Look for me if you need a smile. But apologies in advance if my attention is on the many eligible young men in the crowd."

Alice laughed. Her sister's divorce had been finalized for quite some time now. "Good for you for getting back out there."

"You too, Al. I'm proud of us."

Her sister disappeared down a hall that'd lead to the courts. Alice passed through the door into the dressing room.

"There you are," Teach said. "You ready? Margaret is fast, strong—"

"Younger."

Teach waved her off. "Stop acting like you've missed your shot, Alice. It's annoying. And it's only your fear talking. The best is ahead of you. Mark my word."

Alice took a steadying breath. "Okay, okay. Let's get me ready."

Winning that day was about more than winning the California championships, and hopefully endearing herself to her hometown crowd once more; it was proving to Dr. Commons that she was ready for the US Championships and all that went with it by going east. The cross-country travel. The grueling string of tournaments before Forest Hills. Then Forest Hills itself.

Ready, Alice stood at the entrance to the courts, stretching one quad and then the other. Margaret stood behind her, both of them waiting to be announced. Neither of them spoke. Neither acknowledged the other. This portion of the match could be rather uncomfortable with both opponents pulsing with adrenaline, nerves, and competitiveness.

Finally, the introductions began, and Alice pushed through the door and into the stadium. Instantly, Alice wanted to puke. Teach was clapping. Hazel was clapping—and smiling. But there weren't many more following suit. Until Margaret's name came over the loudspeaker. The crowd erupted.

Alice dipped her head, walking faster, turning the handle of her racquet around and around in her grip. She focused on the feel of the smooth wood in her hand. It settled her. Once more, her racquet was familiar, an extension of her arm.

From her side of the asphalt court, Alice shot her opponent a confident grin. Margaret had a great net game, but what had Teach said?

"Don't let her use it. Make her work hard to get to the ball by keeping your ground strokes low and fast."

Strategy. Precision. Skill. Strength. Once upon a time, Alice had been cocky.

Thirty minutes later, after she dispatched Margaret 6–1, 6–1, she was feeling cocky again.

Alice and Hazel sang the whole way home, feeling drunk with happiness. Climbing the worn cement steps to their home together, Hazel waved around a phone number she'd gotten while Alice hoisted the large trophy above her head. Her mother was once again in the doorway, beaming with pride. Dan was at her side, holding up a sweating glass of iced tea. "To Alice Marble!" he cheered.

She was back.

ELEANOR TENNANT
WE REGRET TO INFORM YOU THAT WE HAVE
DENIED ENTRY TO EASTERN TOURNAMENTS
FOR MS MARBLE STOP
US LAWN TENNIS ASSOCIATION

To: US Lawn Tennis Association
From: Dr. William J. Commons, MD, PhD
Date: July 1, 1936

Dear Mr. Myrick,

I am writing on behalf of my patient, Ms. Alice Irene Marble, of whom I have been treating since January 1935. It is in my professional opinion that Ms. Marble is fit to play tennis at a competitive level, should appropriate measures be taken for her health. Please see the attached medical records to support my recommendation.

Sincerely,

William J. Commons

Dr. William J. Commons, MD, PhD

ELEANOR TENNANT
WE AGREE TO ADMIT MS MARBLE INTO EASTERN TOURNAMENTS STOP
IF SHE CAN PHYSICALLY COMPETE AGAINST MEN STOP
US LAWN TENNIS ASSOCIATION

Alice was irked. “What does that even mean?”

“I made some calls. That knobber Myrick is making you pass a little test even though you’re officially number one in California and have the support of Dr. Commons. If you can play four straight days against men and live to tell about it, he’ll deem you as physically fit to play in the remainder of the tournaments.”

Unbelievable. That man could sure hold a grudge. No other female player had ever been asked to do such a thing. But her irritation faded, replaced with a shrug and a resolve to prove herself. “All the papers say I’m playing like a man. Might as well play *with* them.”

Teach chuckled while simultaneously shaking her head. “That’s the spirit, I suppose. Guess we should hit the road then, huh?”

Hitting the road meant a long, circuitous trip cross-country in Teach's Buick convertible, stopping in Chicago, Detroit, and Cleveland for Teach to run clinics. They had to fund their trip. Alice's debt to Teach was rising still.

Finally, they arrived in New York for Alice's "test." Heat radiated from the grass courts at Forest Hills, all but scorching her ankles. While Alice kept her jaw tight, her serve quick, cabbage snug against her head, and her eyes on the prize, the four men she played complained of the heat. It was quite satisfying to see rivets of sweat drip from Myrick's jowls onto his crisp, white collar as he watched on from the stands.

Alice's nondescript expression was nearly impossible to maintain in the final match against Victor Williamson. She just about burst out laughing when Williamson tossed his racquet at Myrick. "Hell, that's it. It literally feels like hell right now." Williamson pointed to Alice. "If she's too sick to play, then I'm already six feet under. I'm done."

Game, set, match, or so Alice hoped. Myrick clearly made up his own rules. But this time he kept his word and let Alice onto the tournament circuit.

She won at Seabright. She won the Women's Invitational Singles title at the Longwood Cricket Club near Boston. She won the National Doubles Championship with Gene Mako.

In Rye, Alice lost to herself. Well, technically Sylvia Henrotin beat her. The same Sylvia Henrotin who played opposite Alice in Paris when she had collapsed. The memory had clung to Alice, the greatest of distractions. It led to the greatest of defeats, Henrotin taking Alice in the finals in straight sets.

It took a full hour before Teach could even look at Alice. Then she let Alice have it. "We've worked too hard, Alice. Too hard. You could barely walk. Now look at you. It's time to put your demons to bed."

"Okay," Alice mumbled, feeling half her age. She coughed, shooting Teach's eyes wide.

"I'm fine," Alice said. "Swear."

Teach's gaze turned steely. "Play today's match today. Yesterday's matches are history. Got it? And drink some damn orange juice."

"Okay," Alice said, with only mild impotence. She knew Teach had a point about her demons.

At the Essex County Club Invitational in Manchester, she put Teach's advice into play against Helen Jacobs. A formidable opponent, indeed. No cake walk at all. But Alice claimed the win.

Which meant Helen would be gunning for Alice hard at Forest Hills. If Helen won there, it'd be her fifth National Championship.

Alice could all but feel the target on her back when she finally arrived at Forest Hills. The target grew as she advanced through the prelims, quarter finals, semifinals, and was staring down a finals match against none other than Helen Jacobs. Nerves shot through Alice like electricity. If it wasn't already unbearably hot, the jitters she felt would've done the trick to ratchet up her body heat. She was fanning herself when she walked into the dressing room, quickly saying, "Pardon me" as she sidestepped a woman.

"Oh! Miss Marble," the woman said. Alice's stomach dropped. She could recognize a reporter anywhere. It was the eagerness in their eyes, the quick, tiny steps closer. "Miss Marble, do you think it's wise to play in such heat?"

"Of course. No reason not to."

There was no way Alice was going to admit cabbage was her secret weapon. The press would have a field day with that nugget of information.

The woman edged even closer. "Don't you think you should get out of the sun and get some rest?"

"I'm indoors," Alice said flatly. "Now, if you'll excuse me."

Alice shouldered past the woman, doing her very best not to shake her head in annoyance. She'd made it only a handful of steps before she heard her name coming from around a set of lockers. "Kay Stammers looks so healthy. But did you see Alice Marble? She looks halfway to the grave."

For Pete's sake. Alice remained out of their sight and touched her cheek, turning toward a mirror. Her face was browned from the sun. She spent so much time squinting into the sun, in fact, that white squint lines circled around her eyes. She certainly wasn't pale. But her skin also didn't have any variation in color.

A familiar face was suddenly beside hers in the mirror, and Alice jumped.

"Jeepers, Kay. You nearly scared me to death." She then frowned, saying, "You *do* look quite healthy."

"I actually came over here because I heard those girls talking and I thought I could help you from looking cadaverous."

"Should I be insulted?"

"No, you should be thanking me." At that, Kay jiggled a makeup bag.

Ten minutes later, Alice's cheeks were rosy, the lines were blended into her skin, and her green eyes popped. "You can call me your fairy godmother," Kay said with a smile.

Alice smiled. "I'll call you whatever you want if this works to keep the press off my back."

Kay leaned conspiratorially closer. "Just beat Helen Jacobs in the finals. She knocked me out in the quarterfinals and that woman has won enough."

"It'd be my pleasure."

It'd be pressure too. Soon, Alice stood uncomfortably behind Helen in the narrow entryway to the stadium and waited for their names to be called.

The loudspeaker began to boom. "Welcome, everyone, to Forest Hills. Today's match will be between Miss Helen Jacobs . . ." Helen shot Alice a confidant look over her shoulder before pushing through the door, much to the appreciation of the thirteen thousand fans in attendance. ". . . Four-time US National Champion and winner of this year's Wimbledon Championships."

Alice bounced on her toes, wishing those very words were attached to her introduction.

"And Miss Alice Marble of California."

That was it; she ignored the fact they felt no need to mention how she was the reigning California champion. Guess that wasn't impressive enough.

And honestly, Alice dismissed it too. She'd never before won a Grand Slam. But there was a first time for everything. She emerged onto the court, raising her hand to the crowd. Thankfully they cheered.

Alice won the coin toss and she'd start with the serve after the women warmed up. Alice growled; Helen not only looked good in her tailored flannel shorts and English-made knit blouse, but she was playing good too.

Alice once wondered if she'd ever be good enough to play on grass or with the hoity-toity girls from the east. Now was the chance to prove herself. She was healthy. Her game was improved with a different grip from before. And she'd beaten Helen just the other week. Her body could do it again.

If only her body told her brain that. For the first set, Alice played on her heels, reacting to Helen's shots rather than predicting them. She was late, off-balance, and sluggish. It was no surprise Helen took the set 6–4. Alice glanced at Teach in the stands. Surprisingly, her coach wasn't leaning forward in her seat, hands in a prayer position. Teach's head was bobbing in an encouraging manner, and she mouthed, "Number one." Then she stood, motioning with her hands, egging the crowd on, inciting them.

Inciting Alice. Everyone loved the underdog.

"Hit to her forehead. Work the net. Mix it up. Make her hurry her shots."

Alice nodded, remembering, focusing. She took the second set. Adrenaline buzzed through her as both women went to the dressing room for the customary break prior to the final set.

Neither Alice nor Teach said a word as they peeled off Alice's sweat-drenched clothes, both their hands trembling. Alice licked her lips, about to ask if Teach had any coaching tips for her.

"Nuh-uh," Teach said. "Neither of us, let's not say anything. Just keep doing what you're doing."

Teach removed the lucky pin from Alice's discarded blouse and fastened it on her new lapel. Then she squeezed Alice's shoulders, staring into her eyes.

So much passed between coach and athlete.

I want you to win, but it's okay if you don't.

I want to win, but if I don't, I haven't lost, not after they all said I'd never be here again.

This is fun.

Hell yes, it is.

The roar of the crowd was deafening. The chair umpire, Louis Shaw, had a heck of a time quieting everyone down enough to begin the final set with a single word: "Play."

The ball moved swiftly on the grass. Alice met each return. She was playing three moves ahead. Long drives deep to the baseline to keep Helen running. Crosscourt chips. Drop shots. She kept the ball away from Helen's backhand, where she excelled. In no time, she'd won the first five games.

Alice had once been the underdog, the stadium behind her. She felt the shift, the cheers for Helen growing louder than the ones for her. Alice took a moment to regroup. She wiped the sweat from her face and rubbed loose sawdust between her hands.

Then she met Helen back on the court. She was bobbing on her toes, already six feet behind the baseline. Alice's opponent was utterly composed, all but salivating for Alice to serve the ball. So how to beat her?

Alice decided on the American Twist, with as much gusto as she could put behind it, to try to catch Helen off guard. Done correctly, the ball started banking toward the right in the air before hooking to the left, then bouncing to the right once it landed.

Lungs filled to max capacity, Alice served, hard, grunting, the muscles in her back bunching before stretching with the effort. The ball banked, hooked, bounced.

Bounced again.

Ace.

"Fifteen-love, Miss Marble," the chair umpire announced.

Alice set up to serve again. Deciding on the same shot, hoping for the same outcome. She served, putting enough spin on the ball so it'd bounce high and to the left of Helen.

This time she returned. It caught Alice by surprise, forcing her into an error.

15–15.

Alice served. Helen lunged—and missed.

30–15.

Alice did another high-bouncing serve, then immediately sprinted toward the net. Helen tried to return the ball down the line with her backhand. But Alice was there. She was ready. She cut off the ball.

40–15.

Match point.

Alice bounced, strategizing. She'd been in this same position three years ago against Betty Nuthall—and lost. This time she'd go for the net.

Alice served, sprung forward, only to realize her mistake. Helen was setting up for a high lob. Skidding on the slick grass, Alice changed direction, racing again for the baseline, lungs aching, teeth gritted.

Alice imagined how she'd return—high, but dropping in bounds—before Helen could get to the ball. Alice had to go for broke. Muscles firing in her legs, she turned, jumped as hard as she could, and made contact.

Alice landed, knees buckling, going down to all fours.

By the time Alice looked up, she only saw the ball bouncing in Helen's backcourt, shagged by a ball boy. Had it been in? Or out?

Then came Louis Shaw's voice: "Game, set, and match, Miss Marble."

The stadium erupted.

CONGRATULATIONS ALICE STOP
THANK YOU FOR SAVING ME FROM HAVING TO EAT MY WORDS STOP
WILLIAM COMMONS

Chapter 27

"Champion of the United States," Alice whispered to herself. She'd made the Wightman team. She won Nationals. Alice blew out a breath, this second accomplishment still sinking in. But it was impossible to deny the newest trophy settled in her lap, bouncing as the Buick rumbled down a road in Missouri. Or maybe they were in Kansas.

"And future champion of Wimbledon," Teach said, taking a hand from the wheel to knock against the trophy, which was somewhere shapewise between a tray and a bowl.

"This is silver, not wood. And you claim to be an expert in all that good-luck mumbo jumbo."

Teach laughed.

"Besides," Alice said, tucking blonde hair behind her ear, "can I not have a moment to feel fulfilled and accomplished before we are onto the next thing?"

"It's a long drive to your mum's house, Alice. Then good ol' Myrick has a full schedule of appearances to show off his shiny, new champion. You'll have plenty of time to revel. You'll be signing autographs left and right. But in all seriousness, you should feel extremely proud. Everyone counted you down and out. But you didn't stay down."

Emotion bubbled up Alice's throat. "No, I did not."

Alice laid a hand on top of the many telegrams she received from her family, Whitey, Marion and William, Carole, and Dr. Commons. And the daily letters from her mother. They had all believed in her, and she'd made it to the top. Now, could she stay there?

She'd been so overwhelmed by that question that before their cross-country trek, Alice had sought the refuge of one of her favorite places, the cinema. She sat in the dark theater, ready to lose herself in *My Man Godfrey*. Newsreels always preceded a show. That one began with grainy black-and-white faces of men named Benito Mussolini and Adolf Hitler. The Germans had elected Hitler their leader by a ninety-nine percent margin, and he'd quickly met with a portly figured Italian to form something called the Rome-Berlin Axis. Alice gave it very little thought, besides how Hitler was a strange-looking little man, before the reel switched to Bruno Richard Hauptmann being charged with the kidnapping and killing of the Lindbergh baby. It made her sick.

She was all too happy when William Powell and Carole Lombard filled the screen. She loved seeing her friend do what she loved.

Which inevitably put what Alice loved in the foreground of her thoughts. Tennis. There it stayed throughout the film and throughout their drive west.

As Teach turned them onto Alice's childhood street, she pushed away the pressure, anticipating mounting at celebrating with her family.

The mayor of San Francisco had big things planned for the next day. There was to be a parade through town, with fire engines, bands, and baton-twirling majorettes. Her family was going to follow in a car, waving, smiling, reveling. And leading it all off would be Dan, a newly commissioned motorcycle cop. But that wasn't what she was most excited for. It was once again climbing the steps to her house, her ma waiting at the top with a beaming smile and open arms.

As they approached, Teach honked the horn.

Dan, Hazel, George, and even Timmy tumbled out the front door. Alice's brows creased. "Where's Ma?" she called, stepping out of the Buick.

"She's inside," Dan said.

Alice's foot caught the bottom step and she fumbled. She righted herself, avoiding injury, but she took the rest of the steps slower. Warning bells trilled in her head that something wasn't right with her ma. She'd noticed physical changes the last time she was home. In fact, her mother quickly redirected the subject when Alice suggested seeing a doctor. Since then, she'd put it out of mind, assuming her mother would tell her anything important in her daily letters. But those letters were never about herself. They only ever mentioned Alice's brothers and sister. What had Alice missed while she'd been preoccupied with her own life?

"Inside?" Alice questioned.

"In the living room," Hazel said. "No one wanted to distract you, Ma especially. She made us all promise."

"Promise what?"

"You'll see."

"All right," Alice said in a weary, low voice, not knowing what else to say.

The lamps were off. It took a moment for Alice's eyes to adjust, until she saw her ma sitting in a beam of light on a couch Alice had seen no less than ten thousand times in her life. It was brown, tan, and white in a checkered pattern. But the couch looked utterly unfamiliar, mostly because Alice barely recognized the woman sitting on it.

"Ma," Alice muttered, hesitating only a moment before rushing forward until she was kneeling before her mother. She couldn't weigh more than a hundred pounds. She couldn't weigh more than ninety, maybe even eighty.

Her ma reached out with a trembling hand to wipe her daughter's tears away. "It's okay, baby girl. Don't cry."

Chapter 28

Now

Monday, March 26, 1945
480 Lexington Avenue, 9th floor, All-American Comics offices

Human beings can be so resilient. Alice often needs this reminder. She lazily taps her pencil on her latest Wonder Women of History comic.

To not be able to see. To not be able to hear. To still be able to speak and read. Five languages, at that.

Lip-reading leading to finger-spelling leading to speaking.

And to think, Helen Keller wasn't born deaf and blind, as Alice had incorrectly assumed. Helen had contracted an illness that led to a high fever that left her disabled at only nineteen months old.

Still, Helen fought to have a life.

Alice is still fighting.

Not losing herself after being told she'd never play tennis again was nearly impossible.

Surviving the progression of her mother's cancer, then her death was incredibly difficult.

But the loss of Joe, on the heels of the miscarriage of their child, almost killed Alice. Afterward, she'd swallowed her doctor-prescribed sedatives. More than prescribed.

Teach found her.

In the hospital, Alice's first thought when she woke up was *no.*

It was the same thing she whispered after the serviceman told her Joe had been killed in action. She repeated that single word, over and over, until the sound became more primal and animal-like. In that moment, Alice's future ceased to exist. The war had taken competitive tennis away. Now the war had taken her husband and her family.

She gave herself six weeks to heal. Then she gave herself another.

"This isn't the sanatorium, Alice," Teach said gently as March ticked on. "There is no magic number. You can keep tacking on six more weeks. Or you can stand on your own two feet again. Like you did before."

Alice's lower lip quivered. "I need more time."

She'd allowed herself to have dreams beyond tennis. Because of Joe, she didn't feel lost without competitive tennis. With Joe, she let a new set of dreams claim her. Wife. Mother.

Now it was gone.

All of it.

And Alice felt lost once more.

But because she'd faced the nearly impossible and the incredibly difficult before, because she recognized she'd have to fight to keep on going, she had to believe she'd be able to overcome this excruciating pain and helplessness.

In time.

She'd heal. She was able to lace up her skates again after Billy died. She'd been able to put one foot in front of the other, one block at a time, after her diagnosis.

Now she puts down her pencil, satisfied with what she's written about Helen Keller. It's not her best work. She likes to think Helen would understand the darkness she currently resides in. Alice's editor will simply be satisfied she's turning it in on time.

She places her assignment on his desk, grateful he's not in his office. Alice is in no mood for small talk. She is, however, in the mood for chocolate soufflé from Joe's and her favorite restaurant. It's a craving that surprises her. Food has been unappetizing since Joe died. When you only ever saw your husband every few months for a week at a time, most of that time was spent breaking bread, in between the sheets, or both.

Alice shrugs into a polo coat, one she'd designed with Best & Company, and into the springtime city air. It's muggy, too warm for the coat over her creamy wool dress. It feels laborious to remove her coat, to drape it over her arm, so she keeps it on, sweating by the time she arrives at Le Pavillon.

The maître d' does a double take. "Miss Marble, it's been too long. Your usual table in the corner?"

Tears threaten her eyes. It was once *their* table. "Yes, in the corner, please."

No sooner does she sit than a woman approaches, hands across her middle. "I don't want to bother you, Miss Marble. I only want to offer my condolences."

The "thank you" catches in Alice's throat. She clears it. Tries again. This is the first time she's been in public this way. It feels entirely too similar to ripping off a bandage, especially as more fans approach her. The "thank you" comes easier the second and third times.

Word had gotten out about the death of Alice's secret husband after Teach cancelled numerous appearances. The press did their usual digging and informing. It's only natural that people want to show her kindness. Still, Alice blows out a breath, steadying herself.

A man in an army uniform approaches next. Every muscle in Alice's body goes rigid. It's a captain's uniform, so similar to Joe's. She swallows roughly but it does nothing to dislodge the unease, the sadness, the anguish rippling through her. "Miss Marble, it's nice to see you out in public again."

"Thank you" comes automatically.

A waiter places Alice's chocolate soufflé in front of her. She expects the man to leave. He does not. Not even after she picks up her fork. Nor when she readies it over her dish.

In fact, he sits down. Without an invitation.

Alice clanks her fork against the plate.

He quickly holds up a palm. "I apologize for the intrusion. I'm with the US Army Intelligence," he says in a soft tone. He reaches into a breast pocket and presents an ID card.

Captain Albert Jones.

He then adds, "We'd like to talk to you. I have no desire to keep you from your dessert but—"

Alice's head rattles. "No, no. I do not wish to know any additional details about my husband's death. I know the Germans shot him down. If I could, that's already information I would eradicate from my brain."

He presses his lips together, then tries, "I only want to ask if it'd be all right to call to set up a meeting."

"A meeting?"

He leans closer. "Yes. I can explain more later."

"About what exactly? Joe?"

"Please expect my call. Tomorrow. In the morning. Tell no one."

Alice hesitates to respond, not sure what to say. Should she deny him? Will whatever he has to say cause her more pain? Or could it act as a sort of balm? Alice lets her gaze pass over Le Pavillon. Being here without Joe has been difficult, but she's also not a puddle on the floor. Maybe she can handle whatever this captain has to say. But what of the part where she should tell no one?

The intelligence man, however, does not have his own moments of hesitance. He stands, repeating, "Tomorrow," and then he's gone.

Chapter 29

Alices paces, stopping every few seconds to stare at the phone. She wonders if a ringing telephone can be likened to boiling water; it won't happen if watched.

She drops into a kitchen chair, picks up a pen to see to some long-overdue correspondence, then does nothing more than once again glue her eyeballs to the telephone. She's glad Teach is out. Alice's odd behavior would be impossible to overlook.

What on earth does Captain Jones have to say to her? And why must no one know?

The phone rings. One would think she'd jump for the handset. But Alice continues staring.

"I've done harder things than this," she says dryly.

And so she holds the receiver to her ear, though forgets the part where she greets the caller.

"Miss Marble?"

"Yes?"

"This is Captain Jones."

"Okay."

"Thank you for picking up. I hope you'll also be receptive to an opportunity. We know how hard you tried to enlist a few years ago and about your short stint with the Office of Civilian Defense. We'd like your help again, Miss Marble."

She twirls the cord around her finger and asks, "How?"

"This is a conversation to have in person."

"Weren't we in person yesterday?"

"At a secure location. Look for a dark green sedan at 57th and Fifth Avenue in one hour."

Curiosity latches onto Alice like a leech. "I'll be there."

In under an hour, Alice is dressed in a dark-gray tailored suit and standing on the corner outside of Tiffany's. Hands in her pockets, she tries to appear casual, however her mind is anything but relaxed.

Does this opportunity relate to Joe in some way? Both men are intelligence. Was, she corrects. Joe *was* intelligence, the same department as Captain Jones. Maybe it has nothing to do with her husband. Maybe she'll simply be asked to play mixed doubles with some out-of-shape general. It wouldn't be the first time. Although it *is* the first time she'll be covertly picked up from a street corner.

A green sedan pulls up.

She waits for a window to go down, a door to open. When neither happens, she reaches for the handle of the back seat. Captain Jones is inside, sans the uniform from yesterday. His suit is actually a similar color to hers.

"Thanks for coming," he says in greeting and motions to the driver. "You are quite the tennis player."

The car begins moving. "Is that why I'm here?"

"In part." He smiles. Alice has seen many in her day. This one is more like a reporter than a friend or fan. Reporters always have an underlining objective or motive. So does this man.

"I'm not exactly a tennis fan," he adds.

"No?" Alice responds, taking the moment to assess him. Dark

hair. Standard military cut. Likely in his thirties. His tailor inferior to her own.

They pass over the Brooklyn Bridge. He tries for a laugh. "I mostly go to matches because I like to watch girls."

Alice's heart leaps into her throat. Her fingers tick toward the door's handle.

"Relax. I'm not a masher, Miss Marble. Just some harmless small talk before we discuss business. In fact, we're here."

The car stops alongside a high chain-link gate. The driver hands out paperwork to a guard, who gives a very official-looking nod in return, and the sedan passes through.

The fact this portion feels professional helps Alice breathe a touch easier—about not being abducted, at least. She doesn't want to be alone with Captain Jones a second longer than necessary. Talk about the heebie-jeebies.

They park outside a warehouse that'd otherwise appear abandoned if there weren't uniformed men walking in and out. Alice is out of the car before the driver or Jones can open her door.

She follows Jones inside, down a long corridor, and into a small wood-paneled room, where a tall man in uniform stands behind a desk, clearly expecting them.

This man is older. Fifties. Hair graying at the temples. Creases around his eyes. Fit looking, like he could play a set without breaking a sweat.

"Miss Marble," the man says with a smile, one so different from Jones's predatory-like grin, "thank you for coming in. You've met Captain Jones. I'm Colonel Linden." He gestures to a chair and Alice begins toward it. "We've been watching you and—"

She stops, alarm tingling through her again.

He holds up a hand. "I imagine that sounded rather indecent. What I meant to say is that we've wanted to approach you for some time, but we've been monitoring you and your well-being to ensure it's the correct time. Yesterday you appeared amiable for Captain Jones to make contact."

Alice lowers herself into the chair, glancing at Jones over her shoulder, making sure he is where she thinks he is. "To what end? Why the clandestine meeting?"

"Clandestine, indeed," Colonel Linden says. "Let's start there. No one can know about our arrangement, should it come to fruition. Not Daniel, George, Hazel, or Timothy. Not even Miss Tennant. Certainly not any of your tennis or Hollywood peers. I must have your word before we go any further. Even if you decide not to help us, this exchange can't be spoken of."

The end of his sentence didn't rise like a question, but Alice knows without a doubt he's expecting her verbal confirmation. She licks her lips. "I can agree not to speak of this meeting. And I can give you my full answer after I know why I'm here."

"I have to imagine you're a worthy competitor on the court."

"The best," Alice says.

Colonel Linden chuckles. "Very well. I'll divulge more. The FBI did a thorough check on you prior to President Roosevelt appointing you to the Office of Civil Defense. In the position, the reports you made for the Bureau were invaluable."

"The reports I typed in Spanish?"

"Yes, those."

Alice huffs a laugh, remembering how she enjoyed feeling like a secret agent, but . . . "I didn't report anything of significance."

After a quick glance at Captain Jones, who Alice doesn't like lurking behind her, the colonel steeples his hands. "You don't know that, nor do I have the liberty to tell you how that information was used. What I can tell you is that the assignment proved you to be trustworthy and dependable. It tells us that we can put you to use again. But I also must warn you that this is very serious business."

"Serious in what way?"

"Dangerous."

The man minces no words.

"All right. What is *this* business? Does it have to do with Joe?"

"We believe this can be an opportunity to avenge your late husband. Is that something that would appeal to you?"

Would Alice like to destroy the bastards, destroy the whole regime that took her husband and her future from her? That has left her feeling lost? Is that even a question?

"Your face says it all, Miss Marble. But to answer your question, no, this does not relate directly to Joe. It does, however, relate to another man you know."

"Another man?"

"And we believe that you, and you alone, Miss Marble, are the only person who can make contact with him and complete this assignment for us."

"What man?"

"Someone from your past."

Jones cuts in, "The one who got away."

They need say no more. There'd only been one other man in her life, long before Joe. At the same moment she conjures his handsome, young face, Colonel Linden says his name. "Hans Steinmetz."

A lover she hasn't seen or touched or spoken to since she was twenty-five years old.

Chapter 30

Then

Saturday, May 19, 1938
Port Authority Passenger Ship Terminal

"Good luck, Miss Marble!"

The high-pitched voice came from within the hundred or so who'd congregated to send Alice off before her trip across the pond to England. In the port's mayhem, she'd misplaced Teach somewhere, likely off touting how Alice won Nationals and now had her eyes set on Wimbledon's silver salter. This year was the year. And at twenty-five years old, there wasn't a moment to lose.

A-ha, the well wishes came from a teenaged girl, who Alice now saw, a dark head of hair and a smiling face appearing each time the girl rolled onto her tiptoes.

"Thank you!" Alice called to her. "Of course," she added, seeing the girl wave a notebook. "Excuse me, Gilbert," Alice said to a reporter from the *New York Times*, edging past him to get to the girl, whose eyes sparkled with moisture.

It astonished Alice each and every time someone reacted this way to her. She'd been the "it" tennis player for years, thanks to her famous friends. But ever since winning the US Championships, her star power had been on the rise. Quite the contrast from the fall the psychic predicted. Like a phoenix, Alice felt like she'd returned to the tennis world with gusto. She'd been invited to countless events, speaking countless times about how she overcame adversity, how she didn't let a diagnosis of tuberculosis stop her, how tennis wasn't only for the wealthy club players. In fact, she told her story of illness, inequality, and comeback to such a degree that Alice began to feel as if she were telling the story of someone else, a fictional character.

Sometimes thinking of herself in a fictional manner was necessary, a way to distance herself from the ache she felt when she thought about moments like her mother's passing. Alice hadn't been there when she died. The rest of the family had been, but not Alice. Her mother had insisted that Alice continue her schedule of tournaments. And why had she listened? The reasons were perhaps too raw, too overwhelming, and too numerous to face head-on. She did, though. Eventually.

Part of Alice didn't want to accept her mother being sick. Another part of her was too scared to watch her mother's decline, knowing every protruding bone, sunken cheek, and labored breath would be etched in her brain. Selfishly, she didn't want to disrupt how well her tennis had been going. For both her mother and herself, she wanted to make Teach's proclamation that Alice would win it all come true. She'd never forget what her ma covertly whispered to Teach that day in her living room.

"I'm putting my daughter and my trust in your hands, Ms.

Tennant. Make her the best, just as you said you would. Give her what I can't, no matter what."

No matter what.

Alice didn't want her mother's words to be spoken in vain. Or for the discussion during Teach's visit to be an overpromise her mother regretted. Then there was the guilt that persistently plagued Alice. The debt she owed her mother and Teach for all they've done for her. Being the best at tennis was the only way to repay them.

When Dan had called to tell her their mother was gone, Alice fell to her knees, all of those reasons and the regret she carried too heavy to stand. She wished she had disobeyed. She wished she'd been at her mother's bedside. She'd chosen herself. That was what she'd done at the heart of it. Now more than ever, Alice *needed* to be crowned the best female tennis player in the world to help justify her choices.

She autographed the notebook, then handed it back to the girl just as the SS *Champlain*'s horn sounded.

"Ah, that's my cue," Alice said to the crowd. "I've got a date with Wimbledon."

***

Alice had been on the ship a number of days, and for those days she followed Teach's strict diet, exercise, and sleep regimen.

"Tonight only," Alice tried during dinner, "can I stay out past curfew? I'm inside my head too much. Too nervous. I need a night to feel like I'm normal without having to watch the clock and have everything be about tennis."

"Ten," Teach said firmly, pronging a tender cut of steak.

"Why not eleven? Why ten?"

"Because ten is your curfew."

"Set by no one other than you."

"So you agree I set the rules. Unless you no longer wish for me to be your coach?"

Alice threw down her napkin. There was little use fighting with the woman, especially when the conversation was only adding to the tension she felt in her shoulders. Still, Teach couldn't help adding more. "Everything I do and say is to help you concentrate on tennis."

Alice knew that all too well, along with the fact Teach was giving up quite a bit of income to travel to London with her. After what happened in France, Teach insisted she go along, money be damned.

Which was fine, mostly. Having her coach to practice with, there for advice and pep talks and all things tennis was grand. Having her coach dictate she leave the ballroom by a certain time, not so much. Staying out an extra hour had no effect on her concentration.

For the past few nights, Alice ran from the ship's ballroom room like Cinderella, holding on to the hand of the boy she danced with for as long as possible before she lifted the hem of her evening dress, racing the clock before it struck ten. On the promenade she'd dash past silhouettes along the ship's rail, past men and women walking hand in hand down the halls, past couples in the midst of more in darkened deck corners. All the while, she'd let her mind wonder. What would it be like to hold, to embrace, to kiss in a similar way? That wasn't something Alice had ever had.

Teach would say there wasn't enough room in her life for tennis and love. She can all but hear the British lilt to her coach's voice. But why not? Why couldn't Alice have it all? Maybe having something else in her life—something more to her life—would take the pressure off tennis. And herself.

***

It'd been months since Alice had lost a match. That was both good and bad. Bad because she could think of little else than losing her streak. Good because her record boded well for her goal of winning Wimbledon.

The tournament had begun.

Yesterday she dismantled the French champion, Simone Mathieu, in the quarterfinals.

Today she had no intention of breaking her streak. It just so happened she was playing Helen Jacobs. When Alice closed her eyes, she could practically play each set in her head, knowing how Helen moved, hit, adjusted, served. She smiled to herself; this had the promise of being a lot of fun. She had the potential to win the finals of Wimbledon.

At least, it started that way, with the roar of the crowd, the confidence in Teach's posture as she took her seat, the adrenaline coursing through Alice's every muscle.

But for reasons beyond Alice's understanding, she was off. Helen made fewer than twelve unforced errors. Alice was a different story, and not for lack of trying.

At one point, Alice strategically forced Helen into a weak lob. In any other match, Alice would have put it away. Boom. Point. But her timing was off. Everything was off. The overhead sailed so far behind the baseline it hit the wall.

Frustrated, she whacked her backside with her racquet. The crowd's response was a mixed bag of cackles and gasps. Alice tried to shake it off, but the whole ordeal left her fazed, and, in what felt like a blink, Helen took the set. Rattled, Alice couldn't find her groove. She did, however, find her temper. The chair umpire was not impressed when Alice—again—botched her usually trusty smash and she reacted by kicking a ball into the stands. Before Alice dropped her head, she saw a dark-haired man catch it.

It was all over after that.

The crowd tittered.

The officials looked down their noses at her.

Alice never got her head in the game.

She lost.

She failed.

Her streak was over.

All her sacrifices for this moment felt like they'd been for nothing.

Alice herself felt like she was nothing.

And Wimbledon officially became Alice's white whale.

Chapter 31

"It's no disgrace to lose to Helen Jacobs," Teach said as they approached the Lawn Hospitality Suite where the Champions Ball was being held. "She's formidable. Did I want that title for you? For us? Yes, very badly. I told literally everyone I saw on that bloody ship and here on dry land that you were going to win. And, chin up, you *did* still win."

Alice let out a breath. "Mixed doubles."

It was something. It was. But it didn't have the same significance as winning a singles title.

Teach sighed too. "Well, you are a champion on her way to celebrate with other champions. And, I'll say it again, it is no disgrace to lose to Helen Jacobs."

A woman beside them, clearly disgruntled, let out a harumph. Alice turned to find Mrs. Wightman, of the Wightman Cup.

"Oh, I didn't know we had an audience," Teach said pointedly.

"Is that so? Alice sure acted like she was performing to an audience when she played Helen. You want to know why you lost, Alice?"

She had a feeling she was going to hear it whether she answered the question positively or not.

"You lost in the very first set, the eighth game. It all unraveled when you started dramatizing yourself all over the court after you missed that overhead. Should have been an easy put-away, right?"

Alice nodded.

"Then what did you do? I'll tell you."

Please don't, Alice thought, especially since a reporter's ears were tuned into this very scene. Actually, more than his ears. He took out a notebook and got to work. Alice could already imagine the headlines. "Alice Marble Gets Thrashing On and Off the Court."

"Instead of getting your head back in the game, you patted your fanny and got a response from the crowd."

"I didn't pat—"

"I don't even want to think about that kick." Mrs. Wightman ran a hand over her brow, her face flushed. "While you were amusing everyone, you netted two more simple shots and all but handed Helen the set on a silver platter. I don't know where your mind was, but it wasn't on winning Wimbledon, that much I know. Even a girl with your natural talent can't win if she allows everything to break her concentration. I'll tell you one thing for certain. If Sarah ever pulled a stunt like that, she would not have me as a coach for a second longer."

"Are you done?" Teach asked. "Because I think you are."

Alice thought Mrs. Wightman could've been done a few jabs ago. Quite frankly, she was tired of adults reading her the riot act and telling her what to do. She hadn't been performing for the sake of the crowds' amusement. Alice felt herself losing all she'd been working for. Her emotions got the best of her, for Pete's sake, and she needed to blow off steam. Alice brushed past both women and the reporter and into the grand ballroom.

She wasn't done blowing off steam. She needed music. And dancing. And a night without tennis.

***

Alice had wanted a single night; she hadn't expected a week. But at the ball, Alice also got an interesting suggestion from Teach's good friend and student Rosalind Bloomingdale. "How about a week to recharge in Le Touquet?"

It was a gambling spot across the English Channel in France.

Teach's face lit up. She was a closet gambler. And now Alice, Teach, Roz, and her son, Alfred, were unpacking in the nicest hotel in town, which happened to possess the largest casino as well.

It also happened to mean Teach would be spending a lot of time at the slots and card tables and not with her eagle eyes watching Alice's every movement.

She waggled her brows suggestively at Alfred while her coach and his mother went on and on about the games they planned on playing. This was their opportunity to live a little. It was a shame Alice wasn't attracted to him. It was his confidence, Alice concluded years ago when they first met at Mr. Hearst's ranch, that was the culprit. She could never be interested in someone who didn't have confidence in themselves. Alfred was twenty-something, close in age to her. He had the dark and handsome down. Just not the tall. And it was clear he was terribly embarrassed by this so-called deficit.

At least he was willing to dash off with her to explore the town and seaport—as long as they were home by curfew. Always that curfew, looming over her.

"Freedom," Alice proclaimed.

"Freedom," Alfred echoed.

She snorted when she caught him talking to a woman his mother would never approve of.

She said not a thing when he cursed like a sailor.

She patted his back when he grumbled about returning to their keepers.

"So don't," Alice told him. "Go in search of that woman you were drooling over earlier. I'll set up camp in the lobby and cut off your mother if she returns before you do."

"You're sure?"

"Positive."

The hotel was chock-full of fancy people doing fancy things. Spinning wheels. Making extravagant bets. Laughing with abandon. Tipping champagne to their lips. The atmosphere teemed with excitement, adrenaline, chance, and sweet-smelling perfume and cologne. Alice loved it.

She planted herself on a silk brocade love seat just outside the flow of traffic and watched the bright-eyed foolish people have the time of their lives. No signs of Teach and Roz yet, most likely frolicking in a part of the casino she couldn't see. But they'd have to walk past her to get up to their rooms.

"Miss Marble?"

Alice startled, and also smarted at being caught people watching. She touched her flushed cheek, saying, "Yes?" as she turned. Her gaze met the eyes of the most delicious-looking man, who had no need for his height to cause any embarrassment.

He smiled. "So it is you. *The* Alice Marble."

Alice snorted. "Flattery will get you everywhere."

"Well, then, please, let me say I admire your tennis."

His accent alluded to two things: very rich and decidedly European. His tuxedo supported his wealth. His tan made Alice think he spent a great amount of time outdoors.

"Thank you," she said, her cheeks heating even further.

"I'd go as far to say I'm your best fan."

She chuckled. So this man was clearly a playboy. She didn't necessarily know the type. She didn't have enough experience with men. But he looked like he could have any woman he wanted; there was a confidence to him. And she'd play along. "Best fan, huh?"

"The absolute best. I do wish Wimbledon had gone differently for you. But next years will be yours, I'm sure."

Alice cocked her head. "Did you attend?"

"I did. I was fortunate to catch a ball kicked into the stands."

Alice dropped her forehead into her hand. She heard the chuckle come from him. When she met his gaze again, his palm was outstretched for a proper greeting.

"Let me officially introduce myself. I'm Hans Steinmetz."

Alice put her hand in his. "I'm Alice."

He bent over their hands, gently kissing hers. Before rising, he looked up at her. "I know."

Oh yes, he was quite smooth, and the room was suddenly a hundred degrees hotter. She refrained from fanning herself. Where was a cabbage leaf when she needed one?

Hans stood to his full height, still ahold of Alice's hand. "Will you have a drink with me?"

Instinctively, her head jerked toward the entrance. Alfred hadn't yet returned.

"Unless you were expecting company already?"

She shook her head like a lovestruck teenager.

"So you will join me for a drink?"

She shouldn't; this man was a wealthy von vivant. As women walked by, every single one of them looked at him, some fleetingly, others more cartoonish.

Hans's attention was solely on Alice.

"A drink?" She'd let herself have this moment, this departure from her normal life. "Why not?"

With a grin, Hans led them to one of the hotel's several bars. This one was located in a quieter area, removed from the overzealous gamblers and accompanied only by a soft piano melody and low chatter. It also still offered a view of the lobby.

The table was small, barely big enough for one, and Alice was very aware how their knees brushed. She was also very aware of his white, straight teeth, his perfectly styled dark hair, his well-manicured nails, even, as he aligned his cufflink.

A candle flicked between them.

The setting was so utterly romantic, so utterly opposite of Alice's life, that she almost burst out laughing. Surely that would've killed the mood.

"What?" Hans said. "You appear amused."

The waiter arrived with their drinks. A brandy for him, champagne for her. Hans raised his glass. "*Proscht,*" he said. "A cheers."

Alice tapped her glass against his, then brought the glass toward her lips, her gaze on her bubbly.

"No, no," Hans said. "When we cheers, we must maintain eye contract. Shall we try again?"

They clinked their glasses. Hans's focus on her was so intense, she squirmed in her seat. She nearly lost herself in his dark eyes. Bubbles erupted down her throat and into her stomach.

As soon as she could, she had to look away. She glanced at the lobby. When she brought her attention back to Hans, his gaze was still trained on hers. "You're good."

"I'm good?"

"Very poised."

"I've had a lot of schooling."

In women?

Alice sipped her drink. "You know, I hadn't expected to meet anyone tonight."

"Even with the way it seems you're looking for someone?"

So he'd noticed her fleeting looks to the lobby, then. "Just promised a friend I'd cover for him."

He raised a brow. "Oh?"

"We have overprotective keepers."

"Keepers?"

She shrugged. "But back to you. What made you come say hello?"

He laughed. "You cut to the quick, don't you?

Alice shrugged, and his grin widened. "Well, you're beautiful. Gold is a nice color on you. I'm pleased to have found you utterly charming. But before now, when I saw you play, you left me utterly impressed."

"You mean when you saw me lose?"

"It was a single match, no? You've won many before. You'll win many to come. But imagine my surprise when I walked into the lobby and saw you, the world's best woman tennis player. How could I not say hello?"

"Again with the flattery." Alice couldn't help but beam, while also a feeling of effervescence washed over her. Blame the bubbly that was half gone. "Though I have a long way to go before I'm number one. I'll have to win Wimbledon for that honor."

"Then you'll get to meet the queen."

"I should work on my curtsy. Do you shake a queen's hand?"

"If she offers. Then firmly, at that."

Alice laughed, sipping more. "Fine, if I win, I'll shake her hand firmly."

"And never turn your back on the queen. It's considered rude and disrespectful."

"All this talk of protocol. It feels presumptions. Besides, I'd rather not talk about tennis."

"Is that so?"

"It is."

Silence—and heat—passed between them. He'd said she was beautiful, charming. She utterly impressed him. If she were being honest, she could say those very same words to him. And right now she was hungry to learn more about him, to entrap those pieces of him in her vault of a brain. "Hans," she said in a low voice. "Your name is not French. German, then?"

"My father is German. But that is not my home. My home is in the most beautiful country in the world."

Alice nodded. "America."

"And she's funny. No, I'm from Switzerland, here on a brief holiday after business in London."

"And after watching me at Wimbledon."

He tilted his head. "I thought you didn't want to talk about tennis?"

"I don't."

"Okay, so what else do you do?"

"We're not talking about tennis."

He laughed. "So much of your life, then."

Alice drank, suddenly uncomfortable with it spoken so plainly. She swallowed roughly. "What is it that you do? Besides approaching women in lobbies?"

"Banking. I work for my father's bank specifically. We do—"

Alice's gaze flicked away as movement caught her eye. Alfred, waving at her like a lunatic. His smile could've lit up the room.

Hans followed her gaze. "Ah, it appears you're off the hook."

"It appears so."

He set down his empty glass. "In that case, the night is beautiful. Should we walk?"

"You want to walk with me?"

"I see no reason why our time together should end. I'm wholly enjoying myself. Are you not?"

She was. In fact, their encounter so far had felt too perfect to be reality. Hans felt too perfect, too polished. This clearly wasn't the first time he approached a woman in a bar in this way.

Yet he had come up to her.

"Maybe we could stay for another drink instead?"

He does an exaggerated cringe. "Sadly, I'm an easy drunk. Only one drink for me. Besides, Europeans are known for their strolls, are we not?"

"But isn't it late?" she asked him.

He checked his watch. "Nearly ten. Also early by our standards."

Alice twisted her lips and glanced in the direction of the casino. When would a handsome Swiss banker ever ask her to take a walk again? "A walk sounds perfect. And no, it is most certainly not too late."

***

The sand beneath Alice's bare feet was cold. She couldn't see the water, but she knew it was there. "Did you keep the ball I kicked?" she asked him.

"I did."

This small fact made her smile. She'd been smiling ever since leaving the hotel. "I truly never thought I'd be taking a walk with a stranger tonight."

"A stranger? You wound me. We're old friends now, aren't we?"

"You seem like someone with many friends."

His head tilted back with a deep laugh. "Alice, now you truly wound me. This is not normal for me. I'm usually surrounded by businessmen. When I can, with my former schoolmates. But mostly

I holiday alone. A breather, if you will."

"Yet you approached me."

"I had no other choice but to approach you."

Hans stopped walking, taking hold of Alice's arm to stop her too. He used a single finger beneath her chin to tip her head toward his. His eyes were dark. They pierced into her. "I also have no other choice but to do this."

Alice's mind hadn't fully deciphered his intent before his mouth closed on hers. Just a snack of a kiss. "Was this okay?"

"Very," Alice said.

The second time she tasted the brandy he'd drunk earlier. Even more so when he deepened their kiss, the effects of which she felt in her knees. She didn't budge in his embrace, his arms winding tightly around her. Never before had she been sought out. Never before had she been held in such a way. Never before had she been kissed with such passion.

Until now. With Hans.

Would Teach allow her to see him again?

Did it matter what Teach thought? What anybody thought?

This was her life.

Her choice.

She wanted tennis and love.

She wanted what this could be.

The thoughts whirled around her head, when she should've been concentrating on the slow movements of Hans's mouth.

She tossed the complications, the distractions aside. She let the butterflies take flight in her stomach. And she kissed Hans Steinmetz like there was no tomorrow.

Chapter 32

Tomorrow she had to see Hans again.

She had to feel like this again, all but floating across the lobby, after one last giggled kiss. She pressed the elevator button, weightless, filled with champagne bubbles, giddy with excitement. Alice imagined winning Wimbledon would feel similar.

It wasn't until she reached her floor that she came back down to earth. It was well past curfew.

Alice squared her shoulders, lifted her chin. She was no child. She didn't have to answer to anyone. Teach was only her coach.

Her coach, whom she owed everything to.

Who was the closest thing she had to a mother now.

She rubbed her lips together as she pressed her ear to the door.

Nothing.

She turned the key and eased the door open.

Nothing.

No lights were left on.

City lights shone through the window, the drapes still open.

Alice exhaled. Teach hadn't returned to the room yet.

The bubbles, the weightlessness, the giddiness returned as Alice fell into bed, already replaying every moment of the night.

The night she met Hans.

***

In the morning, a very groggy Teach sat across from Alice in the hotel restaurant. Roz was hardly better.

"Late night?" Alice asked them.

Teach took a swig of coffee like it was a shot of liquor. "It's not every day I get to play the tables."

It also wasn't every day a person started to fall in love.

What a delicious thought Alice had zero intentions of revealing to her coach. She hid her smile behind a bite of her toast, then a sip of her tea.

"Excuse me," the bell captain said, approaching their table. "Miss Marble, this just arrived for you."

At first, Alice laughed, confused, as Alfred had just walked up beside the bell captain. Frankly, he was lucky his mother hadn't fretted about his tardiness. The woman would still nurse him if she could. But then the bell captain revealed a long flower box with a single rose inside from behind his back.

Alice's breath hitched. Hans clearly wasn't going to make it easy to keep her secret. Their evening ended with him promising to contact her today. And he had; she knew without a doubt Hans was behind this peach-colored rose.

Roz snatched the box. "Beautiful! Who is it from?" She pulled the card from its envelope. "It says"—she waggled her brows at Alice—"'From your best fan.'"

What a clever man.

Teach chortled. "That could be anyone."

Oh no, it couldn't.

Alice threw her napkin on her plate, her insides on fire. She had to get to her room in case he called. "I think I'll run up and put this in water. See you at dinner."

Teach forced down the coffee she'd gulped. "Dinner?" She dabbed her napkin against her mouth. "What on earth are you doing all day?"

"Alfred and I are exploring more and having a picnic."

Alfred's eyes danced between Alice, Teach, and his mother, the toast he'd only just buttered halfway to his mouth. Discreetly, she kicked him beneath the table.

He cleared his throat. "Let me just take this to go."

Alice beamed.

***

"I'll cover for you, you'll cover for me," Alice suggested to Alfred.

It took zero convincing, the start of a weeklong conspiracy that began with Hans picking Alice up in a green convertible outside the hotel.

The wheels spun against the road as though they'd just robbed a bank like the outlaws Bonnie and Clyde, Alice yelling, "Go, go, go," and Hans going without any explanation.

"The keeper?" he said after they turned the corner.

"The one and only."

He smirked. "She'd like me."

"You are neither a ball nor a racquet. She will not want me playing with you."

"Actually, I have two—"

She pointed a finger at him, though Alice was unable to hide the amusement on her face.

He chuckled, making another turn. They drove through the narrow city streets and onto the country roads. The scenery was more fitting for the sports coat and khakis he wore. Alice had on a sundress. Perfect for the picnic they had planned along the banks of a river, across from a seventeenth-century castle.

"*En Guete*," he said.

Roast duck, liver pate, caviar, a loaf of fresh bread, and a bottle of champagne.

Was this real life?

It certainly felt real every time Hans's lips touched hers.

It felt real when they dined the next day at a restaurant in Stella Plage. Then when their next tête-à-tête took them to a tiny lobster place down the coast from Le Touquet. Then at a tree-shaded, secluded patio café in a small village Alice couldn't even pronounce.

"Can I ask you about tennis yet? Or is it still out of bounds?"

"And he has puns." Alice laughed. "Tennis, thanks to you, hasn't crossed my mind in days."

"Would it be horrible for you if it ended?"

"What do you mean?" Surely he wasn't suggesting he'd replace tennis in her life.

He reached for her hand. "How is it that I can already read your mind? Or maybe it's your face I can read so clearly. I'd never dream of getting in the way of your tennis. I only meant there are whispers of countries that'll soon be bumping heads that may disrupt all of our lives. Tennis for you."

"Bumping heads?" she asked. "Between who?"

"Time will tell. But many fear a war. July's been an interesting month as it is. The Soviet Union is contentious with Japan. Germany is all but seeking out conflicts. German Jews are now banned from working in a number of professions. In fact, if I understand correctly, all Jews in Germany are required to get special identification cards by the year's end."

"For what purpose?"

"Nothing good. Adolf Hitler is an egomaniac."

Alice cocks her head. "I remember him from a newsreel. Him and Benito Mussolini. I didn't get a good feeling about either of them."

"I'm not surprised. When Hitler opened an art exhibition in Munich last week, he made a speech attacking one in London, which includes some banned German art. He called the artists 'cultural Neanderthals' and"—Hans scratched along his jawline, where a hint of stubble caught the afternoon light—"'lamentable unfortunates who plainly suffer from defective sight.'"

"Ouch."

"I bought quite a few pieces."

"Do you collect?"

"Occupational hazard of being around rare valuables the whole of my life."

"Ah, it's making more sense now. You only approached me because I'm invaluable."

He rose an eyebrow. "I dare say not until you win Wimbledon."

Alice's mouth fell open.

Hans bellowed a laugh, turning heads, clasping her hands to ensure her of his joke, but also saying, "Darling, surely you know that's a jest. But yes, back to your question. I do collect, along with my father. Our family vault is home to some incredible wealth."

"You're very rich, aren't you?"

And charismatic.

Magnetizing.

Handsome.

Kissable.

Tempting.

"Very."

Alice laughed, muffling the sound behind her napkin when a

woman locked eyes with her. The woman's gaze jumped between Alice and Hans, a sly smile appearing on her face. Any moment now Alice expected the woman to rise and ask for an autograph. Or perhaps the woman was a fan of bankers. Alice may have to stake her claim.

She leaned across the table toward Hans and spoke in a low voice. "Want to get out of here?"

Her body language, her tone, they both sounded like an invitation.

Hans's expression became wolf-like, hungry. No one had ever looked at her that way before. She wanted it. Needed it. Needed Hans.

And while Alice hadn't initially intended for it to be suggestive, she leaned in farther. "My hotel room?"

"And risk your keeper? I'll rent a room on a different floor. Hell, I'll buy the whole establishment. You're worth it."

"As I said, flattery will get you everywhere."

"I sure hope so."

Hans's hotel room went to good use. Three afternoons in a row.

In those precious, stolen hours, Alice felt like they were the only people on earth. The two of them, sharing secrets . . .

Hans was irrationally scared of spiders.

Revealing fears . . .

For Hans, it was that he would become like his father, who was on wife number four; for Alice, that she won't ever be the best in the world.

Falling into inside jokes . . .

It was now physically impossible not to see a green chair without laughing, a joke that doubled as a secret.

They talked about everything, except what exactly came next for them after this holiday. Oh, they had talked *around* it. Hans mused he'd lock her away in his castle. Alice joked how it sounded like the beginning of a story where a damsel in distress would be rescued from a tower. Hans posed more seriously how he'd never get in the way of her tennis. She said just as seriously how she wanted both her career and Hans. But they never spoke about what their future actually looked like or how it would work.

And for the moment, Alice was completely content to continue falling in love. Currently falling more in love with his backside as he walked stark naked toward his hotel room door.

There'd just been a light knock before a note had been slipped beneath the door. Alice fluffed the pillow, propping her head for a better view, as he retrieved it.

"It's addressed to you, *mon amour*."

His love. Her breath caught. But she quickly found it. Never one to mince words, so much like her coach in that way, she let the question pour out. "I'm your love, huh?"

Hans slowed his walk. He tapped the small white envelope against his free hand. "I didn't know you spoke the language."

"Not well. But I know a little. *Un poco*."

"That's Spanish." He shook his head, knowing full well she was being playful. "Would that be all right, though, if you were my love? I've never met anyone like you, Alice."

She yanked him toward her the remainder of steps. "More than okay considering you're also mine."

That did it. Those words elicited the hungry look Alice had seen and experienced an obscene amount of times over the last three days.

He maneuvered his body overtop of hers, his interest in Alice without question. Locks of his dark hair dangled, nearly touching her forehead. Alice arched into him.

He shook his head, enamored. "Your stamina is incredible."

"I'm training to be the best tennis player in the world."

"I'm glad to aid in your training."

He repositioned an arm, the note he'd retrieved and Alice had all but forgotten, crinkling.

"Ah," she said, reaching for it.

"And just like that, she's moved on."

Alice laughed. "Never."

But she was curious. These afternoon trysts were top secret, after all.

Turned out, it would have been better if she'd ignored the little white envelope. It contained information she didn't want to know. Information that because she now knew it, she could no longer live in their fantasy land.

Alice shut her eyes and released an expletive that likely made her poor mother roll over in her grave.

Alice,

Teach knows. You made the society pages.

Alfred

Chapter 33

It was the woman from the café, the one who smiled slyly. She didn't want Alice's autograph. She hadn't been interested in Hans. She'd been eager for a story about tennis's darling and Switzerland's golden boy. Both notable in their own way. Alice had seen enough reporters in her life. She should've recognized the woman for what she was, a gossip columnist.

She trilled her lips, absolutely dreading what was to come: a confrontation with Teach. Sweat had gathered on her forehead by the time she reached their hotel room.

Alice was so nervous she almost knocked.

"Don't worry, it'll be all right," Hans had told her before she left his room, placing a soft kiss to her forehead.

The man was a gorgeous fool. Teach was going to have an adult-sized cow.

Alice eased into the quiet room, much like she had a few nights ago. She caught her coach's reflection in the bathroom mirror, putting on lipstick.

Teach went still, only her bottom lip colored. Alice swallowed roughly.

Their eyes met in the glass. Her coach's were icy, the blue of them seemingly darker than usual. Alice had never seen her coach so angry. Her jaw was tightly set. Her brows were furrowed. She lowered the lipstick and breathed, teeth clenched, only through her nose.

Every instinct in Alice's body told her to retreat. She could be out of the room in an instant—she was known for her speed—and back in Hans's room, in his arms.

But she'd eventually have to face her coach. It was not like she could get back to the States without her . . . Not like she could continue with Hans in secret forever . . .

And every minute worsened the situation. As it was, it was nearly dinnertime and Teach probably saw the story hours ago, Alice guessed while Teach had her habitual afternoon cuppa. That left ample time for Teach to brainstorm the dressing down of a lifetime while she readied herself for dinner. Hell, her coach likely practiced in the mirror.

Alice wasn't enough of a dolt to defiantly raise her chin, but she tried for an even voice as she said, "Say something."

"You want me to say something?"

"Pretty sure that's what I just said."

Teach widened her eyes in that way that all parental figures know how to do. "You're not going to like what I have to say."

"Just say it already."

"Fine." Teach slammed her palms against the bathroom vanity, forgoing the lipstick, only her bottom lip painted. She whirled toward Alice. "Tell Steinmetz it's over."

"No."

"No?"

Alice crossed her arms. "No."

"Girl, you better rethink *all* of this." Teach gestured from Alice's challenging expression all the way down to her locked knees.

"And while you're at it, you may want to do something about those buttons."

Alice's hand flew to her chest, where her blouse's buttons were indeed mismatched, a result of how quickly she'd dressed.

Teach's head shook now. "I can't believe you'd do something so stupid as sleep with him."

"For God's sake, I'm twenty-five years old. I needed somebody!"

"Needed somebody? Who was there when you were sick? When everybody thought your career was over and even you didn't believe in yourself? When your tennis tanked and prick reporters were writing fake obituaries about your career?" Teach said in a low, warning voice.

"I said I needed *somebody*. I already have a coach. And you sure as hell never let me forget it."

"You may be twenty-five years old, Alice, but you act like a child. You are naive, sheltered. You don't live the life of a normal twenty-something. You live to play tennis. It's what you said you wanted and it's what I've given you. I made it possible for you to focus on that, on the thing you love most in the world. Unless you now love this Steinmetz more than you love tennis. Is that it? Is *that* it, Alice? Maybe you *don't* need a coach if a man is what you really want."

This question wasn't rhetorical. Alice could see in the desperation in her coach's voice and face, in how she stormed out of the bathroom and began pacing back and forth in the narrow space between their two beds.

"I don't know," Alice said finally.

Teach whirled again. "You don't know? Are you being serious right now? You're out there screwing strangers"—Alice cringes—"At the risk of getting pregnant, when you're at the top of your bloody game. Remember forty-love? Remember how I taught you it's a pivotal moment? Right now, Alice, you're a point away from winning it all. But if you give anyone a foot in the door, they can score. Again and again. They can take it from you. Tides turn fast in tennis. Haven't I taught you this? Are you willing to risk losing it all when you're sitting at forty?"

"Teach, please . . ." Alice's mouth had gone bone-dry. She'd pushed too far. Tennis was everything. She just wanted Hans to be something too. "I'm sorry."

"You're sorry? So it's over then? No more Steinmetz. We're in agreement."

The thought of ending things with Hans nearly brought Alice to her knees. Tears sprung to her eyes while her fists tightened. And her coach knew her well enough, even without words, to know that Alice didn't want to give up Hans. That she was about to try to reason with Teach to keep seeing him.

"No." Teach shook her head, pacing again. "Absolutely not. And frankly, I'm confused. We've been fighting to make you the best for nearly ten years. You've known Mr. Playboy for all of ten hours."

"It's been more than—"

"Yet you're acting like you're in love." Teach threw up a hand. "This feels like a joke." She laughed. "Has this been some cruel joke after all?"

Teach's dismissal was infuriating. Why couldn't it be love? "Queen Victoria and Prince Albert both recorded in their memoirs they fell in love almost instantly."

"Queen Victoria and Prince Albert had a carefully orchestrated future. Have you and Steinmetz even talked about the future?" A smug little grin appeared on Teach's face. "So, no. If you had, you'd be snapping off my head with whatever grand plans the two of you have made. But do you know who has plans? You and me. We have goals. Are you going to let a man distract you from those?"

"He wouldn't be a distraction," Alice insisted.

"He already is."

"We're on holiday."

"And after holiday? Will you be thinking about winning another championship and finally winning Wimbledon? Or will you be thinking about the next time you'll see Steinmetz? For what? For him to hurt you? They'll all just hurt you. They're not worth it. I'll say it one last time, Alice. There is no place in your life for tennis and men! If you don't believe that, I'm wasting my time with you. So tell me, am I wasting my time? Do you want to win Wimbledon? You've had your fun the past few days. Now end it. Tell him it's over. Or find another coach."

The threat landed as if Teach had crossed the room and slapped her across her face. Alice rubbed her stomach, feeling physically ill at the thought of Teach abandoning her.

But if she couldn't lose her coach, it meant she'd have to lose Hans.

Teach had given her an ultimatum.

Teach or Hans.

Hans or tennis.

She chose tennis.

***

Alice sat on the edge of the hotel bed, her head in her hands for nearly an hour. Teach had stormed off, saying how she needed a drink with Roz.

Now Alice stood outside Hans's hotel room, dreading what she had to do, furious with herself that her desire to win and her guilt for all Teach had done for her were a stronger force than the love that'd grown for Hans.

The smell of his talc powder met her as soon as she entered his room. He stood only in a towel, water droplets dripping from his hair, a suit laid out on the bed.

"Hans," she said softly.

"Alice, darling, I don't like how you've just said my name. How about you reenter and say it again, with more joy, then I'll whisk you out to a fancy dinner where we'll listen to grand music, we'll order chocolate—your favorite—then go dancing."

"I can't."

"You can't? Or you won't?"

"Both."

Hans ran a hand through his damp hair. "Listen, you leave the day after tomorrow. We'll continue to dodge her until then. I'll visit the States in a few months' time. By then she'll have calmed down. I'll talk to her, tell her I have no intention of ruining your career. I'll tell her we love each other. Would any of that be a lie?"

Alice shook her head. "No. I do love you, Hans."

"So what is it, then?"

"She won't ever understand. It's black and white for her. We can't see each other anymore."

Yes, he stood there in a towel, exposed. But it was how the hope drained from his eyes that made him appear incredibly vulnerable. And hurt. "Teach and tennis mean more to you than I do?"

Alice ran to him, throwing herself into his arms, her head against his chest. "No. Please don't think I don't care for you. I've never fallen in love with anyone like I have with you. Not ever."

She felt the weight of his head as he lowered it atop hers. "I don't doubt you care for me. But I also know I cannot win."

"She's done so much for me. She saved my life, Hans, and she's made me the champion that I am. I can't do this to her."

"So you'll do it to me."

Alice couldn't see his face. She didn't need to. She was glad she couldn't, until the weight of his head lifted. He stepped back, his arms unwinding from her body, Alice immediately feeling the loss of his touch. Hans's words came quietly. "I hope our paths will one day cross again." Then he turned away, leaving Alice with only a view of his back. She longed to reach out and touch the nape of his neck where his hair had grown longer during his holiday. In bed, she had run her fingertips through it rhythmically.

She opened her mouth to say something. What, she didn't know.

But then Hans said all that was left to say. "Goodbye, Alice."

***

She cried all night.

She didn't try to hide it. Alice wanted Teach to hear it from the bed over and know the sacrifice Alice had made. She still wanted both tennis and Hans.

By the morning, she knew she had to see him again. Was it selfish? Yes. But she'd thought of one more thing she needed to tell him.

Rather, it was a question.

Perhaps an unfair question. But one she needed to ask nevertheless, to try to make them work. To salvage her first love.

After she gathered the courage to go to him, she found his hotel room door ajar. Sounds of movement came from inside. Heart pounding, Alice pushed the door wider.

She'd run to him. She'd throw herself into his arms. She'd ask him.

Startled, a maid looked up. "*Bonjour, mademoiselle.* May I help you with something?"

Alice flicked her gaze over the closet, the dresser top, the bathroom vanity. Empty, bare, cleared.

The tears came then. Hans was gone.

Chapter 34

"Why don't we loosen the reins on the voyage home?" Teach suggested. "No need to be back in our stateroom until midnight. When we're home, we'll get serious again."

Alice only stared at her. Unbelievable. "Ten is fine."

She had no desire to dance with anyone but Hans. She wondered where he was, what he was doing, if he was thinking of her the same way she constantly thought of him. Every rotation of the steamship's engine took her farther away from him and any chance of closure to their whirlwind romance.

Alice considered writing him a letter. But all she knew was his last name and that he was from Geneva. He could be found, though. The question was, did he want to be found? He'd left the hotel immediately. If he wanted to, she'd be easy enough to track down. All he'd have to do was contact the tennis association.

Again, if he wanted to.

No telegrams arrived on the boat.

None were waiting when they disembarked in New York. Or when they arrived back in California.

No letters came either, not over the next few weeks of training. Alice would never admit it, but he *had* become a distraction, by not being able to have him.

Tennis.

She'd chosen tennis, Alice reminded herself.

Now she had to make that choice worth the pain of letting Hans go.

Soon the National Championships at Forest Hills was upon her.

Alice quickly advanced to the semifinal round, where she was to play Sarah Palfrey. They were friends, but they were also rivals, Alice beating Sarah at championships back in 1932. It was what originally put Alice on the map, the first time an "unknown" had beaten a seeded player.

"Alice Marble Upsets Sarah Palfrey in Brilliant Match," the papers had written.

A year later, Sarah had stopped Alice in her tracks in the Seabright semifinals. But a few years after that, with Gene Mako at her side, Alice had wrestled the National Doubles Championship away from Sarah and Don Budge.

Then came last year's Wimbledon, where Alice and Sarah won as a doubles team.

Now both women were using championships to gauge what a singles title at Wimbledon could look like this year.

Who was playing well?

Who was in a slump?

Who would be the most formidable opponent?

Alice wanted to be the answer to that last one. She was eager to face Sarah again at Nationals. The night before their match . . . in fact, for six days prior, a hurricane had dropped cat-and-dog amounts of water on the turf, leaving the surface unplayable. Today they'd finally take the court.

Alice bounced the ball, getting a feel for it on the still wet court. The rebound was lower. The weight of the ball was heavier. It'd be a slower match. Alice reviewed Sarah's game in her head. Right-handed. Known for her one-handed backhand. Also known for an unorthodox wrist action that robbed her forehand and service of power.

Alice, too, robbed Sarah. She won the first few games and was up 5–1. Though Sarah wasn't about to lie down. She took on an aggressive style and won nine games in a row, claiming the first set and a head start on the second.

Breathe and focus.

Focus and breathe.

The roar of the crowd made it difficult. Alice looked to Teach while the umpire worked to quiet the stadium. Teach mouthed, "Do or die time."

She nodded to her coach.

Then she resolved to break Sarah's serve.

She did.

On her own serves, she gave Sarah everything she had. Sarah didn't give an inch, the game still in her favor, a point away from a 4–1 advantage in the second.

That wouldn't do. Alice wanted the headlines to read how she played brilliant tennis, as brilliant as she ever had shown at Forest Hills. Sarah could be called a formidable opponent; that'd be fine to include. But there was no other option but an article that proclaimed how she was playing tennis that was simply invincible in its power and control. It spurred her on.

Even when the game was at 40–40, and Alice had to fight through multiple match points, she kept her eye on the prize. She secured the win.

5–7, 7–5, 7–5.

A hard-fought victory.

She needed it madly. She needed desperately to be on the right path to being the best in the world.

New York Times

Sunday, September 25, 1938
With finesse, strength, and stamina that makes her medical history a distant memory, Miss Alice Marble took down Miss Sarah Palfrey, the number four seed, in the semifinals. The match may as well have been the finals. Marble dismantled Nancy Wynne, the Australian champion, in only twenty-four minutes, barely missing the record of shortest women's singles match. That honor still remains with Miss Suzanne Lenglen, who beat Miss Molla Mallory in twenty-three minutes in the 1922 Wimbledon final.
Marble does, however, join Lenglen in achieving a triple crown. Marble and Don Budge won the mixed doubles championships and Sarah Palfrey put her singles loss aside to play and claim a doubles victory alongside Marble. That's three for three for the marvel, Alice Marble, who left Forest Hills as the number one seed in the country. Now the question all tennis enthusiasts are wondering: Can she claim number one in the world?

DEAREST ALICE STOP
WIMBLEDON IS YOURS STOP
ALL OUR LOVE AND SUPPORT STOP
MARION AND WILLIAM

"Nope. No. This won't work."

"What won't?" Alice asked her coach, nearly running into her back. Teach had stopped abruptly outside their room at the Hyde Park Hotel. Alice stifled a yawn. If only Wimbledon was stateside. Though then it wouldn't be called Wimbledon. There'd go the history. The elegance. The prestige. She yawned again.

Teach was pointing at the room number like it was a serpent about to attack.

"Miss Tennant, what's wrong?" the bellhop asked, urgency in his voice, yet a practiced smile still maintained on his face.

"I'm sorry, this just won't do."

"What won't?" Alice asked again.

"Allie, the room number."

812.

Teach widened her eyes. Alice still didn't get it. Her coach's exasperation was almost comical. Or maybe Alice was overtired and would laugh at just about anything at this point.

"If you add up eight, one, and two, it equals eleven. Come on, Allie, you *know* eleven is an unlucky number for you."

Her childhood friend Billy died when Alice was eleven.

Her mother died on the eleventh.

Her father's car accident occurred in the eleventh month of the year.

Eleven days after her collapse in France, the doctor had said she'd never play again.

She lost Wimbledon last time in the year '38, which totaled eleven.

Teach had been going on and on about how '39 should erase all that bad luck.

Alice squeezed the bridge of her nose. She was equal parts annoyed with Teach's superstitions but also resigned to the fact there was no getting her coach over this. They had to get through it. She pressed harder, trying to wake up her brain to find some type of solution.

"How about," Alice began, blowing out a breath, "we alter the room number? I know that sounds absurd." She looked to the bellman. His smile hadn't yet slipped, though Alice could only imagine what was going through his head. "During our stay, could we flip over the 2? Unscrew it, then screw it in as a 5? That eleven becomes a fourteen."

Surely something positive happened to them on the fourteenth at one point or another. Alice began wracking her brain, but fortunately Teach let out an enthusiastic, "Yes!" followed by a sudden, crisp clap that made the poor bellman startle.

Somehow his smile grew larger. A defense mechanism, most likely. "Of course," he said. "Let me see to that right away."

He bowed and backed away at a clip, nearly colliding with the bell captain's cart that was piled high with their mountain of luggage.

"There," Alice said. "Problem averted. Now, can I please get some sleep so I'm ready to practice tomorrow so I can win this thing?"

Teach extended her arm, gesturing into the floral-wallpapered room. "What? Do you need an invitation?"

Chapter 35

Mary K. Browne had predicted Alice would play at Wimbledon one day. She had. Alice was about to again. This wasn't the first time she set her eyes on the words of Kipling, the ones above the double-door entry. But this time they read differently.

If you can meet with Triumph and Disaster and treat these two imposters just the same

She'd experienced triumph and, soon after, a downfall. She worked hard after each and every one of her disasters.

Now she hoped to find success.

She'd personified Wimbledon as her very own white whale, which could easily slip through her grasp if she didn't seize it this very year. Months ago, Hans had spoken about contention between the Soviet Union and Japan, about German hostility, mainly from their leader, Adolf Hitler. Now France, Britain, and the Soviet Union were spending these summer months trying to forge a pact. One the newspapers didn't speak of with confidence.

Could there be a war on the horizon as Hans had predicted? Could that war disrupt her life, her tennis?

Alice soldiered a breath and pushed through the entry. Teach followed, knowing Alice needed this time alone in her head to focus.

If only she didn't become distracted by every dark-haired man she passed, daring for one to hold out a single peach-colored rose. Hans may've been in attendance last year, but the chances of him being there again . . . Alice couldn't let her mind go there.

"You ready, Allie?" Teach asked, coming up beside her.

"I will be."

***

In order to win Wimbledon, Alice needed to be the best of a hundred and twenty-eight players.

The draw put the women into a top half and bottom half.

The top half didn't mean better, not exactly. But it did mean that the number one seed and the number two seed were placed in opposite halves. They'd also play on different days, something spectators greatly appreciated.

There'd be four rounds of play. Anyone who won all their matches moved on to the quarterfinals. Then the semifinals. Then the finals, God willing.

Alice arrived as number one, a seeding that gave her a pep in her step. Helen Jacobs was number two, a seeding that kept Alice grounded. The two women had battled more than once over the years. At least there was no chance of seeing her until the very end, if they both made it that far.

It helped that Alice had a bye for round one.

It felt wonderful to sit in the crowd, legs crossed at her ankles, knowing she was already in the next round as she watched Sarah Palfrey versus Mary Norman.

Sarah won.

In round two, Alice faced Britain's Ruth Kirk. And if the roar of the hometown crowd was any indication, they wanted Ruth to win.

It added more pep to Alice's step when that didn't happen, winning in two sets: 6–3, 6–2.

Dora Beazley, also British and also with the support of the stadium behind her, made Alice sweat a little more: 6–4, 6–3.

In the fourth round, Alice's dominance over France's Arlette Halff resulted in a chant of her name. *Finally*. And now that she'd won over the crowd, she needed to win the whole damn thing.

"Don't let it go to your head, Allie," Teach warned. "Yes, you're seeded number one. Yes, the opening rounds were a cake walk for you. But Jadwiga Jedrzejowska just won convincingly. You'll be going up against her in the quarterfinals."

Alice rubbed her lips together. Jadwiga was a baseline player with a strong forehand. She covered the court well, always looking for opportunities to attack.

The night before the match, Alice played it in her head. She hit the ball deep into the court. She varied the height and spin of her balls. She brought Jadwiga to the net using drop shots. It was the aggressive net-rushing style that Teach taught her that often had the press saying she played like a man.

On game day, Alice put Jadwiga away in two straight sets, no need for a third.

"Well done," Teach said. "But don't let it go to your—"

"I'm not." Alice closed her eyes, not believing what she was going to say next. "My next match is on July fourth. I know that."

She knew seven plus four equaled eleven.

She knew how Teach felt about that number.

She also knew she'd either face Hildegard Sperling, who'd won the French Championships three years in a row, or Mary Hardwick, whom she'd played in the Wightman Cup when the Americans faced the Brits.

As unfortunate luck had it, later that day, Hildegard won.

The fourth came. Alice had a few hours before their match, hours she spent in the stands, too tense this time to cross her ankles, watching Sarah Palfrey and Kay Stammers in their semifinal match. Alice's head went back and forth, the women evenly matched. Nerves churned in Alice's stomach, knowing that if she won later that afternoon, she'd face one of them.

Either Sarah, who'd love nothing more than to make Alice eat grass after beating her at championships.

Or Kay, who was always a bridesmaid, never the bride, gunning for her first finals win.

In the end, Kay triumphed.

Alice stood, replaying the final point through her head, questioning if Kay would've gotten her on that last ball down the line too, when the skies opened. It began to pour.

She sought refuge in the dressing room, slowly changing from her street clothes into her game wear. She'd yet to put on her wool socks. In wet conditions, most of the men wore spiked shoes to keep their footing. Alice didn't like them. She preferred socks *over* her shoes. She wouldn't win any fashion awards, but she'd keep her traction. And when one pair became too soggy, she'd switch into a new set. She had a half dozen pairs in men's size eleven. Teach thought they were a size ten.

An attendant popped her head into the room. "Still raining."

Then a few minutes later. "Still raining."

The next time the attendant came, Alice beat her to it. "Let me guess, still raining?"

"Yes, there's talk of your match being put off until tomorrow. But don't leave, not yet."

Alice nodded. "Have you seen my coach?"

"No, sorry, Miss Marble."

A second attendant entered the dressing room. "It's been called, Miss Marble. Your game has been rescheduled for tomorrow."

Alice sighed. She'd be stuck with nerves bouncing around her stomach for another night. The lead-up to a match was always exponentially more unsettling than the game itself.

She thanked the attendants, then began packing her things.

Teach walked in, looking like a drowned rat who'd just stolen a load of cheese. Alice snorted. If she was a betting woman, she'd put ten on her coach having just been out in the storm doing a rain dance, successfully at that.

Chapter 36

Alice ate when she was nervous. Bored. Upset. She was what you'd call an emotional eater.

With her match against Hildegard Sterling postponed, her body moved on autopilot to the hospitality tent. The table was full of delicious-looking little sandwiches and sweet cakes. There was a silver tea set. It was all very British.

She helped herself.

Ten minutes later, there was nothing left on her plate but crumbs. She sipped her tea. Her knee still bounced whenever she thought about her delayed match, but a sleepiness had come over her to help dull some of those nerves.

A woman burst into the tent. "Thank goodness." She blew out a breath. "There you are, Miss Marble. The chair umpire has decided you'll play after all. You're due at Centre Court in five minutes."

Alice nearly spat out her tea.

"That's not possible."

"What . . . what do you mean?" the attendant asked, clearly at a loss for how to handle a hesitant player.

Alice released her own breath, though hers wasn't relief. It was acquiescence. "Never mind. I'll be there." What other choice did she have?

Hilde hadn't just eaten her bodyweight in tiny sandwiches. She was ready to play. She had no reason to default.

Alice ran for the dressing room, stretching one arm and then the other above her head. She hoped to stretch out her stomach as well.

Teach was waiting for her there.

"I'm here, I'm here."

She said no more. No way was she going to confess to her coach she felt ten pounds heavier. Her movements as she dressed were abrupt, sharp, laced with fury. She'd likely just cost herself—and Teach—the semifinal match. She prayed that at the very least she wouldn't throw up on Centre Court.

"Good, you have on your pin," Teach noted. "And hey, the fact it's our country's independence can't be poor luck, right? Now remember, when you get out there, wave hello with your racquet so everyone gets a good look at it."

A few months back, Alice and Teach both had the opportunity to design their own signature racquets with Wilson Sporting Goods. Now the pressure was on to sell them.

But so was the pressure not to lose.

Alice snapped back, "Do you want me to win or do you want me to sell sporting goods?"

"Can you not do both?" Teach followed the question with a coy smile.

Alice wanted to vomit. She was nearly out of breath as she skidded to a stop at the entrance to the court and nodded at Hilde, who looked just as shocked—but not as disheveled—at the sudden match start.

It wasn't until Alice's name was being announced and she

stepped out onto the court that she realized she forgot her wool "traction" socks.

She cursed.

It wasn't until she was seven games in that she realized she'd forgotten to take off her warm-up sweater.

That she didn't curse at, because those seven games had all been her wins. And the wins kept coming.

Maybe the less-than-ideal circumstances freed up Alice's mind to just *play*.

Maybe she was having a phenomenal day.

Maybe Hilde wasn't. Her usually stoic nature made it hard to tell what she was thinking.

But Alice won 6–0, 6–0.

There was little doubt what Hilde thought about that.

There was even less doubt when Alice entered the dressing room, leaving Teach to deal with the press, and found Hilde with her head in her hands, her cheeks wet with emotion, the most emotion she'd ever seen the woman display.

How many times had that been Alice? She'd let that remain rhetorical. Hesitantly, she sat beside her opponent on the bench.

Hilde clenched her jaw, and Alice questioned leaving her be, but then Hilde said, "I've never been beaten like that before."

No animosity. No poor sportsmanship. Simply shock. And likely a whole lot of disappointment in herself.

Alice had been there before too. She bumped Hilde with her shoulder. Mary K. Browne had done this once for her. "I've sat where you're sitting many times."

Hilde's head bobbed until a tear tracked down her face. "I'm getting older. My coach and I decided this would be my last Wimbledon." Then the woman was sobbing.

Alice couldn't help it, she cried for Hilde too.

The door opened and a woman came in with a wave of noise. It was Lady Crosfield, a society woman who also dabbled in tennis. She stopped short, her brow wrinkling as she studied both Alice and Hilde. "My goodness, ladies, did you both lose?"

Alice snorted a laugh while the jest at least ended Hilde's tears.

"Hilde, dear," Lady Crosfield said, "there is absolutely no room for tears. No one could have stopped her on this particular day. Alice, you were truly magnificent."

Alice wanted to vocalize her gratitude but only smiled her thanks. Then she gripped Hilde's hand and squeezed.

The press had a field day with Alice's win against Hilde, calling her *Miss Marvel* instead of *Miss Marble.*

"Those reporters love their play on words, don't they?" Alice remarked to Teach.

"They love *you.*"

"For now they do."

One said she'd played like a man but looked like a goddess.

Truly, Alice's confidence didn't extend that far, but who was she to stop someone from comparing her to Athena or Circe? She wouldn't mind being a magical being who could transform her next opponent into a silly pig.

Or better yet, she'd be Nike.

The goddess of victory.

That'd suit her just fine.

The next day she went on to claim another semifinal victory with Sarah Palfrey as her doubles partner, and she was about to win again with Bobby Riggs in mixed doubles when she stretched to hit a smash and felt something in her stomach smart.

She stopped short, taking inventory of herself, as the hit found its mark, giving Alice and Bobby the point. Brows scrunched, Teach gestured to Alice in a "what's going on?" manner.

Alice ignored her.

Nothing.

Nothing was going on.

She bent, ready to receive the serve to put the game away. And she did.

The next morning Alice woke in agony. She couldn't sit up. She touched her stomach and winced in pain. "Teach!" she yelled, panicking.

The next bed over, Teach shot up, her head on a swivel. "What? What is it?"

"Teach, I can't move."

"What do you mean you can't move? You have the finals of Wimbledon in a few hours."

Alice gripped the sheets, squeezing, fighting for composure. "I need a doctor. I think I pulled a muscle."

This wasn't happening.

Her mind flashed to Hilde, head in her hands, crying in the dressing room, saying how it'd been her last chance at the finals.

Teach's voice was urgent. "Don't move an inch, Allie. I'm calling now."

The hotel doctor came straight away. "When did you start feeling pain, Miss Marble?"

"Yesterday during my mixed doubles match."

She ignored the whip of Teach's head toward her.

"Was there a particular moment when you aggravated the area?"

Yes, she explained.

Teach now glared. "And you didn't tell me after the match?"

She answered her coach's question, yet kept her words directed at the doctor. "It smarted when it happened, but afterward it felt fine. I didn't see the need to mention it and cause any hysterics."

Teach narrowed her eyes. "I am not hysterical."

"Hmm," the doctor said. "As you suspected, Miss Marble, you have a torn stomach muscle. It likely began to swell after the fact, significantly while you were sleeping, and here we are now."

He glanced at Teach. She was pacing.

"Miss Tennant," he said, "will you help me sit her up? I want to tape around her abdomen to try to increase blood flow and reduce the swelling."

Alice grunted with the movement. She didn't want to scream or let on how bad even sitting against the headrest felt . . . because then her next question would sound even more nonsensical. "Can I play?"

The doctor had been rustling around in his bag. He froze, the roll of tape in hand, at Alice's question.

"I'm in three finals today," Alice explained. "I can't default in any of them. There are too many people I'd be letting down."

Alice still couldn't look at her coach's face. She kept her focus trained on the doctor. He sighed. "It'd be foolish and very painful."

She nodded to the tape. "Make it tight."

Chapter 37

"You certainly can't expect to play your best."

That was what the doctor had said to Alice after she insisted on playing. She was about to step foot on Centre Court for the finals of Wimbledon with crippling pain, severe doubt, and a coach who was usually optimistically mouthing off to the reporters but who now looked like a puppy who'd been kicked.

Oh, and she was going against Kay Stammers. Top seeded. British, with the fans behind her. Healthy as a horse. Dismantled Helen Jacobs in the semifinals. And desperate for her own single's win.

Of course she was also completely congenial. "You've perfected the color in your cheeks, Alice," she said with a wink when they met at the net prior to the match.

"I learned from the best." Alice could be congenial too. But with those niceties out of the way, Alice headed toward the court to warm up. The day was gray and cool, but a waterfall of sweat dripped down Alice's neck and back almost instantly. She felt too warm all over, but especially where the tape was wrapped snuggly around her midsection, as if her skin were on fire.

During warm-ups, she moved as little as possible. She didn't practice her serves. She hit only a few balls. Alice hoped Kay saw it as confidence; she knew nothing of Alice's injury. The press didn't know either. Teach said it'd be used as a weapon, a weakness, a target. Alice had gotten the point. She held up her hand for Teach to stop after she'd said, "A major disadvantage."

But also, if Alice lost, she wanted no excuses to spoil Kay's first singles victory.

The toss went to Kay. "I'll receive first," she said.

Alice would begin with the serve, and her mind buzzed with why Kay made that decision.

Maybe she was nervous.

Maybe she wanted to get a feel for the court speed.

Maybe she wanted the pressure to begin on Alice.

Maybe she hoped Alice's serving rhythm wouldn't be perfected this early on in the match, especially since Alice hadn't practiced her serves.

Alice circled her lips and blew out a long, hard breath. To think, such an exhalation was impossible after she collapsed in France. Still impossible in the sanatorium when everyone and everything around her suggested her career was over.

Those days were hard.

Today would be hard too.

She slapped a smile on her face, raised her arm—and racquet—to the crowd, and let their reaction wash over her. She may not be the hometown favorite, but there were many out there who were rooting for her.

Alice looked to her coach, aching to see optimism there. Teach had her head down. But right before Alice turned away, her coach's head shot up, their eyes met, and Teach gave her a thumbs-up.

She bobbed her head. In her mind, she played her serve, Kay's return, her return. Satisfied, she bounced the ball, feeling the painful tug in her stomach muscles.

Then she served.

Dark spots burst in front of her eyes. She fought the wince but couldn't stop it. She only hoped Kay was too focused on her return to notice. The ball came back at Alice down the line. She hit it, but she had to stretch for the ball. A second wince.

She had to stop showing the pain. She had to ignore it. There was no cutting out the heel of her shoe in this scenario.

She couldn't get to Kay's return in time.

Alice gritted her teeth.

She dropped the first game.

Miraculously, she took the second.

With a growl, she lost the third. That left at least five more to go in the first set.

Every time she twisted her body to hit the ball, pain seared through her, seeping from her stomach into her arms and legs.

Step and swing, she told herself. Step and swing with her whole body. Find her rhythm. She'd given up so much to be there. She'd worked too damn hard to let a muscle pull stop her.

She wouldn't look at Teach.

She wouldn't.

Then she did. She couldn't help it.

Teach sat stiffly, rubbing her lips together, as nervous as they came.

On her baseline, Alice leaned forward, weight on her toes, showing everyone, including herself, she was ready for Kay to serve.

Fault.

Alice bounced in place, then got back in position. The second serve came in quickly, giving her a heartbeat to react, but she found it with her racquet, the vibration almost unbearable. Alice returned it low and flat. It worked. It was worth the pain.

She found her rhythm, throwing in chops and slices to keep Kay guessing. Kay didn't win another game in the set. They all went to Alice. 6–2. The first set was hers, but darkness crowded the edges of her vision. Her breath came ragged. She fought the urge to bend in an attempt to ease the feeling of daggers stabbing again and again in her abdomen.

No way in hell did she want the match to go to three sets. She needed to win this match in two. A third set meant a ten-minute break. It meant losing her momentum. It meant her body fully realizing the agony she was putting it through and calling it quits. Alice was dangling from a cliff, and if she stopped, she'd lose her grip. It'd be a long, long fall.

The number of games in their first set was even so they didn't change sides. Alice was happy to stay where she was as they began the second set. She didn't hear the crowd. She saw nothing but Kay.

And she served.

Alice served and played and served like it was her very last chance at being the best in the world.

And it very well could be.

Alice thought of Hilde and how they were nearly the same age. Then of Hans and of his prediction. She promptly put him out of mind before she began searching for a dark-haired man in the stands. The crowd had grown quiet, enamored, in awe.

Alice focused on each individual play, only knowing that Kay had yet to win a point in the second set.

Nor would Alice let her. She hit a backhand down the line, catching Kay out of position. With a small smile and a shake of her head, Kay began walking toward the net.

At first, Alice didn't know why. Had the chair umpire called for a pause in the game? She looked up at him. Then, for the first time, over at the scoreboard, where the numbers were going up.

6–0.

She'd done it. She'd won. Alice whirled toward the roaring crowd, a stabbing burn filling her stomach one final time, to meet Teach's gaze. Her coach was on her feet, already caught up in a mass of reporters and well-wishers. But Teach bobbed left and right, fighting to meet Alice's eyes. Never before had Teach smiled like that.

Seven years ago, Teach made the biggest gamble of her life. And it just earned out. Alice's victory was Teach's victory.

And now . . . they were the best in the world.

Her debts had been paid, to her mother, her brother, her coach.

Alice hugged her racquet to her chest as tears fell. Filled with the feeling of champagne bubbles, giddy with excitement, she approached the net weightlessly, where Kay pulled her into a tight hug. "Time for you to meet my queen."

This must be make-believe, a well-directed film. Alice must've just paid her fifteen cents to be transported to another reality, surely not the girl who grew up playing in public courts with barely two dimes to rub together. But then a man was introducing himself as Joseph Kennedy, the American ambassador, and he'd taken Alice's arm and was leading her toward the Dowager Queen Mary, dressed in all white from her head to her toe. Alice had never seen someone more regal looking.

"Your Majesty, Miss Alice Marble," Kennedy said, introducing her. He stepped back, making way for the two women.

The queen's violet eyes held Alice's, and for a moment she panicked at the protocol of meeting royalty.

Hans flashed through her head, a conversation they had upon first meeting.

"I should work on my curtsy," she had said to him. "Do you shake a queen's hand?"

"If she offers," Hans had said, amusement on his handsome face. "Then firmly, at that."

Alice had laughed. "Fine, if I win, I'll shake her hand firmly."

The memory was a punch to her gut that Alice could barely tolerate. She'd given him up for all of this. She'd told herself again and again she had to make losing him worth it. Now there she was, standing in front of the queen, who smiled at her, small crinkle lines forming around her lips. At the same time she extended her hand to Alice, Alice curtsied.

"Sorry," Alice muttered.

The queen smiled demurely. People likely made a baboon of themselves in front of her on a daily basis.

"Thank you for a fascinating match," Queen Mary said in a low, confident voice. "And I like your cap."

"My cap?" Alice said, touching her head. "You can have it."

A blip of a laugh slipped from the queen. "That's quite all right. I have plenty. Please, enjoy your victory."

"Thank you," Alice said, no short of three times. Not wanting to take any more of the queen's time, she began to walk away, then realized she'd turned her back on royalty. Mortified, heat filled her cheeks. "Your Majesty," Alice said, turning around, "I apologize."

Suddenly Kennedy had her arm again. Bless that man. Together, they backed away, a look of amusement again on the queen's face.

They'd taken only a handful of steps before the reporters swarmed.

"How does it feel to be the World Champion?" a reporter yelled.

"Outstanding," Alice said. "Best feeling in the world."

Flashbulbs popped, blinding her.

In the flash of darkness, she saw Ma's face. Emotion thickened her throat. Her mother would have been so proud. She imagined Dan double-gripping the radio while ignoring his police duties, eating up every word. He'd been the first to put a racquet in her hands. Lastly, she remembered Hans's confidence that she'd be the world's best.

How could one body contain so many emotions? She welcomed the peppering of questions from the press. She barely said two words before someone else asked another. What was she even saying? She didn't know.

Teach bum-rushed the crush of reporters, wrapping her in a hug, Alice not feeling an ounce of pain, the adrenaline coursing through her too strong.

"That's it for now," Teach shouted to the reporters. "She still has two matches to play. Alice will have plenty of time for interviews after she wins those too."

Teach angled Alice toward the dressing room. "Holy cow, Allie, you were wonderful." Her sheer excitement caused a tremble in her voice. "I don't know how you did it. I'm so proud of you."

"Proud of us," Alice said.

"I always knew you could do it."

"Not without you, Teach," Alice said. "But hey, can we please be done with the rules now?" Alice beamed. "I mean, we did it. I'm the best."

"Yes, we did. No more rules, Allie. Cross my heart. But opinions, you better believe I'll still have those." Teach winked. "Like how you really should be seeing a doctor right now. But I also know Bobby's waiting for you if you're up for it."

Alice mentally thanked the adrenaline keeping the pain at bay. She'd pay for it later. But right now she had no intentions of letting down Bobby in mixed doubles.

She didn't.

Nor did she let Sarah down in the women's doubles.

Alice claimed a Wimbledon triple crown.

She was the best women's tennis player in the world, and Alice felt like nothing could stop her now.

Evening News

September 1, 1939

This Country Is at War

Chapter 38

Now

Tuesday, March 27, 1945
US Army Intelligence offices

Come again? It's lucky Alice is sitting down. She assumed Colonel Linden would bring up Joe. She suspected their clandestine meeting would be about him.

But about a former lover?

About Hans Steinmetz?

Someone she hasn't spoken to in six years.

Someone she sacrificed on her path to success.

"I see by your expression, Miss Marble, that you were not expecting to hear his name."

"No," Alice said in a choked voice. She said it again, stronger. "And I'm not sure why you'd bring up Hans. We didn't exactly keep in touch."

"I see." Colonel Linden glances over Alice's shoulder at Captain Jones. By the time Alice twists, whatever silent communication that passed between the two men is over. She hates that Jones has lurked behind her this entire time.

She hates that he called Hans "the one who got away."

Is he?

They may've last seen each other those six years ago, but she thought about him on her road to winning Wimbledon, after winning Wimbledon, every single time Teach put Alice in a situation where she had to choose tennis, reminding her she hadn't picked him.

He never wrote. He never called. Alice was guilty of the same. Then she met Joe. Joe, whom she desperately loved. But she'd desperately loved Hans once upon a time too.

"Do you need a moment?" Colonel Linden asks.

She can only imagine the emotions that just passed over her face. She shakes her head, refolds her hands in her lap. "No, I'm fine. What does Hans have to do with me? You said that I alone am the only person who can make contact with him. Why?"

"Straight to the point," the colonel says. "I like that. I'll be blunt too. He's unmarried. We think you're the one who got away for him. Which means we think he'd be receptive to hearing from you."

Unmarried . . .

The one who got away for him too . . .

Alice uses her thumb and forefinger to pinch on either side of her eyes. "And why would he need to hear from me?"

"I'll remind you that this is classified information. You cannot tell Miss Tennant, your siblings, any friends, any colleagues. Even if you decide not to help us, you cannot speak of any of this."

Alice nods. "Yes, I understand that. What I don't understand is why the sudden interest in me seeing Hans again."

Another moment passes between Colonel Linden and Captain Jones, then the colonel says, "We believe Mr. Steinmetz is working with the Nazi party."

Alice startles.

"And we'd like you to go undercover to try to secure proof that our assumptions are correct."

Chapter 39

Colonel Linden said so much with so few words. Alice's brain tries to catch up. "You think Hans is working with the Germans?" she asks. "And you want me to go undercover to incriminate him?"

She's still unclear how she is the only one who can do that.

The colonel's expression is stoic. "Yes." He pauses a beat, then says, "We have reason to believe Mr. Steinmetz is an important link to many high-ranking Nazis."

Alice quickly interjects, "So you don't know for sure?"

"To the best of our knowledge, he's aiding them, and the Germans can see the writing on the wall that they're going to lose this war. The smart ones are taking the riches they've wrongly acquired—gold, jewels, paintings, currency, anything of value—and are smuggling it into Switzerland. When the Nazi members run after Germany surrenders, they'll be able to set up dynasties in places like South America, where no questions will be asked as long as they can pay."

Alice feels sick. "Hans is allowing the Nazis to keep their treasures in his bank?"

"That's what we have reason to believe. What we don't have is proof to pin anything to the wall. We suspect that he keeps records of these transactions in a private vault, like his vault at home, rather than at his bank. I'll stress again: this is serious, dangerous business. But it's a chance to get evidence we can use to stop the Nazis from getting away and reorganizing in a new country. Nobody wants to fight this war a second time."

And have all the deaths be for nothing, Alice thinks. She rubs her temples again. Yesterday she'd been minding her own business, trying to gain some normalcy at her favorite restaurant with her favorite dessert when Captain Jones approached her. Now she's here in some abandoned-looking warehouse being asked to help implicate an ex-lover, one who's crossed her mind over the years more times than she'd like to admit. And, oh, she can't tell a soul about any of it.

"Why me?" she has to know. "You say I'm the only one who can do this. Why is that? How do you even know about Hans and me?"

Jones says, "You two were all over the European tabloids," at the same time Colonel Linden says, "Because of tennis."

Alice ignores Jones and keeps her focus on the colonel, who says, "Yes, your relationship was well-documented, considering the brevity of it. When we looked into his background to find an angle in, we recognized your name. You've been on the intelligence's radar ever since your day of trying to enlist at every armed forces office possible. And then, of course, you helped with the president's fitness program. As far as tennis, I believe we can use it as a very simple cover. That's mainly why we have chosen you for this assignment. We'd say you are playing a number of exhibition games in Switzerland."

"And then what? I somehow bump into Hans and reignite whatever was between us, when he very well could hate my guts?"

"We're hopeful he'll be receptive," Linden says. "Though the reigniting only need be believable so that you can gain access to his home vault. Do you think Hans would be amiable to running into you again? We weren't able to discern from the gossip columns the reason for your relationship ending. Was there an argument?"

Alice runs her tongue over her top teeth. This conversation is stirring up so many memories and emotions, all on the heels of a very paralyzing and difficult few months after the loss of her child and the death of her husband.

"Miss Marble?" the colonel asks, his voice kind. "Do you need a moment?"

"I'm fine," she says instinctively. She prolongs a blink, gathering herself. "Your question . . . No, there was no argument, not really. My coach talked me into ending it with Hans. He didn't like it, but he didn't argue. He simply left. We were both hurt. But we loved each other. Our split was heartbreaking but not mean-spirited."

"You haven't communicated since 1938, that's correct?"

"Yes."

"Do you think Mr. Steinmetz would see you if he could?" he asks again.

"I don't know. You said he was unmarried?" She clears her throat, recalls that he said how he hoped their paths would one day cross again, then decides, says, "Most likely."

But did she want to see him? She loved Joe more than anybody. But Hans . . . he was her first love. When she thinks of him, there's only good. They weren't together long enough to ever argue, to disagree. It was only rainbows and unicorns. If he sees their relationship the same way . . . She changes her answer. "I think he'd be open to seeing me." Her shoulders rise and fall. "But do you know what you're asking me? He's not just going to open his vault for me. Not to mention all of the old emotions that'll surface. And so soon after . . ."

"Yes," Colonel Linden says, "we imagine this could be hard. It's worth repeating. This assignment may not directly relate to your late husband, but it's an opportunity to avenge his death."

So he's playing that card again.

Alice couldn't lie, it's as effective now as it was the first time. Would she like to help destroy the regime responsible for her husband's death? For essentially the death of her future? Yes.

Does she want to do that at the cost of seeing Hans again?

Could an answer be both yes and no?

"We'd train you," the colonel says. "We'll teach you everything you need to know. Then we'll send you to Switzerland for some well-publicized matches. You're a charismatic woman, Miss Marble. We think it's likely Hans will see your name in the headlines and come looking for you."

Heat settles into her belly, and she shifts uncomfortably in her seat.

"If you say no," he adds, "we'll understand."

Jones scoffs behind her.

Alice says, "I need time to think about this."

"Tomorrow, then?" Linden says. "I'll call you."

On the car ride back to her apartment, Alice had suspected Jones would open his big mouth and try to convince her, but the ride was eerily quiet. Until Alice reached for the handle to get out.

"We need you," he said simply. "Just seduce the guy. Wouldn't be anything you haven't done before."

She narrowed her eyes but otherwise bit her tongue. She did, however, slam the door upon exiting.

For the remainder of the day, Alice moved through a fog.

This morning, the fog has yet to lift.

Her thoughts oscillate from Joe to Hans and back to Joe. Could she do this for Joe? Could she spy on Hans, only to betray him? Does he deserve that?

Maybe, if he's working with the Nazis.

The thought disgusts her. It also doesn't align with the man she fell in love with. A love she once regretted letting go, which made her willing to defy Teach when she had another shot at her happily ever after—with Joe. In a strange way, Hans led to Joe. And now Joe is leading to Hans.

She could do this for Joe. Perhaps at the risk of her own life. What would happen to her if she was caught spying? What if she didn't know Hans as well as she thought she did? What if he's different now? Or what if the Germans get their hands on her?

Alice puts down her mug of coffee. She's been drinking it absently while her brain works on overdrive. She does not need any more caffeine.

The phone rings at the same time Teach comes into the kitchen, a bag slung over her shoulder. "I'll get it," she says.

Alice, half raised out of her seat, slinks down. She pulls her bottom lip between her teeth and listens. She watches as Teach says nothing more than hello, then shrugs. "No one is there. Guess it was a wrong number." Teach drops her bag by the door; she has a clinic to run this morning and checks the pot for coffee. She frowns at Alice. "You left me with the dregs."

"I can make more for—" she starts to say.

The phone rings.

Alice rises so quickly the chair nearly topples. "Hello?" she says into the receiver.

"Miss Marble, good. If you're not alone, say, 'I think you have the wrong number.'"

She does.

Teach spares her only a glance as she reaches for the coffee grounds.

"Thank you, now, do you have a decision for me?"

She assumes its Colonel Linden. If it was Jones, he'd probably say something arrogant, pompous, or crude.

Does she have an answer for him?

It has taken an entire pot of coffee to be able to say this, but, "Yes."

"Yes, as in you'll help us?"

"Yes."

She has nothing else to lose, and it'll be a second chance to help her country. Unfortunately, it'll also be as second chance to hurt a man she already hurt years again, a man who may or may not be guilty of anything at all.

"You have our gratitude, Miss Marble. A car will pick you up at two o'clock tomorrow. Same place. I'll set up a training schedule for you. There's a lot to learn and not much time to learn it. Before I go, I need verbal confirmation that you agree not to speak of this call, our previous meeting, or anything going forward.

"Yes."

"Okay, then. I'll see you tomorrow."

Alice returns the phone to the base, the reality of what she just agreed to setting in. Spying. On an ex-lover. Overseas. Teach will most definitely have questions when she goes to pack her bags. And when she has to explain away all the time she'll spend training.

"Who was that?" Teach asks.

"A wrong number."

"You sure said yes a lot."

"They kept asking if I was sure a Rebecca Jones didn't live here."

Alice's first lie, a name she fabricated from midair.

Teach snorts. "Relentless." She opens a cabinet, closes it. Opens another. "Are we out of filters?" She shakes her head. "Maybe this Rebecca rented the apartment before us."

Alice shrugs. "Anyway, need help with the clinics today?"

The perfect way to salve her growing guilt until she's off to Switzerland.

"What I need is coffee."

"I'll run out and get you some."

Teach raises an eyebrow at that. Alice will have to do better. Arousing suspicion with Teach is one thing. But with Hans. With the Germans. That could mean the difference between life and death.

Chapter 40

Soon Alice has a routine. She likes routines. Routines are expected, controlled. Every day she plays tennis in the morning with Teach. Then, under the guise of taking business classes at New York University, she slinks off to the warehouse in Brooklyn to train. At night she dines with her coach, keeping the focus on tennis.

Tennis techniques.

Tennis strategies.

Up-and-coming players.

Possible exhibitions.

She really leans into that last one, building a story around how she'd love Teach to keep an eye out for anything she can play in.

"I have an itch," Alice says.

What she doesn't say is how an "opportunity" will soon fall in their laps. Alice just isn't sure when Linden will call upon her.

Today as she walks into the warehouse, she asks another agent a question she's been thinking on a daily basis. "Dave, I can't be the only person here training, right?"

She's never seen another soul besides Jones, the colonel, and the young man she was told to call Dave, who happens to be the size of

Goliath with the hair of Samson.

He smiles coyly. "As a precaution, we stagger our recruits and trainees. If anyone were to see you, they'd recognize you. Your cover, and essentially your mission, would be instantly blown."

"But there are others here?"

Dave smiles a second time.

"What's on the agenda today?" she asks him.

So far, her training has been a blur, likened to that device in filmmaking where a montage is run, going through a sequence of moments. Hers began with how to use a .25 caliber automatic with a six-shot clip in the handle and one shell in the chamber. Not her favorite. "Easy to conceal. Small caliber, but it can kill," Alice was told.

Maybe the gun could kill, but could Alice?

She immediately put a pin in that question and chased her uneasiness with a quip. "Well, my coach has certainly made me a killer on the court."

She disliked the joke as soon as it left her mouth.

Map reading went better. A cinch, in fact, with her photographic memory. She knew Geneva's roads inside and out within minutes.

Picking locks, identifying booby traps, and disarming explosives went moderately better, Dave praying she never actually encountered a bomb. "Explosives are usually set up to kill an intruder without disturbing the safe or its contents," he warned.

Even hand-to-hand combat in an honest-to-god padded cell went more smoothly than her introduction to a gun. Wrestling Dave was a challenge, seeing as they were so unfairly matched. But under his tutelage she learned to use his bulk against him and send him flying in a variety of throws. It was quite satisfying.

"Today," Dave says now, "we're target training."

"With a gun?"

"Unless you want to somehow discreetly carry a bow and arrow."

Alice sighs and follows Dave into the shooting range.

"Now, we've gone over the gun," he begins. "It's a peashooter compared to the weapons most of our operatives carry. But it's the best gun for you. If you ever have to use it, you'll likely be in close quarters."

Like in Hans's home?

She shakes the thought away and focuses on her gun. She hasn't grown any more fond of it. Her .32 is still ugly and sinister-looking. Still, she wraps her hands around the heavy steel the way Dave taught her.

"Good, now stretch out your arms and aim."

Not far away, perhaps half a court's length, is a line of paper targets.

"Fire," Dave instructs. "Fire," he repeats when Alice hesitates. "You're going to need to fire. Your life could depend on it."

Alice blows out a slow, controlled breath—and fires.

She hits the bull's eye. Not dead-on, but toward the outer ring.

"Not bad, Miss Marble."

"Alice," she corrects, and not for the first time.

"I prefer Miss Marble."

"Yet you're Dave? That feels a bit unbalanced."

"You're stalling," he says.

He may have a point.

Alice stretches out her arms and fires again.

"Better."

He points to the next paper target. "Now go again."

And again, and again, and again.

They move on to a man-sized cardboard silhouette.

"Picture that as a Nazi who just put the pieces together that you're an American spy. He's out for blood. Your blood."

Alice's brow knits together. "I'd rather not paint such a vivid picture if that's okay with you, Dave."

"Life or death, Miss Marble. Life or death."

"Fine," she grumbles. "That's a Nazi who wants to kill me."

"Perfect." Dave pulls out a stopwatch.

Alice's hands lower. "What are you doing with that?"

"Cooking you dinner. What do you think I'm doing? I'm going to time how quickly you can shoot and reload. We've gone over all of this. Now it's time to put it into practice."

"Fine," she grumbles again.

Alice has been in some stressful, high-intensity situations. A tennis ball flying at her at one hundred miles per hour is no joke. She's had to react quickly, both in mind and body.

She can do this.

Dave the Gentle Giant is expecting her to do this.

She aims, fires. Fires again.

Two tiny holes appear in the heart of her target.

She shoots a third, fourth, fifth, sixth time.

Her target now suffers two head and groin wounds.

"Good! Reload!" Dave barks, eyeing his stopwatch. "Life or death. Life or death."

"So you've said," Alice says through gritted teeth as she pulls a clip from her shoulder holster and reloads her gun.

A small smile spreads on her face. She did it within seconds, and now Dave's head bobs in approval. "Remember, nothing fancy, just shoot for the body until he drops. Or in this case, until you need to reload. In either case, you run. Reload as you go."

Alice shoots again, lowering her hands when she's done to find the target peppered with holes.

"That'll do the trick, Miss Marble. Now let's do it all again, this time with the lights off."

***

When Alice isn't being thrown against padded walls, hitting balls on the court, and dodging Teach's questions about how her classes at NYU are going to help her tennis, she's preoccupied with what could await her on her mission.

She's preoccupied with Hans . . .

Who may have no desire to see her. If he does, she'll have a job to do. She doesn't want to hurt him—again.

There's also the fact Linden has called her assignment dangerous a number of times. What circumstance would cause Alice to stick her thumbs into a person's eyes? Or shove the heel of her hand into someone's nose, ramming his bones into his brain? Or crush a windpipe with a chop of her hand?

"A kick to the groin is useful," Dave has told her. "But not very original. A man is likely to suspect such a thing from a woman. But those other ways"—he whistled—"Those can do some serious, unexpected damage. They'll save your life."

She never imagined she'd learn such things.

Now she only hopes she won't ever have to use these newfound, deadly skills.

She arrives at the warehouse on an unseasonably warm spring day. Sweat gathers on her forehead. She pulls at the long-sleeve blouse, the fabric sticking to her skin. To maintain her ruse, and thanks to Dave, Alice has had to wear long-sleeves during her morning tennis with Teach. Bruises cover her arms.

"Miss Marble," Alice hears.

She spins to find Colonel Linden and her brow raises.

"This way," he says, motioning.

So no Dave today?

He leads Alice into his office. Jones is there. His presence makes the office seem too small.

"What do we have here?" Alice says, directing her attention to a smattering of photos and papers on the colonel's desk.

"What we have here is the final step," Linden says. "You know your way around Geneva, and you know how to stay alive. Now you need to know the ins and outs of Mr. Steinmetz's estate."

He spreads out the photos.

It's the first Alice has ever seen the castle, beyond her imagination. During their time together, Hans had described it in detail. A mini fortress perched upon a hill, high walls, a tall central tower, gabled roofs, a stone facade flanked by vineyards, gardens, and rocky crags. A chapel that Alice knows is painted with ancient frescoes, even though its unseen in the photographs.

Her eyes land again on the tower. Hans's playful words about locking her up in his tower are a chokehold on her emotions.

She's grateful when Jones slams down blueprints, covering the photographs. He uses ashtrays to keep the corners from curling.

"Here's the inside," Jones says.

"How'd you get this?" Alice asks.

"Mostly it's guesswork," Jones says causally.

"Educated guesswork," Linden adds. "We acquired blueprints from recent remodelings in the area. Many of the structures built in the 1600s have a similar floorplan. A wide central hall with a drawing room on one side," he says, tapping the blueprint. "A formal dining room on the other. Then, here, a grand staircase leading to the rooms above." He presses on the rendering of the staircase. "Under it is where we suspect there's a doorway to the basement. There's likely a wine cellar down there, and, making another educated guess, that is where his vault will be."

Alice offers, "With his transaction records."

"That's right," the colonel says.

"I have it memorized."

Colonel Linden leans back in his chair, amusement crossing his face. "I wish we had you earlier in the war."

Alice snorts. "I tried."

"That you did. But we're fortunate to have you now." He points to the blueprints, exactly where he suspects the vault to be. "Think you can get here?"

"I will certainly try my best."

"When you do," he says with confidence, "photograph the records. You'll be provided a camera, small enough to conceal."

"You'll have to show me how to use it."

"That can be arranged before you go."

Alice cocks her head. "Why do you think he'll have these records at home instead of at his bank? Wouldn't security be better there?"

Linden nods. "Yes, but at home he has discretion. His household staff has been working for his family for many years. Generations, even. They're very loyal. Employees at the bank come and go. They can be bought off. Some may even be Russian agents. The Russians want this information too. We suspect they have men watching Steinmetz, his house, his bank. No one wants the Germans escaping the country with their stolen fortunes that could put them back in power. Speaking of power, the Russians want that too. I wouldn't put it past them to loot Steinmetz's vault for their own military use. It's hard to know who to trust, especially during times of war."

A chill runs down Alice's back. She distracts herself from the uncomfortable feeling with a question. "Will it be only me over there?"

On the court Alice prefers singles every time. But it certainly puts the wind up her to think about shouldering this all alone. What if she gets in trouble and her thumbs, hands, kicks don't work?

"We have others in place in the area as well."

Alice nods in relief.

Linden smiles. "We'll keep an eye on you, but you can't count on anyone coming to your rescue. It's the reason why Dave has been so . . . thorough . . . with your training."

Alice runs a hand over the bruises on her arm.

Linden puts a new photograph in front of Alice. "This'll be your contact while you're in Geneva. The one keeping a distant eye on you."

The man is willowy with a gnome-like face. A heavy beard.

"His name is Franz Regenbogen. He works as a goldsmith on La Grande Rue near the Hotel Les Armures. That's where you'll be staying, by the way."

Alice pulls the map from her memory and knows exactly where that is.

"He's there if you need him. But I'd rather you don't contact him until you have the records photographed. Once you do, bring the film directly to Franz. Then get to the airport. Your job will be done and we'll get you out as soon as we can. There will be an army transport waiting day or night, any time you arrive."

Alice has been immersed in training, yet now, in this moment, it truly hits her what she's signed up for. This isn't squaring off with a petulant man like Myrick. This is potentially facing the Nazis, the Russians . . . an old lover who may want absolutely nothing to do with her. She centers herself, just like Teach has taught her. "When do I leave?"

"Great question," Linden says, glancing at Jones. "One I'm

pleased as plum you're asking. We were worried about your mental state when we first began. Loss is not easy to overcome. It's only been a few weeks, but we see a change in you."

"I have something to fight for again," Alice says, refusing to let her voice crack.

Linden presses his lips together and nods. "As far as timing, the war is winding down. We have to move before Hitler's own officers kill him and all the rats run for cover. You leave Monday."

Alice's brow scrunches. "And today is?"

With such little variation in her weeks, she's lost track. This happens; Alice gets so hyperfocused on the moment, the play, the point, that it's all she can see.

"You have two days, Miss Marble," the colonel says.

"Time to tell that coach of yours about the cover assignment," Jones chirps in.

Alice startles at his deep voice, and not for the first time. She really wishes he didn't hover behind her in her meetings with Linden.

Colonel Linden scratches along his jawline. "Do you think Miss Tennant will pose a problem? We can stage a call, inviting you to Switzerland as a guest of the army."

Alice shakes her head. "No, it's fine. I'll give her the details. But she'll expect a contract."

Is Alice looking forward to lying—more—to her coach?

Not a chance.

Does having Linden pave the path make her feel like a coward?

Absolutely.

And right now, with who knows what's in front of her, it's no time to let fear rule her.

Chapter 41

I'm confused."

Honestly, Teach's response could have been a lot worse.

On the sidewalk, her coach sidesteps a woman with a pram. "Why didn't they talk to me?"

"I guess they saw me first? I don't know. I had just walked off the court. You were talking to Mary."

Part lie, part truth. Alice runs her damp palms down her practice shorts as nonchalantly as possible. "It's just for a few weeks. A few exhibition matches for them."

"For the army?"

Alice nods, quickening her pace to match Teach's, which is accelerating based on her current emotion: agitated. "That's right. They've coordinated with our tennis association and Swiss Tennis. Strengthening bonds through tennis or something like that."

"Very well, but there's no way I can make it with a single day's notice," Teach argues. "We'll have to turn them down. I haven't even seen a contract yet."

Alices dodges a puddle. "But you know I've been wanting to play in some exhibitions. The contract can be figured out later."

"We'll find you some tennis to play. I've already put feelers out.

But Switzerland? Tomorrow? That's a pile of horse—"

"I want to go."

"But I *can't* pull this off, Alice."

"I know you have students. I can go alone."

"Can you?"

And just like that, this squabble is about more than going to Switzerland; it's also about Teach having too firm a grip on Alice's decisions.

Alice stops dead on the sidewalk. It takes Teach a few paces to realize.

She turns back, throws up her hands. "What are you doing?"

"I'm going," Alice says, holding her ground.

"There's a war on!"

"Switzerland is neutral."

"Really, Alice? This is preposterous!"

So is yelling back and forth on the streets of New York City. Alice snaps back, "I'll send you a postcard." Then she starts walking the opposite direction. Frankly, she's not sure where she's going. Their apartment is the other way. But she'll figure it out. In fact, Le Pavillon for a chocolate soufflé sounds like the perfect destination.

Switzerland may be neutral. The skies to get there are not. But with a white-knuckle grip much of the way and with visions of Joe being shot down haunting her every breath, Alice arrives unscathed.

From within the US Army transport, all of Geneva stretches below her and the seemingly endless summits of the Alps stretch before her. Her first glimpse of the mountains, so beautifully white against the blue sky, are a balm for her nerves.

The city lies at the tip of Lake Geneva, a shade of blue that deserves its own name. Even the more exotic-sounding blues like azure, cerulean, or cobalt feel too pedestrian.

As the plane descends, small wrinkles become roads that snake across the earth and through the mountains.

No sooner does Alice land than she's whisked away in a vehicle, bound for Chamonix.

Hans's chateau is in Chamonix.

Alice's knee bounces as she's driven along the roads she's memorized from her training. She recognizes the various escape routes Colonel Linden taught her. She knows the exact moment they pass the roadway that'd take her to Hans.

Yet he's supposed to find her.

What is she doing? It all suddenly feels like a mistake being here. Acting a fool. Playing a spy. She broke both their hearts. And a heartbeat later, he was gone. There was never any closure, for either of them. Why had Linden and Jones assumed he'd want to see her? Why did she agree that they might be right?

Alice is a stupid woman with too much confidence. Either that or she's living in a dream world. Alas, it's too late now; she's already gone halfway across the world. Her driver stops in front of the Hôtel Les Armures.

"Here we are, miss. Quite a few have turned out for your arrival."

As in, the press.

But maybe Hans? Would he have come immediately upon hearing she's in town? So many others have.

"Thank you," she says, straightening her blouse and tucking her hair behind her ears. She climbs from the car, acting as if she hasn't just spent countless hours traveling. She's wrinkled. Her mouth feels stuffed with cotton. Her legs are fatigued despite sitting all day. She licks her lips, but they're still too dry. She'll have to work with what's got.

Alice hopes Hans likes what he sees. The question is, is it merely for the assignment or because she *wants* him to be attracted to her after all these years? Her stomach flips at the thought. Thank goodness playing lefties with a killer backhand has prepared her for this very moment. Immediately, she scans every face for Hans. Would he look similar, only older? The same dark hair, dark eyes, tanned complexion? There are men, some handsome, even. But no one holds a candle to the dashing face Alice conjures from her memories.

Alice is approached by one person after another: local tennis figures, local political figures, newspaper columnists. But no wealthy bankers.

She turns on the charm, smiling big, laughing freely, talking boldly about how she has plans to win. Alice pulls out every trick in the book so she'll make the headlines.

She waves, wiggling her fingers, as she finally heads inside the hotel and to the lavish suite the tennis association has booked for her.

Face down, she falls onto the plush bed. With a groan, exhausted from her put-on smile and travel, she checks her wristwatch. Dinner in an hour. It's another opportunity to get her name plastered across the headlines like a beacon.

But as she's walking toward the restaurant, she passes by the hotel bar. The setting stops Alice in her tracks. For a moment, her heart pauses. How serendipitous would it be if she sat down, if Hans approached her? If only her mission could start on such an easy foot. She'd welcome the ace.

But no, Hans does not walk into the hotel like he'd done upon their first meeting. By the time she retires to her room, her emotions are frayed. She draws back the heavy drapes. In the distance, the mountains glow in the moonlight. She peers in the direction of Hans's home. Does he know yet? Will he come for her? Will she have the courage to see her mission through?

She curses. Those questions will keep her up all night.

***

Desynchronosis barely allows for any sleep as well.

Alice wakes the next morning feeling as if she hadn't slept a wink.

She's thankful for a busy routine or else she'd dawdle. Instead, she's up, dressed, and meeting the tennis pro of the local club in the hotel dining room for breakfast.

Two cups of coffee and one slice of buttered bread later, they're off to the indoor courts at Parc des Eaux-Vives for Alice's first match.

Her opponent, Ingrid, is young and powerful. Her serve could create envy in many of the girls back home. Alice handles her swiftly.

It gets her name in the papers.

She attends a luncheon after.

Then a party that evening.

More press coverage. More headlines.

Alice does this three days in a row.

Do you know what it doesn't get her?

Hans.

Maybe he saw her picture and didn't bat an eye.

Maybe he immediately stashed the newspaper in the trash.

Maybe he didn't see the coverage at all.

She twists her lips as she bounces the ball on day number four of matches. Another young girl, Emilia, waits on the other side of the net.

It's 40–0.

Forty-love, which Teach has always warned Alice is the most pivotal point in any game. She's a point away from winning the game, which'll win her the set and the whole shebang. Either she shuts out Emilia with her next serve or she gives her opponent a foot in the door. It could be all Emilia needs to kick it down.

"*Tides turn fast in tennis,*" Teach said.

Alice knows what she has to do. Emilia loves the slice. She offers Emilia an easily handled serve. Ball back on Alice's side of the court, she hits it deep and low with an ample amount of top swing.

The ball bounces in bounds. Emilia can't get to it in time.

The umpire signals Alice is the winner.

Smiling, she shakes hands with Emilia, smiles for the cameras for the umpteenth time, then makes her way toward the dressing room.

A girl steps in front of her. "Miss Marble," she says politely. "This is for you."

She presents a single long-stemmed, peach-colored rose to Alice.

And a card.

Apparently tides can turn fast off the court too.

Chapter 42

Alice's heart pounds.

Hans has found her.

He sent the same gesture he had while they were in France.

That has to be a good sign, right?

Still, she cannot bring herself to open the card.

But she must.

The Steinmetz family crest is at the top.

The neat handwriting speaks of confidence.

You're more beautiful than I remembered. Have dinner with me. I'll be at your hotel at 7.

Hans

Alice closes her eyes, a smile smarting on her lips. She's done it.

***

Alice only brought five evening dresses with her.

She's tries each of them on five times each, until she decides on the red one that shows off her figure and best accents her blonde hair and warm skin tone. It also has cap sleeves and matching gloves, which go a long way to cover her fading bruises.

Alice attaches her pin to her dress, a risk to the fine fabric, but she's in need of any luck it can give her. Hans's note seemed friendly enough, but would he still hold any resentment toward her? She's running a matching red shade of lipstick over her lips when the hotel phone rings.

She checks her watch. It's ten to seven.

"Hello?"

"I'm downstairs," says a deep voice she instantly recognizes.

Alice blinks, hoping her heartbeat can't be heard over the line, and sinks onto the edge of the bed. "You're early."

"It's been years. I didn't think ten minutes made much of a difference."

Alice bites her bottom lip, unable to decipher his tone. "I'll be right down."

The hotel's staircase is wide, as if made for grand entrances. With each carefully placed footstep, she prays she won't trip. It's not until she's at the bottom that she finally looks up. And she sees him, one leg crossed over another, casually sitting on a wingback chair, his dark blue suit deepening the shade of his brown eyes. His thick, dark hair droops over his forehead, curling slightly at the nape of his neck.

She's twenty-five again. She's overcome with an instant attraction. She wants his time, his attention. But does he want hers? Will her assignment be over in a snap if this dinner goes south?

Hans stands. "Alice," he mouths, his teeth white against his tanned skin, she guesses from him spending so much time outdoors during the recent skiing season.

She smiles, encouraged by his reaction, and quickens her pace toward him. Alice stops short, slowing, nerves firing on all cylinders. She takes in the details of Hans now.

There are touches of gray along his temples. Laugh lines hug his eyes. He seems taller. Perhaps because she's used to Joe's slightly shorter height.

Joe . . . the reason she's come. The Germans took him from her. And Hans may be working with them. She has to spell it out for herself. Alice wagers it won't be the last time, a thought that forces a rough swallow. Then: "Hello, Hans. You look handsome as ever."

A smile adds lines that flank his mouth. Then he bows over her hand, pressing his lips lightly to her gloved hand. "Flattery will get you everywhere."

A laugh slips free. "Using my line against me?"

"Not against you, Alice. Never against you." His words hang between them until he adds, "I never thought I'd see you again."

"Even though you hoped our paths would cross once more?"

"I said that, didn't I?"

Alice nods.

He asks, "Are you glad for my dinner invitation?"

"Are you glad I've infiltrated your country?"

He smiles again. Amusement? A defense mechanism? Simply being civil? In his business, he must interact with many types of people. Then he asks, "Shall we eat? I'd like to show you my home."

"Your home?"

"Geneva."

Alice nods. "Yes, of course. I'd like that too."

Hans holds open every door in their path—the hotel's, the car's, the restaurant's—until they're sitting at a small table in a candlelit room. Hans is so smooth and polished, and again she wonders if he's pulling out the stops for her or if this is a learned behavior he does for everyone.

"I come here often," he says.

"With someone special?" Alice asks, trying to add a teasing note to her voice.

He steeples his hand, his gaze intent on hers. There's the slightest twitch to his nose before he clears his throat, settles his napkin across his lap, then meets her eyes again. "There were times, yes. But I've always remained unattached."

Alice's lips part as past conversations surface in her head. "You never married?"

"No."

She knew this. She was given this intel. Yet she asked it to set up her next question.

"Because of your father?"

"Yes. He progressed to wife number five since I saw you last. When I wed, I want it to be just that once. The only woman I ever saw myself marrying slipped from my grasp six years ago."

The way his says this is laced with sadness, but also a flash of anger. She removes her gloves in the darkened room, one, then the other. Alice's cheeks heat as Hans's intense gaze flicks to her empty ring finger. She decides to squash the elephant in the room. "I married. Only within the past few years, actually. I'm a widow now."

Their drinks arrive. A glass of champagne for her, a snifter of brandy for him, just as they had ordered in Le Touquet.

"Still only one drink for you?"

"Still an easy drunk, yes." He raises his glass. "*Proscht.*"

Alice, hand a bit unsteady, taps her glass against his. She stares deeply into his eyes, knowing it is part of his toasting tradition. It earns her a warm smile. The first smile that feels more friendly than diplomatic. "So you remember?" he remarks.

"There's a lot I've never forgotten," she says honestly. The single rose. The drinks. The toast. The familiarity of him.

Their gazes hold, one heartbeat, two, three, until Hans sips and puts down his glass.

"I'm sorry for your loss, Alice."

"I am too."

"But I'm not sorry tennis has brought you here. After you told me you didn't want to be with me—"

"Hans . . ."

"Please, let me continue."

"Of course," she says in the tiniest of voices.

"I won't lie. I was very hurt. I was angry. But underneath it all, I still loved you. Perhaps I tortured myself because I've followed your career. The world's best." He snorts. "As if I held any doubt you'd get to the top."

"I had to get to the top, more than ever. To make saying goodbye to you worth it."

"And was it? Was it worth it?"

"Please don't ask me that."

"Would that be unfair of me?"

She shakes her head. "No."

He takes a long draw of his drink, licks his lips, twirls his glass. He sets it down, a loud clink against the wood table. Alice can see him rein in his emotions. "I saw you play a few times."

A statement that could make a woman choke on her champagne. "You did?"

He nods, laughing softly at her reaction. "Yes. In England."

"But you didn't approach me?"

He only raises a brow, as if saying, "You know why."

"Because of my coach. She was with me."

He nods again. "Please tell me she's not hiding behind a plant in the corner."

Alice laughs. "It's only the two of us."

His head cocks. "Curious, the headlines I've seen over the years never mentioned a husband."

"Government secret," she says with a wink.

He laughs softly, no doubt taking her truth as an attempt at levity. She's glad to see him softening, more of the Hans she remembers shining through. His next comment holds no animosity as he says, "I'm surprised your keeper allowed it."

"We almost came to blows."

His gaze drops from her, and her stomach pinches at how he must've taken her response. His words confirm her worry. "Well, when you truly want something, you are relentless."

"Hans . . . ," Alice says gently. "I wanted you. I was younger. I hadn't achieved my goals yet. Joe came after I did. You were before. And when I met Joe, I knew I couldn't make the same mistake twice of choosing only tennis. But please know I wanted you. I wanted you very much." She steadies herself with a breath, then reveals, "I went back to your hotel room, not even an hour later. I regretted ending things. I had a question to ask you." She bites her bottom lip. "Over the years, I wondered how you'd answer. I don't know if it'd do any good to know the answer to it now."

"There's a Swiss proverb, 'Great consolation may grow out of the smallest saying.'"

"So I should ask it?"

He bridges the distance between them, reaching across the table to take her hand. "Please."

"I wanted both tennis and you. I was going to ask you if I could have both. If you'd be wherever I was playing. If you were part of my normal, and I wasn't anticipating when I'd see you next, I could show Teach you weren't a distraction."

There would've been tennis. There would've been Hans. They would have coexisted in her life.

"You were going to ask me to give up my work and my life here to follow you from match to match?"

"It sounds foolish. And extremely selfish." She closes her eyes, opening them to find Hans with the smallest hint of a smile on his face.

"I may have said yes. It's hard for me to say with certainty now. But I know I would have tried to make it work between us at the very least."

"I would have been very grateful. I wanted it all."

"When we're forty, love, we'll look back and realize we have everything we've ever wanted."

Joe's words burst into her head. She doesn't know what to do with them.

"Past tense," Hans points out. "Everything you're saying is in past tense. *Wanted.*"

Heat overcomes her. Could she want him now? Could she . . . when she's here to aid the US government, when Joe has been a catalyst for her agreeing to this mission, when Hans may or may not be on the wrong side of history?

An expletive explodes in her head. She thinks she does still want him.

Chapter 43

Wanting Hans and needing to complete an assignment is complicated. To say the least.

At the end of the night, after both their walls slowly crumbled, he took Alice's hand and pressed his lips to the inside of her wrist. "I want to make you happy again, if you'll let me. Have dinner with me tomorrow?"

"Of course," she said, not missing a beat, her heart hammering in her chest. If he had asked to come to her hotel room, she wouldn't have been able to resist. Instead, he acted like a gentleman and they said their good nights at the entrance to her hotel, with only that kiss to her inner wrist.

After, their eyes met. "At my home."

That's when the conflicted feelings kicked in. His home is exactly where she needs to be to begin her snooping. It's exactly where she wants to be to get to know the man Hans is now, someone she hopes is not actually in association with the Nazi party. She tried to level her warring emotions with a joke. "Oh, you're going to cook for me?"

He laughed. "You wouldn't want that. Chef will prepare a meal for us."

His chateau is immediately familiar upon seeing it, a medieval-looking castle on the outskirts of the mountains, overlooking Geneva. The photographs Linden showed her must be recent, down to the budding springtime flowers and grapevines.

Hans offered to pick her up, but she insisted someone from the tennis association could give her a ride.

She uses the oversized knocker in the shape of a fox's head.

"Greetings," a man says, opening the heavy-looking door. "You must be Miss Marble."

Alice is led into the foyer.

Only moments later, Hans appears. He doesn't wear a suit, tie, or vest but a linen shirt with a camp-style collar.

He looks relaxed, comfortable. His smile is easy, welcoming.

"Alice," he says, pulling a bouquet of roses from behind his back. "For you."

She smells them momentarily before the butler offers to put them in water.

"Should we begin with a tour?" Hans asks her.

She nods eagerly. She *wants* to see where he calls home. She *needs* to determine where he could be keeping his records.

They begin by going down the wide central hall. When Hans reaches for a doorknob, she already knows it's to the drawing room. A beautiful one, at that. The room is filled with old tapestries, antiques, and works of art. Tall windows let in the day's final rays of sunlight and overlook formal gardens that Alice knows will be spectacular during the full bloom of summer.

Her mind flashes there, to the summertime, walking through the gardens, her fingertips trailing through the petals.

"Is everything all right?" Hans asks her.

She nods, plastering on a fake smile. "It's stunning. I'd stay forever if I could."

"That could be arranged."

He's joking, she concludes. An indulgent host trying to make her feel comfortable.

"Let's continue this way," Hans says, gesturing toward the door. Next is Hans's office, equally as opulent. Then the den.

"And the library," Alice says, knowing it to be the final room on the downstairs level from the blueprints she studied.

Hans pauses, hand on the doorknob. "Have you been here before?"

She panics at her slipup and playfully smacks his arm. "A lucky guess. Most libraries are on the main floor."

"In some. Many castles have the library on the same floor as the guest suites."

Alice knows this. That's how it is at Hearst Castle. Her guest suite had been next door. "Oh," she says simply. "Well, let's have a look inside. I'm a fan of books."

"So I remember," Hans says.

"This is impressive," Alice remarks, slowly rotating to take in the room and seemingly endless amount of tomes. She crosses to one of the shelves and tilts a spine toward her. "Drat, no secret passageway."

"Not on account of that book," he says coyly.

Alice raises a brow. "I bet this place has a dungeon."

She's probing, something she feels is worth trying after his playful retort.

"No, no dungeon," he says, leading them out of the library and into the central hall. "However, we have one of the finest wine cellars in the country." He motions to a doorway under the grand staircase that's all but hidden due to the paneling of the wall and door.

"Oh, I should like to see—"

"Mr. Steinmetz," the butler says, in full uniform, a black suit with a white-and-black bow tie. "Dinner is ready."

"Thank you, Brunner."

The formal dining room holds no surprises. A grand table. Tapestries. Chandeliers. The food is just as opulent. Silently servants come and go, appearing at just the right moment to serve the next course, only to vanish until needed again. Never once does Hans ask for them. But he lavishes them with gratitude and praises for a job well done.

Alice surmises they are just as loyal as Linden suggested. She could envision Hans stowing away his secrets in his massive home with Brunner and the other servants not batting an eyelash.

"Tell me," Alice says, wanting to make up for lost time, needing to ferret out other details, "what have I missed, besides the addition of a few fine lines?"

"Fine, indeed," he says with a smile, his laugh lines, now familiar, appearing. "I must say nothing overly exciting. My father passed away a few years ago, making all of this mine."

"My condolences," Alice says. "I lost my mother too."

"I'm sorry we share that similarity. After France and after his death, I threw myself into work, as I assume you've thrown yourself into tennis."

She nods. She did. She had to make giving up Hans worth it. That thought alone quickens her heartbeat. The next question she knows she needs to ask adds to it. At dinner the previous evening, she'd been so caught up in their reunion that she didn't press about his past—or any associations with the Germans he may have now. But she wades slowly into it, asking, "And the war, how have you fared?"

He dabs his napkin against his mouth before setting it again in his lap. "Better than most. You know Switzerland is neutral. As such, we have become a very stable, neutral financial center during these unique times."

Alice props her chin on her hand, slightly tilting her head. "So you work with both sides?"

"You make it sound so nefarious, darling. It's nothing like that. Ah, dessert," he says, a tray suddenly presented at his side. "Shall we?"

"I will never turn down chocolate," Alice says, part of her relieved not to poke anymore into a possible connection with the Nazis. Until she knows for certain, she can tell herself that Linden and Jones are wrong in their accusations. And what if she finds his vault and discovers there's nothing inside? That'd clear his name in full. What could that mean for her? For them?

She's won it all in tennis, a triple crown at Wimbledon, the number one female player in the world. Could she prove herself this one last time? Could she win again in love?

What an exposing, terrifying, and optimistic question to allow herself to ponder. Immediately, a hand to her chest, she shakes her head. The question surprises even her and stirs a pang of guilt; Joe's been gone only just shy of six months.

But this is Hans, she reminds herself, setting her gaze on him across the table. These aren't new feelings. They were simply dormant and now have been reawakened.

Chapter 44

To want a man who may be on the wrong side of history.

Alice is back to that complication.

She needs to locate his vault, get into it, and find nothing incriminating inside.

She licks her dessert spoon.

"Alice," Hans says, patting his napkin to his lips. "Stay the night."

She snickers. "Just as forward as ever."

"No." He shakes his head. "Forward would have been me asking to visit your room the first night. Somehow I found the fortitude to kiss only your wrist. I'm afraid all fortitude is lost, especially with what you're doing to that utensil."

Alice's cheeks heat while the spoon stills in her mouth.

"Alice . . . ," Hans says, in a tone that's almost painful-sounding. "Stay the night."

***

"Darling?" Hans asks, confusion in his voice.

Alice lay in his arms. Up until a few moments ago, she'd been quiet. Being in bed together was like muscle memory, picking up where they'd left off. Everything, all of Hans, feels like a resuming of before.

Hans strokes her hair. "Darling?" he says again.

Alice is crying. Sobbing, actually, the cadence of her cries quick and strong enough to shake her body.

Hans holds on tight, not letting go until she's more or less blubbering. She wipes a hand under her nose, then he lifts her chin, forcing their eyes to meet. "Have I hurt you?"

"Of course not."

"I noticed the bruises and wasn't sure if I was too—"

"Occupational hazard. One of your Swiss girls sure knows how to smash a ball."

"Then what is it? Did I disappoint you?" he asks, as if the weight of the world sat directly upon him. "What have I done wrong?"

"Nothing," she says. "And you should know better than to ask if you've disappointed me. You can't."

But could he, if he's helping the Nazis squirrel away wealth?

"Then why are you crying?"

She shudders a breath. "I'm happy. You said you want to make me happy, and I am. I feel alive for the first time in months. But I'm also sad."

"We'll work on the sad part," he says, kissing her softly on the top of her head. "This is a second chance."

Like another serve after a fault, it's a second chance at love, yes. But it's also Alice's second chance in this war. It's that *second* second that is sobering. How easily she forgets why she's here.

The soft kiss on the top of her head comes again. "I've an idea. I'll warn you it's another forward one."

"I'd expect nothing less."

"Let's move you out of your hotel and into my house."

Alice's eyes widen, but she tries to cover it with a joke. "Your house? You say that so casually, as if this isn't a castle."

"Fine, my castle. Move into my castle. Your matches will last for—what—four weeks in total? Stay in comfort. Better yet, stay longer than a month. Stay as long as you want."

***

It's too much. Too much guilt. Too much confliction. Too much hope. Too much regret. Too much sadness.

So Alice tells Hans she needs time to think about it and avoids it all.

She's on the third day of ignoring the messages the bellhop delivers to her from Hans on her way into the hotel after her tennis matches.

Those three days, tennis has been her only focus. It's nothing new. She's good at it. Focusing on tennis is a hell of a lot less confusing. In fact, it's straightforward. She has a job to do playing against the young Swiss athletes at the Parc des Eaux-Vives.

In her hotel room, Alice drops her head into her hands. She also has a job to do for the intelligence office; her actual reason for being in Geneva. And, as if taunting her, Linden's words hammer inside her head.

"We believe that you, and you alone, Miss Marble, are the only person who can make contact with him and complete this assignment for us."

It's times like this she wishes she didn't have such a good memory. But she does.

So Alice reads the latest message from Hans instead of slipping it into the desk drawer like the others.

I can't do this again.

***

Alice picks up the phone, her grip tight, rattled at the thought of losing Hans a second time. But maybe him dejecting her and Alice going back to the States is the best outcome—for them both.

"I'm sorry," she says instinctively upon hearing his voice.

"I need more from you than that, Alice."

Not darling, but her name.

She swallows roughly.

"I needed time to think and to get my head on straight. It's all happening so fast—"

"The last few days of silence haven't felt fast."

"I know, I'm sorry. Ignoring someone you love isn't fair. It's not a solution."

"That you love?"

"Yes. I loved Joe, but that doesn't mean I ever stopped loving you, Hans."

"I must say I am relieved to hear it. That head of yours, were you able to get it on straight after all?"

"Yes," she says, instilling confidence into that single word that she doesn't feel. In fact, it's complete fiction.

By not saying yes to Hans and accepting his invitation to his home, she feels like a traitor to her country.

By saying yes to Hans and sharing his bed, she feels like a traitor to her late husband.

By saying yes to Hans and using it as an opportunity to scour his home, she feels like a traitor to Hans.

Her head is anything but on straight.

Alice sighs, her gaze flicking to the makeup bag that holds her gun, camera, and tools and says, "Ask me again."

"Alice, will you move from the hotel and into my oversized home?"

"Yes, I'll pack my bags and be ready within the hour."

Chapter 45

Alice clips on an earring, catching a glimpse of Hans in the dressing table mirror.

Their rooms are adjoined, the door separating them open.

A servant knots Hans's bow tie. His regard meets hers in the mirror, and he winks.

That wink. Her knees would melt and give out if she wasn't sitting.

After moving into his home, the days have stretched into a week, then three. Suddenly Alice has only a final week of her cover story.

"Almost ready," she calls out, loud enough for him to hear.

"I'd never rush perfection."

She snorts, shaking her head. Tonight, getting ready for a party Hans is obligated to attend, is the longest she's actually spent in her bedroom.

"It's yours, darling," Hans said the day she moved in her things, "but I hope you'll decide to spend the majority of your time in . . . there." He held her in his arms and flicked his foot backward to push open the door to his room.

"Decision made," Alice had said, a silkiness to her voice.

Now she clips on her final earring, straightens her necklace, smiles at her reflection, then stands to join Hans.

The soirée is at the Argentine Embassy. Before entering the ballroom, she smooths a hand down her pale-blue gown. It's a gift from Hans, a terribly expensive one. He wants her to look her best. Likewise, she wants to look her best for him. Still, upon receiving the dress, she had to ask, "How much did this cost? It's too much."

"I'm a very wealthy man, darling, and getting wealthier all the time. Nothing is too much."

"And all of this? The dress, the necklace, the earrings, the house . . . it's all from owning a bank?"

"My bank holds many valuables that people pay me a great amount of money to safeguard."

The answer got under her skin.

It's still under her skin now as she enters the ballroom ripe with dowagers and debutantes. The amount of sparkling jewelry is blinding, dulled only by the many penguin suits in the room. Nearly every tuxedo is identical, yet Hans still stands apart. He offers Alice his arm, and she clings to him as the receiving line inches closer to the Argentine ambassador and his wife. Alice's head jerks toward an accent she places as German. And now that she knows there are Germans here, it's all Alice can see . . . there, and there, and there.

"It's okay, darling." Hans gently presses a finger to her forehead. "Slow down whatever is happening in here. You think so much, two plays ahead. Let's just enjoy the here and now, where this is no war. Only friends."

"Friends?"

"The Swiss do not get involved in these periodic European purges."

His words settle on her like an ill-fitting tennis shoe. But it's not the Swiss who've risen her blood pressure. "No." She nods toward a German. "That is not a Swiss man."

He waves his hand, thinking of a new word. "Neighbors, then."

"Neighbors who kill people," Alice says between clenched teeth.

"The Americans have killed people too."

Alice stops walking, so abruptly the woman behind her catches Alice's heel. They both mumble an apology, but Alice is quick to return her attention to Hans. "The Americans did *not* kill my husband. *They* did."

Hans's eyes track again to where Alice is looking with a fury. He blinks, long and hard, then says in a voice only for them, "I'm sorry, I'm being insensitive. But please understand that the people in this room mean you no harm. They meant your husband himself no harm. We are businessmen, not politicians. Not soldiers. It's very important to me that you do not upset them. You'd do me a great favor to remove the hostility from your expression."

She rescinds her hand from his arm. "Of course."

"Ah, Mr. Steinmetz," the ambassador says.

It's their turn to shake his hand. The ambassador kisses Alice's. "Miss Marble," he says, "I'd heard you were in Geneva. It's lovely to meet you. It'd be even lovelier if you'll come to play in Buenos Aires one day soon."

"Thank you," she says politely. "Perhaps after this war concludes."

"Then we shall wish for a speedy resolution."

At that, the ambassador turns his attention to Hans and Alice turns her attention to the ambassador's wife. Pleasantries are exchanged between the women. Alice catches something about three hundred million German marks being softly spoken between the men.

As they step away from the ambassador, a server presents a tray of champagne. Alice snatches a flute and takes a large sip. Hans rises an eyebrow.

"Let's dance," he says, taking the glass, having a sip of his own, then placing it on a passing tray. "A better way to lift your spirits."

On the dance floor, Alice does immediately feel lighter. Only, not enough for her not to question Hans on what he was talking about with the ambassador.

"Just business," he says, spinning her.

She twirls back. "Of what kind?"

He sighs. "You are relentless on and off the court. It's part of your intrigue. The rumor—an exaggeration, I'm certain—is that we Swiss hold more than three hundred million German marks in our banks. The ambassador has a strong interest in that wealth being invested in his country after the Germans lose."

"In South America?" Alice questions, goose bumps erupting on her bare arms.

"Buenos Aires, yes."

This isn't proof of what Linden has said, Alice tells herself. Circumstantial, at best, considering Hans didn't point a finger at himself. Instead, he'd spoken of Swiss men, as a whole, engaging with the Germans.

"Hans," she says, "I have to ask."

"If I have German money in my bank?"

She nods, no longer dancing, but still clutching his hands.

"I also have money from men fleeing the French Revolution nearly two hundred years ago. Everyone wants a nest egg. I've never hidden from you that I'm a banker."

"*Also* . . . so you do have German money in your bank."

"Darling, like I said, I'm a banker. I do not worry about where the money comes from."

Alice's heart is breaking; she now knows she cannot put off her assignment any longer. Hans is working with the Nazis. He's on the wrong side of history. It's now up to her to gather the proof to condemn the man she loves.

But can she do that?

Chapter 46

Years of losing matches and wanting to throw her racquet at her opponents' heads have taught Alice control.

So throughout the rest of the party, she smiles.

While Hans drives them home, she doesn't act like anything is amiss.

When she hands off her jacket to Brunner, apologizing for keeping him up, her voice doesn't reveal any unease.

As she follows Hans up the grand staircase to his bedroom, immediately above where she knows the cellar staircase is located, she doesn't let on that her mind is buzzing about how to get down there.

Maybe she's a better spy than she's given herself credit for.

She cuts through Hans's bedroom to get to her own, where she removes her layers of jewelry, makeup, and clothing.

In her slip, she sashays back into Hans's room, cursing herself because—yes—she knows what she needs to do tonight, but also—damn—she can't help loving this man.

He's sitting in a wingback chair idly reading a newspaper in nothing but his trousers, one leg crossed over another. It's not the first time she's seen him barefoot in the three weeks they've played house together. But there's still something so intimate about seeing him without his dress shoes and fancy socks. They lay discarded on the floor, next to that evening's jacket, white ruffled shirt, and black cummerbund. There's also something about his bare chest, a man who clearly takes care of himself, that is remarkably sexy.

Alice refocuses, like she's done so many times during a match.

She crosses the room to him, laying a hand on his shoulder before wrapping one of the curls that tease the nape of his neck around her finger. "How about a nightcap?"

"I've already had a drink at the party."

"No, you've had a few sips. And that was hours ago. Have a nightcap with me? Tonight was a lot."

He palms her cheek. "We do have the best wine cellar in the country."

"Shall I fetch us a bottle?" she's quick to offer.

"The staff can do it. Don't you lift a finger."

"It's late. I feel bad."

"There are at least two staff members on call every evening for our needs. Tonight that includes Brunner. He's yet to garage the car and has other odds and ends he's likely doing. Besides, he's more than capable of selecting for us."

Brunner is indeed very apt at it. The wine is delicious. Obvious notes of red currant and raspberry, with a hint of strawberry.

A fire crackles in the fireplace. In her own chair, Alice has her feet, crossed at the ankles, propped on the arm of Hans's wingback. She sips slowly, barely letting any wine pass her lips.

They don't talk. Not at first.

Hans lets his head fall back, his eyes closed, only opening them to sip his Pinot Noir.

"This is good," he remarks.

"From your grapes?"

He smells it. Takes a sip. Rolls it around his mouth. Concludes,

"I have no idea."

A laugh slips free of Alice.

"There, finally," Hans says, "a genuine response out of you."

"What do you mean?"

"I know you, darling. You've been putting on a show all night. I'm sorry this evening was a lot for you."

She repositions so her legs are beneath her, both hands clasping her wine glass. "It was. More than I wanted to hear, I guess."

"You're referring to the German marks here in Switzerland?"

She takes another small sip. "Yup." And stands to retrieve the bottle from a side table. Hers is only half empty, but she tops it off, hoping Hans doesn't notice the small amount she's imbibed. She moves to Hans's empty glass. He tries to put a hand over it, but she gives him a pointed look, and he allows the pour.

She's returning the bottle to the table when he says to her back, "I didn't answer directly when you asked me if I had Germany money in my bank."

She faces him. "I could do the math."

"Yes, well, I wanted to explain further. With everything that happened to Joe"—hearing his name come from Hans's mouth nearly has Alice spilling her drink—"I can understand your vitriol toward the Nazis. If it makes you feel any better, I have them by the balls."

Alice finds comfort in curling up in her chair again. "What do you mean?"

"Those miscreants are stockpiling their fortunes with me." He smiles wolfishly, then bookends his remark with a large sip. "All along I've been charging them insane amounts of interest to protect their money. Most of them will never get out of Germany when the war ends. If I were to guess, most will be arrested and never see their investment. It'll remain mine."

There's that wolfish grin again.

"So all along you've been playing a game with them? You don't like them either?"

"What's to like? In fact, I loathe them for the pain they've put you through."

"Thank you," Alice says, then a thought slices through her. If not for Joe being killed by the Nazis, she never would have rekindled things with Hans. She never would have given up Joe willingly. Never. But now that she has Hans, she's happy. It makes her even happier to know he never had plans to give the Nazis their money.

Their stolen money . . .

Alice screams internally. How had she lost focus on that salient detail? All along she's known where the Nazis acquired their wealth, but she'd only been focused on Hans and the Germans.

Hans asks her, "What is it you're thinking?"

"I'm relieved you've . . . how did you put it? . . . got them by the balls."

But is she really? This assignment has grown larger than avenging her husband. It's about an entire group of people. Hans may be able to overlook the origin of the money in his bank, but she cannot. During this war, so many Jews had their wealth, their jobs, their homes, their *lives*—if the rumors are true—stolen from them. It makes her sick to think that Hans is a part of that. Earlier, he boasted about the money his family accumulated while people fled during the French Revolution. For years, Hans and his family have benefitted from the loss of others. And he has no intention of changing his ways.

The dress she wore tonight, the jewelry, this wine she's drinking is at the expense of others.

Hans tilts his glass, watching the deep red liquid slide back and forth. His words are slightly slurred as he says, "I don't like being in cahoots with anyone, if I'm being honest. Governments can be unreliable. You don't always know who you can trust." He pauses, his eyes trailing over Alice. Then he adds, "It's why I've put none of their fortunes in my bank."

Alice cocks her head. "Then where is it?"

"Here, darling. Right beneath you."

Her mouth falls open.

She's about to try to cover for her reaction, then realizes it's a normal response, spy or otherwise.

Hans laughs. "I know," he says. "To think I'll get the better of them—in an extravagant way."

She forces a smile, what Hans wants and needs to see. But all Alice can see is the Jewish families who've been plundered. Hans said it himself earlier: he doesn't worry about where the money comes from. She shakes her head, acting as if astonished with his scheme. "But is it safe in your private vault? I mean, I assume it's in a vault and not just lying about in the cellar."

"Of course I have a vault. And yes, my dear, it's very safe. I've a key to get in, but otherwise the vault is protected by explosives." Hans makes a demonstrative gesture with his hand and an exploding noise.

Alice smiles. "You're drunk."

"I've told you I'm an easy drunk."

Yes, he had, and it's the very reason Alice suggested the nightcap, why she refilled his glass. Why she'll do it again once his current glass goes empty.

It doesn't take long.

Nor does it take long for him to fall asleep, giving Alice time to think.

And think.

And think.

A tear rolls down her cheek.

The idea of deceiving him makes her physically recoil. But now that she knows for certain about his vault, she has to go through with her mission. It's not Hans's money. Nor can it ever be hers.

Chapter 47

Hans snores lightly, his chest rising and falling.

How innocent and peaceful he looks.

How happy they could've been together.

But it's the fact he's sleeping without a care in the world, with God knows how many German marks in his vault, stolen from others, that makes her choose the alternative to being with Hans—a second time.

Alice wipes away the wetness on her cheeks and turns toward her room. There, she shrugs into a robe and then palms deep into an upper shelf in the armoire until her hand blindly hits the makeup bag she's hidden there.

Her camera, gun, and tools.

In her bureau, buried within her unmentionables, is her holster.

She straps on the shoulder holster, then slips in the small automatic gun. The camera and tools go into the pockets of her robe.

The plan is simple. Get into the safe without getting blown up, take photos of his transaction book, and be back in Hans's room before he stirs. In the morning, she'll act as if she's going to tennis, but she'll go to Franz Regenbogen at his goldsmith shop on La Grande Rue instead. Once her contact has the film, she'll get to the airport.

Again, simple. Yet her throat is thick with nerves. And sadness. She can know Hans is wrong. She can know she can't choose him. But she can also know her heart aches at the thought of losing him. Hurting him. Betraying him.

But doing the right thing is important. She is the only one who can do it.

Alice reminds herself of both sentiments, the ticking of the clock feeling as if it echoes in her silent room.

She needs to act—now.

Hans is still asleep. She can see him through the open door.

Alice pokes her head into the hallway. Brunner has likely retired to his room. She pictures him reading by the fire, at the ready in case he's called upon. She wishes she knew who else was on call this evening. The maid, cook, deputy butler, valet, footman, groom? The second on-call house staff could be anyone—and anywhere. Though Alice is fairly certain the cook lives with her husband in a cottage off the estate.

So what to do if she runs into Brunner or any of the staff? The answer fits smoothly into her simplistic plan: she's visiting the cellar for another bottle of wine.

"Don't be silly," she'll say. "It's so late. I wouldn't think of asking you, Brunner."

Alice nods and takes a step into the hallway. The runner is blessedly thick, and soundless.

She begins creeping down the wide staircase, sliding her hand down the polished wood banister. But her hand catches, on account of her sweaty palms, and a squeaking sound fills the night.

It feels loud enough to wake the cook all the way in her cottage.

Alice holds her breath, listening intently for any other noises. She waits an entire minute. Two minutes, even, before she takes another step.

The staircase betrays her with a creak. She pauses again. Resumes. Pauses. Her heart is beating so rapidly her head gets dizzy. She grips the rail tighter, fully lifting her hand before gripping again. Her movements are laughably demonstrative. Though nothing about the moment is funny. All fantasies of being spy-like have vanished.

Still, she makes it to the bottom and quickly turns, padding barefoot toward the hidden door beneath the stairwell.

Alice tilts her head back and thanks the Lord when it opens soundlessly. She closes the door, putting herself in darkness.

Alice once read that eleven percent of adult Americans are scared of the dark. She now knows she's included in the statistic. Her breath comes quicker, and she releases an expletive for not thinking to bring a flashlight.

How is she going to defuse an explosive blind?

Alice also once read that a heart rate of 120 to 140 beats per minute is considered dangerous. She worries hers is getting close.

She could go back upstairs, slip into bed, pretend this never happened. But as soon as she thinks it, she knows it's not an option when there are thousands, maybe hundreds of thousands, maybe millions of Jews and others who've been targeted by the Nazis and who can't pretend it never happened.

Alice takes a step. The steps are cold and stone beneath her bare feet. She runs a hand along the wall, also stone, until she reaches the bottom. There's a sharp bend in the hallway and, to her utter relief, a light has been left on. Like a moth, she follows it toward its source. The damp air puts goose bumps on her arms and she pulls her robe tighter, feeling her gun press into her chest.

The light leads straight to the wine cellar, the amount of wine inside mind-boggling. She's about to step away, to look for a door she must've missed, when she freezes. Voices.

Alice presses herself against the wall and into a shadow, knowing full well she can still be seen. This isn't a childhood game of hide-and-seek where she closes her eyes and believes herself to disappear.

The voices come again—above her.

From a vent.

She listens, recognizing Brunner's low voice. And a second softer, more feminine one. It doesn't matter who. What matters is that if she can hear them, they'll be able to hear her. From the sounds of their movements—the scrape of a chair and the clang of dishes—she assumes they're in the kitchen.

At any moment, Brunner or Mystery Woman could decide to check on Hans to see if he needs anything.

At any moment Hans could wake. He'll notice her missing. He'll go in search of her.

There isn't any time to waste.

She pads back the way she came, her head on a swivel looking for an entry to the vault. One would think it'd be big, metal, and obvious. What Alice hadn't expected was an oak door, recessed into the stone wall. She'd gone right by it before as she followed the light.

She runs a hand over the ancient wood, stopping when her hand hits the knob. It's locked.

Protected by explosives.

Hans had told her that much.

He'd also mentioned a key, one she wishes she had. She curses herself for not taking the time to search his belongings. It's too late now.

With a deep breath, Alice bends closer, examining the keyhole. Her brain is slightly fuzzy from the wine. She physically shakes herself, a scientifically proven way to clear her head. She's being silly. Why does she do that when she's nervous? She needs to focus. It always comes back to focus in tennis, in life, when trying not to get yourself killed.

The greatest risk, she remembers Dave telling her, is compromising the lock or subjecting the door to a sudden shock, like trying to ram it open. It'll blow this door, but there'll be a second protecting the vault. The intruder would be killed without disturbing the safe's contents.

But if she can successfully pick the lock . . .

A hammer mechanism won't release within the lock and set off the booby trap.

And kill her.

She questions one last time whether she should go back upstairs and search for the key, perfectly made to raise the pins inside the lock and align them exactly at the shear line, allowing the plug to rotate—and open the lock.

She runs a hand through her hair.

No, no time.

"God bless, angels keep," Alice whispers to herself.

Then she targets the keyhole.

"*Most locks use between six and eight pins, although some have as few as four or as many as ten*," Dave told her back in the warehouse.

Here's hoping this one has as few as four, hence easier to pick and less likely to blow off her head.

She removes her tools from her robe pocket and lays out the various sizes of picks in front of her. In her left hand she takes the tension wrench. In her right, a twelve-thousandth size pick.

Alice blows out a breath and brings up a mental picture of the lock in her mind. There's the keyway, where the key goes into the plug—the turning portion of the lock. The key's wards—or teeth—push against the spring-loaded pins when inserted. While applying pressure with her tension wrench to the keyway, she'll push up pins one by one with her pick, the tension wrench keeping them from falling down again. When all pins are set and align with the shear line—the lock-turning mechanism—the lock will open.

She reviews the steps again, practicing with her hands in the air. Even now she thinks of tennis, the mental practice something she does with her opponents.

"Okay, Alice," she mouths and uses the sleeve of her robe to wipe the perspiration from her forehead. "Let's play."

She pauses one last time, listening for any sounds, then gets to work.

"First things first," Dave instructed, *"figure out which way the lock turns."*

Alice inserts her tension wrench into the keyway and gently turns to the right. Then applies torque to the left. It's easier to go right, which means the lock will open in that direction.

"Okay," she repeats again to herself. "Easy does it. Just the right amount of pressure with the wrench." Alice's tongue slips out while she works. Once the tensioner is in place at the bottom of the keyway in her left hand, she tries to slide the twelve-thousandth pick inside with her right. It gets caught. Too big. Keeping the tensioner in place, Alice swaps out for a thinner pick, a ten-thousandth.

It drags but goes all the way into the keyway where she touches each pin, testing the resistance of their springs.

"Got you, pin three," she says, identifying the pin that resists more than the others. It's her first binding pin.

"The inner workings of a lock are delicate, Miss Marble," Dave had warned.

"I know, Dave. I know," she murmurs under her breath, barely audible.

She works pin three little by little to lift it, until the tension wrench turns the plug very slightly. She blows out a breath. Pin three is in place.

Now to find and solve the next pin while keeping the tension wrench in place. If it moves, she'll have to start over from the beginning.

She bobs her head. Inserts her pick and feels a binder on two. Her next target. Only, her fingers are damp with sweat. She removes the pick, wipes her right palm down her robe, then goes to insert it again, the pick bending.

"Oh, no you don't," she whispers through gritted teeth. "Get in there."

The ten-thousandth snags but goes back in.

She lifts pin two into place. Alice has solved pins three and two, committing the image of them to memory.

"Keep track of your solved pins, Miss Marble. It'll save you time if you need to start over. Sometimes time is of the essence."

She glances toward the stairway. She listens for voices. Brunner and the woman servant aren't in the kitchen anymore. Or at least she can't hear them. Does that mean they've gone to bed? Gone to check to see if Hans needs anything?

Alice puffs out her cheeks, then focuses again on the lock.

It feels like it takes an eternity, but she finds two additional binding pins, sets them in place, then—hallelujah—the lock opens.

Alice twists the knob to the door and braces herself.

"Don't count your chickens before they hatch."

Dave's final advice.

But nothing explodes. The door swings open, revealing another door. A very vault-looking door. This one with no lock, just a large circular knob.

She's in.

She's done it.

Thank you, Dave.

But then Alice's head whips behind her. She hears voices. Footsteps too. Neither are coming from the kitchen. They've got to be in the central hallway. Right above her.

Chapter 48

The household knows Alice is not where she is supposed to be. Of course she has no way of actually knowing that. But it's what her gut is screaming at her.

She could stop here. She could come back later, pick the whole ridiculous lock again. Or she can take her chances. Continue. Maybe get caught. Hopefully succeed.

Succeed, she decides.

Alice heaves the vault's knob to the right and yanks open the heavy door, cursing the groaning noise the movement makes. She steps into the dark vault.

The camera won't work without light. She pats the wall until she finds a switch. The sudden brightness of the room is blinding. The vault's contents are even more so.

An entire wall is lined with stacks upon stacks of gold bars. Head shaking in disbelief, she walks toward them, unable to stop herself from reaching out. As if burned, she yanks back her hand. Each bar is imprinted with the unmistakable swastika of the Third Reich. Seeing the disgusting emblem fortifies her resolve to do what needs to be done.

She scans the rest of the room. Paintings. Large packages

wrapped in heavy brown paper. Another wall of neatly stacked and neatly numbered boxes. The vault has little room to move around, but she maneuvers to one of the numbered boxes.

It could be booby-trapped. But she risks slowly lifting the lid.

"Oh, Hans," she murmurs, her heart dropping. Inside is a mess of jewelry—rings, bracelets, necklaces, tie tacks, buttons, studs. At the end of a heavy gold chain is the—also unmistakable—Star of David.

"Why?" she whispers.

Why can't Hans understand that possessing these is wrong?

Until this moment, she still had a sliver of hope that she'd find nothing incriminating in his vault. That hope is gone.

She fishes in her robe pocket for her camera, snapping a shot of the boxes' contents. But it's Hans's ledger, ripe with every one of his transactions, that Linden wants from her.

The ledger is in plain sight on one of the shelves.

Inside, German names and columns of figures paint an undeniable story of Hans's enterprise.

She flips the pages to find only deposits, no withdrawals. Just line after line, in Hans's precise handwriting, of detailed lists of valuables and the numbered box in which it could be located.

The amount of stolen family heirlooms in this very room is sickening. And what of those families? Where are they now? What happened to them after the Nazis ransacked their homes?

"I'm sorry, Hans, but you are guilty by association."

Alice photographs the first page. Then the second. Third. Fourth. Her heart races with each click, imagining the sound vibrating through the house. If Hans wasn't already awake, he is now. If Brunner wasn't already onto her, he is now . . .

There's no talking her way out of this if she's caught in Hans's vault.

She flips a page. *Click.* Footsteps above her. She fumbles the camera, her hands trembling. Flip. *Click.* Flip. Footsteps. She pauses. *Click.* Flip. *Click.* Alice can't remember the last time she breathed. In total, she captures twenty pages.

How is it there are still so, so many more?

"I'm a very wealthy man, darling, and getting wealthier all the time."

That's why.

What she has should be enough to nail the Nazis—and Hans. She wishes this moment didn't feel so bittersweet. She just found the evidence to incriminate the Nazis who took her husband and her future from her, after all. But she can't help mourning another future she's only just begun to experience, one that has made her genuinely hopeful again.

Alice's throat is thick as she eases out the vault's opening, closes the door as quietly as she can, and slips through the wood door she picked open, scooping up her tools along the way. As if she'd never been there. Slowly, she climbs the stairs, pausing every few steps to listen.

"Miss Marble," she hears in the Swiss accent of the staff.

Alice curses, but then retreats down the steps, racing to the wine cellar to grab whatever bottle is closest. She runs now, not bothering to be quiet. She can still get upstairs. She can still pretend she only came for wine. She can still wake up beside Hans one last time. She can still give Franz Regenbogen the film. Then get the hell out of dodge.

"Miss Marble!"

Alice takes the stairs two at a time, barreling through the door. "Yes? I'm here. Hello?"

The maid is in the hallway, a hand flying to her chest. "Miss Marble, there you are."

"Alice!" Hans calls from somewhere upstairs.

Brunner appears. "Where have you been? Mr. Steinmetz—"

Alice holds up the wine.

But Brunner's not looking at the bottle. His eyes are wide, shocked, confused. When she raised her arm, her robe shifted. When her robe shifted, her shoulder holster—her gun plainly in sight—may as well have flashing lights on it.

"I can explain—"

"Sir, come quickly!" Brunner yells.

Muted footsteps sound upstairs on the carpet runner.

This isn't how it's supposed to go. Not at all. Alice was going to leave a note. She'd lie through her teeth in it, but at least she'd try to soften the blow of leaving Hans a second time.

Now, what choice does she have . . . than to flee?

Alice throws down the wine, red liquid and glass flying everywhere.

And she runs.

She runs for the door, her robe behind her like a cape. Alice heaves open the heavy door and stumbles outside. Thank the Lord, Hans's Mercedes still sits under the portico in the glow of the lamps. The keys would be in it; they always are until one of the servants moves it to the garage.

"Alice!" she hears at her back. "Wait!"

The confusion and hurt in Hans's voice turns her stomach. The confusion and hurt on Hans's face is even worse, when she spares a final look back.

"I'm sorry," she tries to say, but her words only come out strangled. She's sobbing by the time she yanks open the car door, slips inside, finds the keys in the ignition.

Alice hates cars. She has ever since her dad's accident. Even more after the army kid drove her off the road. Hated cars with a passion when that drunk driver ran into her, causing her miscarriage.

She hates that, soon, she's going faster than she's ever gone before. Down the winding drive. Through the open gate at the bottom. Along the highway that'll lead to Geneva—and Franz Regenbogen.

A few sips of wine be damned, Alice's body feels completely sober, on high alert, both hands firmly gripping the wheel. She blinks away her tears. On her right, the mountain is an impenetrable wall. On her left, the roadside falls off into nothing but darkness. It's too much like Panama.

Alice slows, knowing there's very little margin for error on these narrow, winding roads. Only the sport car's two pinpricks of light guide her way. She slams her palm against the wheel, furious that everything has gone so wrong.

Maybe it's cowardly of her, but she'd been hoping to slip away without seeing the pain on his face. But either way—if she'd had the opportunity to write the false letter or not—she'd have broken his heart.

Alice is over being a spy. She tugs the gun free from the holster and throws it on the passenger seat. A flash of light catches her eyes. There, in the rearview, she sees it. There's a car coming up behind her.

She wants to believe it's a coincidence, but it's too late and the car is gaining on her too quickly for that.

It has to be Hans.

She pushes harder on the accelerator, fully accepting the fact she's a coward. Alice's head whips to the side as she reads a street sign her headlights caught.

GENEVA 10K

Six miles.

It'll be a miracle if she doesn't drive herself off the road. She throws the wheel left and right, turn after turn. Whenever the road straightens, she floors the gas.

Hans doesn't seem to take his foot off the accelerator at all.

His headlights are so close now they are blinding whenever she looks in the rearview mirror.

Alice curses, evaluates. Maybe she should stop. There's no way she'll be able to outrun him. And what is she going to do, bring him straight to Franz's door? Confess that she took photographs that'll incriminate him?

Hans pulls up beside her.

"Hans!" she yells as they go around a dangerous turn side by side. "You're going to kill us!"

Not that he can hear her.

Alice risks a glance at him, her brow immediately furrowing. It's not Hans. It can't be him. She knows every angle of his face. The man is motioning for her to pull over. Alice glances whenever she can, searching for any recognition through the darkness.

"Jones?" she questions to herself. Colonel Linden didn't mention Captain Jones coming to Switzerland. In fact, he said the opposite. But once her mind accepts it's him, here, in Geneva, she's certain of it.

He's still motioning for her to pull over.

"Okay, okay," she says, taking her foot off the gas. Jones wouldn't be her first pick to come to her rescue. She'd take just about anyone over him, in fact. But she's more than happy to unload the film on him. She's mostly relieved it's not Hans.

Not yet, at least.

Another pinprick of light appears in her rearview mirror.

She slams on her breaks, her tires spinning out, the car nearly going over the edge. Her knees are wobbling as she falls from the Mercedes, already calling to Jones, "I have the film!"

"That's a good girl," Jones call back.

Alice fights the urge to get back in the car and try her luck without Jones. She's never liked him. But he'll have to do. "Take me to the airport!" she yells, starting toward him.

"There's been a change of plans."

"What do you mean?" Frantic, she points toward the approaching car. "Hans is almost here."

"That's not Hans."

"What?"

"Give me the film."

Jones's delivery has never been the best. Pompous-sounding. Thick with innuendos. But this time it's a demand. It's cold. It doesn't sound like they're on the same team.

"No," she says instinctively, taking a step backward, laying a hand over the pocket of her robe. An expletive slips free when she realizes she's all but draws Jones a map about where the camera is.

"Stop wasting time on that bitch," someone shouts.

Alice startles.

She hadn't realized anyone else had been in Jones's car. But now that her eyes have fully adjusted to the darkness, she sees the shadow of another man.

"Who's that?" she shouts at Jones. Better yet. "Who are you?"

The slimiest of smiles appears on his face.

A double agent, that's who he is. Not working with her and Colonel Linden, but against them.

And he's charging at her.

Alice turns to run but trips. She lands hard on the ground. In a heartbeat, Jones is on top of her, trying to flip her, trying to get the film. She slams back her elbow, exactly like she's been taught, connecting with Jones's face, and she scrambles to her feet when his weight rolls off her.

Alice makes it two steps before she's whipped backward, Jones catching the tie of her robe. One shoulder, then the other slips out of the thick cotton as she struggles to free herself. She realizes too late the camera goes with the robe. She makes a play for grabbing it, but Jones is faster, yanking the robe fully under an arm while pulling his gun with his other hand.

Alice goes to do the same, but her holster is empty, illuminated by the second car that's quickly approaching.

"Just shoot her," Jones's partner yells.

She stares at the weapon. The hairs on her neck rise.

He'll do it. He'll pull the trigger. She can see it in his eyes.

Tires screech. A shot rings out from the new car.

Alice is still standing, the bullet not meant for her; Jones is ducking for cover.

Adrenaline kicking in, Alice turns. She runs.

Another shot is fired.

Alice is still running.

Another shot.

Still running.

A third shot.

Searing pain shoots through her body, and the ground rises up to meet her.

Chapter 49

Alice knows exactly where she is. The white walls, the white sheets, the white metal bed frame. She's been here before, more times than any human should have to endure. A hospital.

"Welcome back," a voice says.

Alice startles, wincing in pain. She should've expected someone would be waiting for her to wake. She never would have guessed who, though: Colonel Linden. She croaks out his name, clears her throat, then adds, "What are you doing here?"

Alice follows the question with a surveillance of herself. An IV is secured in her lower arm. The rest of her arm, her torso, and her second arm are in a hard bandage. She couldn't move if she wanted to. But should she be worried about him? Could she trust Linden?

"I'm here to check up on you," he says. "I came to your rescue, but was too late."

She tries to sit up. A poor decision. She can't, and it only causes a surge of electric pain throughout her body.

"Easy now," Linden says, inching closer, then settling into a bedside chair.

She eyes him warily, then decides to just come out and say it. "Jones was a double agent. Are you?"

"I am not." He shakes his head solemnly. "But you are right about Jones. I've gone through it a million times in my head. I worked with the man for more than two years and never suspected him of working with the Russians."

"The Russians," she parrots.

He sighs. "Everything changed last week. Jones insisted you were taking too long and demanded a transport to Geneva to move things along. After he left, I worried he'd push you into something you weren't ready for, so I got on the next plane. I was going to scrap the mission and pull you out if I had to. But I was too late. I had men watching the roads from the chateau. They saw you leave, Jones go after you, then the standoff between you two. We believe he was trying to intercept the film to give it to the Russians. My men killed him and his partner, but not before Jones took a shot at you."

"Where?" Alice asks, looking down at her bandaged body. It had all happened so fast and the searing pain had felt like it engulfed the entirety of her.

"In your back."

Alice took a quick, excruciating intake of breath. "My back? Am I going to—"

"Your shoulder, more specifically. I don't know all the details, only that the bullet didn't hit your spine or any organs. It all makes me very squeamish, in fact."

"You, Colonel Linden?"

"We all have our weaknesses. What matters is the doctor worked his magic and says you'll heal completely. He has you fully outfitted in a cast. But you'll be feeling like yourself in no time."

Unbelievable.

"I'm sorry, Alice," Linden goes on, using her name for the first time ever. "I knew this assignment could be dangerous, but I never imagined you'd end up here, Jones would be dead, and we'd have nothing to show for it."

"You didn't recover the camera? I had it in my robe. Jones took it."

Linden's jaw tightens. "Last thing he did before he was shot was open the camera to expose the film. If they couldn't have it, neither could we, I suppose. Jones always was an aggressive man. We were hoping the film would be salvageable, but the headlights were enough to destroy the negatives."

Alice closes her eyes, exhausted, disappointed, remorseful. She had failed. She did not meet expectations. She did not prove herself capable of completing her mission. She struck out, three for three. And for what? She poses the question aloud, "So it was all for nothing?"

She sees Hans's face as she ran from him. She recalls the pages of names of the Nazis who'll get away with their loot. She can vividly see the numbered box and the Star of David emblem.

Her eyes shoot open. "I can still help you."

"Miss Marble, you've done enough. Now you need to rest—"

"No," she says. "Get me a pen and paper."

Linden's face tells her he clearly needs more of an explanation.

"I can see every page I photographed. Remember my eidetic memory?"

He stands. "I'll get a stenographer in here right away."

When he arrives, Alice provides page after page of Nazi names that were listed in Hans's ledger.

Hans.

"What will happen to him?" she asks Linden after her work is done and her hospital room on the US Army base is once more calm.

"Honestly? Probably nothing. But we expected that. Best-case scenario for us is that he'll cooperate and hand over the holdings of his vault. Best case for him, and I imagine he's a clever man, is that he'll find a way to protect himself. The list of Nazi names you provided is only a starting place. Mr. Steinmetz will likely deny doing any business with them without any hard proof."

"Do you think he'll assume it's me who gave you the names?"

Linden pats her hand. "Like I said, he's a clever man. And unless another ex-lover fled his house last night . . ."

"Was that a joke, Colonel Linden?"

"My very best. Now, rest up. As soon as we can get you out of here, we'll get you back to the States. We'll have someone keep an eye on you for a bit, but I believe you'll be safe on our home turf." Colonel Linden smiles. "You and I, our paths won't cross again, but I'm grateful—and I know our country is grateful—for your service."

Alice's brow creases. "That's it, then?"

"That's it. In fact, none of this ever happened. You came to Geneva for the exhibition, which the Swiss believe ended early because of an emergency back home. The journalist will print nothing. Miss Tennant has been informed you'll be extending your visit because of an inflamed cyst that needs to be removed from your back. Someone from the Tennis Lawn Association is taking care of her . . . I mean, that situation, for you. In the meantime, the servicemen and women here at the hospital are sworn to secrecy."

Alice lets his words sink in. He offers her a final smile and turns to leave, but she stops him with a question. "Can I write him? If I'm careful with my words. Can I try to . . ." What would she try to do? Apologize? Assure him she loved him?

"I'm sorry, Alice. And if he tries to contact you, you cannot respond."

"He won't," she says, knowing it in her heart. "He can't trust me anymore."

"It's for the best."

Alice puffs out her cheeks, annoyed with the wave of melancholy that washes over her. She'd chosen her assignment over him. It was forty-love and, in that pivotal moment, she went for broke, fighting for something bigger than herself, for someone *other* than herself. Alice believes it's the first time she's ever done that. She likes how it feels, the warmth that washes over her, and she resolves to do more of it.

Epilogue

Sunday, August 16, 1964
The Newport Harbor Hotel
Newport, Rhode Island

Alice smiles, clipping on an earring, one of the final touches. That evening she expects to receive a loud reception. She was equal parts surprised, honored, and—okay—relieved to have recently received the news that she'd be inducted into the Tennis Hall of Fame at the age of fifty.

When Alice thinks back, especially on the days, weeks, and years that followed her time after the war, it's astonishing how they bleed together, one into the next.

She had a falling-out with Teach, and years later a reconciliation. Alice was no longer a naïve, yielding Eliza Doolittle to her coach's demands and control, reins Teach had promised she'd loosen. An estrangement was bound to happen after so many years of their power struggle. But to this day, Alice is thankful for the chance that woman took on her.

After the war, she played in exhibitions but never in another Grand Slam, letting her victories at Forest Hills and Wimbledon stand as her last appearances. Maybe it's that she didn't want to tamper with her winning record. Maybe the need to constantly prove herself began to feel silly after the war. Perhaps it was a little of both. That's okay, a person never stops growing. And grow Alice did, from a fireplug who so desperately needed people to notice her to a woman who's never told a soul about her real reason for being in Switzerland.

A few years after the war, she rounded out her Wonder Women of History column, writing seventeen in all, with her final comics about Sojourner Truth, Abigail Adams, Evangeline Booth, Madame Marie Curie, and—finally—Emma Willard, the woman who started it all before Alice even knew her column would be a thing. All she knew was that Emma's story needed to be told.

She took more lovers, who will go unnamed, thank you very much.

She had a lung removed. Fortunately, she's gotten by with one.

She worked on a film, coordinating tennis scenes.

She even took classes to become a practical nurse and a receptionist—something she did for eight years that had absolutely nothing to do with tennis.

While she no longer played competitively, she played socially and then decided to coach. To think, the talent she's had a hand in shaping over the years. More than two hundred students, in fact, but two stood out above the rest.

Billie Jean Moffit, soon to be King after her recent engagement, had champion written all over her from the jump. And Darlene Hard was an exemplary player when she won—and even when she lost.

Alice recalls such a moment during the 1957 Wimbledon tournament, when Darlene was beaten by Althea Gibson in only two sets. Yet Darlene's smile matched that of Althea's. It's a victory that warms Alice. She likes to think she had a hand in Althea playing in that very match.

When Alice caught wind that Althea, an African American player she'd never met, wouldn't be allowed to play in the National Championships, she couldn't *not* say something. Especially when the stance of the US Lawn Tennis Association committee was that Althea couldn't play because she hadn't sufficiently proven herself.

Oh, that got under Alice's skin.

Miss Gibson hadn't proven herself?

Miss Gibson didn't belong?

It hit too close to home. Like how Myrick put Alice through the wringer—and into the hospital—in order for her to get on the Wightman team because she wasn't like the other girls.

Or how she had to prove she should be paid the same amount as her male counterpart. What had she told Icely all those years ago? *"I don't care if he's a man and I'm a woman. Last time I checked, we're both human beings, deserving of the same opportunities."*

So Alice wrote an editorial piece for *American Lawn Tennis.* People paid their fifty cents and read how Alice thought it was unfair that Althea was expected to prove herself in tournaments she wasn't even invited to. Do the math there . . .

But if Miss Gibson was given the chance, then maybe, just maybe, tennis would add another great champion to its history. Let Althea be judged by her skill and not the pigmentation of her skin. That was all Alice wanted to get across. And she did. Althea was allowed to play. It took a few years, but she became the first African American to win a Grand Slam. A year later she won both Wimbledon and the US Nationals.

Alice likes to think she cheered the loudest when Althea received her trophy at Forest Hills.

Somewhere in all those years, Alice turned forty.

"One day when we're forty, love, we'll look back and realize we have everything we've ever wanted."

Alice pondered Joe's words. They made her smile. He may be gone, but he wasn't lost to her. She thought of him often and his use of *love* stuck out to her. A quote from George Sand, a French novelist, came to mind.

"There is only one happiness in this life, to love and be loved."

Alice has had both. More than once. Many times over. It's funny, in tennis, love means nothing. But in life, love is everything. And Alice has loved fiercely—people, moments, and a game.

After leaving Switzerland, she never contacted Hans. He never contacted her. He'll forever remain a what-could-have-been, a regret, a name she has never said aloud again.

It doesn't mean that she doesn't think of him, or, she'll admit, that she doesn't hope to one day be handed a single peach rose. She'd ask him if he'd have done anything differently all those years ago during the war.

A year after victory was declared, the Nuremberg Trials came to a close, where more than two hundred stood trial for everything from aiding in concentration camps to stealing Germany's wealth. Soon after, Alice received a handwritten note in the mail. There was no signature.

Thank you for Schmitz, Kugler, Ambros, Krauch

She remembered the names; of course she did. To this day, she still can name those in Hans's ledger. To this day, she also wonders how the end of the war affected him. Switzerland signed an agreement to pay 250 million Swiss francs toward the reconstruction of post-war Europe. In return, the Allies waived various claims against Swiss banks. What's more, the Swiss government pledged to identify and return any assets that once belonged to Holocaust victims.

Alice likes to think the retribution make a difference.

She likes to think her time in tennis has too.

Her old doubles partner Donald Budge will be beside her that evening at the Hall of Fame ceremony, along with George Lott, Sidney Wood, Frank Shields, and George Adee.

The kicker: she'll be inducted by Van Alen, the president of the Lawn Tennis Hall of Fame, with the assistance of none other than her old "pal" Myrick.

That man almost broke her.

Alice is proud that she didn't let him.

She's proud of many things.

She clips on her final earring and then her pin from Teach, one of her most prized possessions. Alice stands to leave her hotel room, a car likely already waiting for her outside.

What will be said about her tonight? The mention of her eighteen Grand Slam wins. A world number one ranking. A champion. An ace. A marvel. A spy?

No, no one knows about that last one. Yet it's Alice's time in Switzerland that may be her greatest achievement of them all, something she accomplished for everyone but herself.

A Note from the Author

Learning and writing about real people, especially strong women, is a favorite of mine. It's been an honor to get to know Alice Marble—tennis ace, marvel, and spy—and I hope you've found inspiration in her courage, focus, and doggedness.

While crafting my novel, Alice's memoir was my primary source, a goldmine of emotions, information, moments, and anecdotes. I'd be remiss to not mention that the validity of Alice's words have been questioned. I, too, questioned them at times. Alice likely embellished, misquoted, misremembered, maybe, even though Alice did claim to have an eidetic memory. For example, Alice mentions opponents who would've actually been children at the time. Alice says her first Wonder Women comic was published in 1941, however the publication date is June of 1942. She tells of story of the WAVES, a new women's branch of the navy, an entire year before it was formed. Alice also boasts—more than once—how she won a match in less than twenty minutes. However, at the time, the shortest recorded match lasted twenty-three minutes.

While I did my best to fact-check and amend where needed—Alice really kept me on my toes!—my novel is just that: a novel, though all the moments and experiences I've included in my fictional account—some of it admittedly incredible—have been directly inspired by Alice's memoir. Yes, she claims she got a call directly from President Roosevelt, that she was in multiple car accidents (I even left out one!), and that Jones ended up being a double agent—to name a few.

If you're interested in a nonfiction account or a biography, those exist. I'll be honest, I didn't read them during my research. I drew a line in the sand that I'd take Alice at her word, when possible. It's been a lot of fun.

Regardless of any embellishments or inaccuracies, at the end of the day I think we can all agree that Alice Marble was a remarkable woman, a young girl who felt like she had everything to prove, who grew into a woman who accomplished historic feats on and off the court—even more than my novel includes. For the sake of storytelling, pacing, and to avoid redundancies, I did not include all of Alice's tournament play. I also chose to leave out a moment that occurred prior to my storyline that Alice included in her memoir: an assault when she was a teenager. Alice provided an account of the horrific event. However, it's not something Alice gave significance to in the remainder of her memoir. As a result, I did not feel comfortable interpreting how the assault did or did not affect Alice's life.

I kept my storyline focused on tennis as much as possible, mentioning but not fully bringing to life Alice's friendships or her interests in singing, acting, and fashion design. For example, Alice designed not only her own clothing but also racquets. Her relationship with Carole Lombard was more significant than depicted. Alice was also briefly represented by Frank Orsatti, a Hollywood agent who represented Judy Garland. For a spell, she took on singing gigs. Considering Alice herself said, "The two months at the Waldorf were so different from anything I'd ever done that they were like pages from someone else's life," I chose not to spend a lot of time on these other facets I couldn't fully pay off, instead deciding to focus on two main paths in Alice's life. You likely noticed the shifts in tenses to align with the novel's two timelines. The first is one I like to call Present-tense Alice, which is set during the war years and brings to life non-tennis elements, and the second, Past-tense Alice, which follows the rise and fall and rise of her tennis career prior to the outbreak of the Second World War.

Alice's involvement in the war is something else questioned, largely because Joe Crowley and Hans Steinmetz are names researchers and historians haven't been able to corroborate, to the best of my own knowledge. However, based on what I've gleaned of Alice's personality, I can confidently say I see her taking action. It's why I chose to include and highlight the spy portion of her memoir. There were many "Hans Steinmetzes" in real life. Many Jews used Swiss banks to hide their money from the Nazis, only to later find their money had disappeared. It's been estimated that Swiss banks held over $400 million in Nazi gold, over half of which was believed to have been looted from their victims, including those in concentration camps, to add to their wealth. As recent as 1997, Swiss banks said they had uncovered an additional 21 million Swiss francs (15 million US dollars) that might belong to Jewish victims and their heirs.

I like to think that Alice had a hand in righting some of the wrongs of the Nazi party. In her memoir, she says, "On November 20 (1945), the International Military Tribunal convened at Nuremberg and would continue for almost a year. More than 200 Germans stood trial for everything from concentration camp atrocities to stealing Germany's wealth. Among the names of the accused were some I recognized from Hans' ledger. By helping bring them to justice I had, in a small way, avenged Joe's death."

The novel includes various multimedia enhancements—telegraphs, articles, notes, comics, and letters. While these are inspired by factual events, I've authored them all. A big thank-you to [designer name] for bringing Juliette Gordon Low's comic to life.

Also a big thank-you to . . . to be continued.

Thank you again for reading *Ace, Marvel, Spy.* My goal was to create a compelling, entertaining story to celebrate and shine light on a fascinating historical figure, and I hope you enjoyed reading it as much as I enjoyed writing it.

Acknowledgments

[HOLD 2 PAGES]]

Discussion Questions

[[HOLD 2 PAGES]]

About the Author

Claire Brock Photography

Jenni L. Walsh worked for a decade enticing readers as an award-winning advertising copywriter before becoming an author. Her passion lies in transporting readers to another world, be it in historical or contemporary settings. She is a proud graduate of Villanova University and lives in the Philadelphia suburbs with her husband, daughter, son, and various pets.

Jenni is the *USA TODAY* author of the historical novels *Becoming Bonnie, Side by Side, A Betting Woman, The Call of the Wrens*, and *Unsinkable.* She also writes books for children, including the nonfiction She Dared series and historical novels *Hettie and the London Blitz, I Am Defiance, By the Light of Fireflies, Over and Out*, and *Operation: Happy.* To learn more about Jenni and her books, please visit jennilwalsh.com or @jennilwalsh on social media.

Printed in the USA
CPSIA information can be obtained
at www.ICGtesting.com
JSHW021022190524
63083JS00002B/5